Praise for Peg Cochran's
Cranberry Cove Mysteries

"A fun whodunit with quirky characters and a satisfying mystery. This new series is as sweet and sharp as the heroine's cranberry salsa."
—Sofie Kelly, *New York Times* bestselling author of the Magical Cats Mysteries

"Cozy fans and foodies, rejoice—there's a place just for you, and it's called Cranberry Cove."
—Ellery Adams, *New York Times* bestselling author of the Books by the Bay Mysteries, the Charmed Pie Shoppe Mysteries, and the Book Retreat Mysteries

"I can't wait for Monica's next tasty adventure—and I'm not just saying that because I covet her cranberry relish recipe."
—Victoria Abbott, national bestselling author of the Book Collector Mysteries

"First-class mystery fun."   —*Suspense Magazine*

SOWED TO DEATH

PEG COCHRAN

BERKLEY PRIME CRIME
New York

BERKLEY PRIME CRIME
Published by Berkley
An imprint of Penguin Random House LLC
375 Hudson Street, New York, New York 10014

ISBN 9780425282038

First Edition: July 2017

Printed in the United States of America
1   3   5   7   9   10   8   6   4   2

Cover art: *Morgan County Fair* © Betsy Ross Koller
Cover design by Emily Osborne
Book design by Laura Corless

ACKNOWLEDGMENTS

Many thanks to Anne Perkins of Headacre Farm in Owls Head, Maine, for answering my questions.

1

Dear Reader,

We're almost halfway through September. I don't know where the time goes. We're starting to harvest our fall crop—broccoli, cabbage, carrots, and squash. We have a few apple trees between the house and the barn—a Paula Red and some Macs—and they produce enough fruit for eating and baking but not much else. I've wanted to make apple butter so the children and I picked a bunch of Cortlands over at the Tedfords' orchard. They let us have a couple of bushels every fall in exchange for Love Blossom Farm's lettuce and herbs during the summer. And they're not the only ones— Zeke Barnstable down the road gives us corn in exchange for root vegetables. Farmers take care of one another like that.

Today is the annual county fair and the children are
excited. Well, Billy is—Amelia is doing a good job of
hiding her enthusiasm, which I've been told is normal
for a thirteen-year-old.

Shelby McDonald sighed and hit SAVE on her computer.
She'd started her blog, The Farmer's Daughter, to while away
the long winter evenings on the farm, and it had taken off.
She now had enough of a following to attract some sponsors.
The money came in handy—selling lettuce, herbs, and other
fresh vegetables from the family farm, along with her homemade cheeses, made up the rest of her scanty income.
Fortunately the farm had been in the family for several generations so she didn't have to worry about a mortgage.

She wrote about life on the farm, shared favorite recipes and gardening tips and the antics of Jenkins, her West
Highland white terrier; Bitsy, a mastiff; and Patches, her
calico barn cat who was a champion mouser.

Shelby had grown up on Love Blossom Farm, and except for a brief sojourn in Chicago, she'd lived here all
her life. Her parents had retired from farming and were
touring the country in their secondhand RV, leaving her
to run the farm. Things had been easier when her husband, William "Wild Bill" McDonald, was alive, but she
prided herself on having risen to the occasion to manage
the farm and raise their two children alone.

Shelby was about to turn away from the computer
when she realized she hadn't responded to or even looked
at the comments on her previous blog post. She felt that
part of the popularity of her blog stemmed from her in-
teraction with her readers, so she tried to answer the comments left after each post.

She poured herself a glass of iced tea from a pitcher in the refrigerator. She noticed the rubber gasket around the fridge door was looking worn, and in several places, she had to push it back into position. It would be a long time before she could afford a new refrigerator—she was going to have to make do with this one as best she could.

The window over the sink was open, and the scent of newly mown grass drifted in on a breeze that was warm from the sun. There was a hint of autumn in the air as well—a crispness that hadn't been there even a week ago.

Shelby peeked into the living room. Billy was sprawled on the sofa, his bare and very dirty feet pressed against the back. The furniture was old and worn but Shelby had still taken the precaution of covering it as protection against dirty little boys and even dirtier animals.

Bitsy and Jenkins were stretched out on the floor beneath the open window. Amelia was nowhere to be seen—Shelby suspected she was in her room with her cell phone all but glued to her fingers as usual.

She sighed and went back to her computer, setting her glass of iced tea on the table beside it. Someday she hoped to turn the closet-sized spare bedroom at the back of the house into an office for herself. Her mother had used it as a sewing room, and Shelby had yet to find the time and energy to convert it to her needs.

She scrolled through the comments after her last blog post, featuring a recipe for sweet-and-sour red cabbage.

Shelby, I had to write and tell you how much my family enjoyed this recipe! I served it with roast pork, and it was a huge hit. Even the under fives liked it, and that's a miracle considering they normally refuse to eat anything but chicken fingers and French fries.

XXX Dani

Shelby, love your Farmer's Daughter blog. Going to try this recipe tonight.

Monica

Shelby smiled and wrote a brief reply. As she hit EN-TER, the third comment caught her eye and she paused.

Dear Farmer's Daughter, how dare you steal my family's recipe for German sweet-and-sour cabbage? This recipe has been in my family for generations, brought to this country in 1892 by my great-grandmother Anna Kamp. You are nothing but a fraud. Sign me

"Not Impressed."

Shelby realized she had been holding her breath as she read. It wasn't the first negative comment she'd received—far from it. There was something about putting yourself out on the Internet that encouraged people to speak their minds. Numerous times she'd been told one of her recipes *didn't work* (and she had her suspicions that that was the fault of the cook and not the recipe), but no one had ever accused her of stealing a recipe before.

There really was nothing new under the sun, as her grandfather always used to say—and that certainly held true with recipes. After all, there were only so many ways to cook a particular ingredient. Besides, how on earth would she have had access to the Kamp family recipe?

She knew she should write a quick note apologizing although certainly not acknowledging any theft, but she couldn't bring herself to do it. The idea made her feel sick.

She turned away from the computer. Maybe she would feel up to it later.

iiiiiiiiiiiiiiiiiiiiiiii

Shelby was gathering together the jars of jams and jellies she was entering into a contest at the county fair—blueberry jelly and strawberry jam from Love Blossom Farm's own fruit—when Billy rushed into the room, the dogs keeping pace right behind him.

Shelby had measured him the other day and he'd grown an inch over the summer. He was tall for a nine-year-old and the hems of his denim overalls hovered somewhere above his ankles.

"Can we go now?" he asked, hopping from one bare foot to the other.

Shelby looked him up and down. "Did you wash your face?"

"Yes." Billy nodded energetically.

Shelby stepped closer and stared at his face. "What's this by your chin?" She licked her thumb and scrubbed at the spot—it looked like chocolate.

Billy jerked his head away. "Mom!"

"If you'd washed your face properly, I wouldn't have had to do that."

"I did wash it," Billy protested. "Come on, Mom, can we go now?"

"I'm almost ready. Go call your sister, okay?"

Billy's bare feet slapped against the wide-planked wooden floor of the old farmhouse as he ran to the stairs. "Amelia! Mom says it's time to go."

Shelby heard a noise overhead, which she assumed was Amelia sliding off her bed. Moments later Amelia appeared in the kitchen doorway.

Shelby thought it ironic that Amelia resembled an angel with her halo of curly blond hair and blue eyes. Since hitting her teen years, Amelia had become as contrary as Jack Sparrow, the ancient rooster that patrolled the farm's barnyard. And by all accounts, it would be at least seven more years, when Amelia hit her twenties, before she would become normal again. Sometimes Shelby looked at her and wondered where her sweet, darling child had gone.

"I'm not going," Amelia said, her fingers never pausing in tapping out a text on the keyboard of her phone.

Shelby stopped with her hand halfway to the woven basket on the kitchen table. "Why not? You love the county fair."

Amelia scowled. "That was before. I'm not a kid anymore, you know."

A sharp retort rose to Shelby's lips but she resisted the temptation.

"There'll be rides and cotton candy and pigs and horses," Billy exclaimed, barely able to stand still.

Amelia turned her scowl on him. She gave an exaggerated shiver. "I'm too old for those things."

"That's too bad," Shelby said. "Because we're all going to the fair and that's that. Your brother has entered the riding competition and we all have to be there to cheer him on."

"And Mom's entered her jams and jellies," Billy said as he worked his finger into a hole in his overalls.

Shelby felt tears prickling the backs of her eyelids. Billy still wore his feelings for her on his sleeve even if Amelia acted as if she wanted nothing more than for Shelby to disappear in a puff of vapor.

"Fine," Amelia said, and flounced out of the room.

2

Dear Reader,

There's something about the county fair that still excites
me even after all these years—the animal judging, the
pie contest and tractor pull, and all the rides that spin
you around or turn you upside down . . . or both! When
we were children, the fair was always a highlight of our
year, second only to Christmas. The best part was when
the sun began to set and darkness descended. The
blinking lights on the rides and the game-of-chance
booths seemed even brighter then and there was always
the feeling in the air that magic could happen.

A long line of dusty cars snaked down M16, which was
little more than a dirt road. The drivers were waiting to turn
into the field that was being used for parking for the fair.

The air conditioner in Shelby's car had given up the ghost several years ago, and the interior was hot with the sun beating down on the roof from a cloudless sky.

Her children and she rolled down all the windows although the dust kicked up by their tires was threatening to choke them.

"I'm hot," Amelia whined from the front seat without looking up from her cell phone.

"Are we almost there?" Billy stuck his head out the back window to see how much farther until they received the signal to make the left turn into the makeshift parking area.

Shelby had their tickets tucked into the sun visor and reached for them as they got closer. Matt Hudson stood at the head of the line of cars. He had a green canvas money belt tied around his waist. Matt was the owner of the Lovett General Store, and Shelby and Matt were good friends—he'd helped her paint and renovate her mudroom in the spring to eradicate some really awful memories.

Matt made it clear that whenever Shelby was ready, he was eager to take their friendship to the next level. While Shelby sometimes yearned for male companionship, she wanted to be sure the timing was exactly right—and so was the man.

Slowly Shelby inched up the line of waiting cars. Matt smiled when he saw her and bent down so that his head was level with the window.

"I thought I might see you here. My volunteer stint ends in an hour. I hope you'll let me buy you an ice cream and try my hand at winning you a stuffed animal?"

"Sounds like fun."

Matt bent lower. "Hi, Billy. Hi, Amelia."

"I'm going to be in the riding competition," Billy answered. "You've got to come watch."

Amelia didn't bother to look up from her cell phone.

Dear Reader, even though it's been a few years, Amelia is still taking her father's death hard. She thinks that by dating I would be trying to replace him, which couldn't be further from the truth. There is no replacement for Bill McDonald. He was my first love but hopefully not my last.

Matt took their tickets, straightened up, and waved them on. The car bounced over the rutted field as Shelby followed instructions from a young man in khaki shorts and a blue T-shirt with *Lovett County Fair* on it. He waved her into a parking space next to a bottle green van.

Shelby turned off the car and removed her seat belt. She opened her door carefully, not wanting to hit the car next to her—they were packing them in like sardines and there wasn't much space between the vehicles.

The familiar aroma hit her as soon as she stepped out of the car—the scent of manure, hay, and livestock. She took a deep breath—she loved it. It reminded her of happy times—coming to the fair with her parents and falling asleep from sheer exhaustion on the way home; coming as a teenager with Bill and walking arm in arm, oblivious to everyone else.

She retrieved her basket of jams and jellies from the backseat and, with Billy running ahead of her and Amelia trailing behind, made her way across the field toward the entrance to the fair.

The noise was nearly overwhelming—the cry of the carnival barkers, the squeals of the children, and the braying of various farm animals. A Ferris wheel dominated the vista. Shelby knew from experience that at the top there was a view of the entire fair and the green patchwork of farms beyond.

The hint of manure was still in the air but had been joined by the aroma of popcorn, hot dogs, and cotton candy.

Amelia soon took off with a girl she knew from school, looking excited enough despite her original protests, and Shelby dropped Billy off at the stables so he could get ready for the equine events that would be coming up shortly.

Shelby followed signs toward where the cooking contests were to take place. The tent was abuzz with feminine voices arguing over the placement of the entries—pies, cakes, jams, and jellies.

A woman rapped her knuckles on one of the long trestle tables. "Quiet please, quiet," she said in her fluty voice. "Let's put the pies over here"—she indicated a sweep of tabletop to her left—"and the cakes over here."

"Coralynne," a woman in denim capris and a county fair T-shirt called out. "Where do you want the jams and jellies?"

Coralynne turned toward the sound of the woman's voice. Her chins quivered as she pondered the question.

"How about here?" Shelby asked setting her basket down on a corner of one of the tables.

"Perfect." Coralynne beamed.

Shelby removed the jars from her basket and arranged them in a neat row. Labels affixed to the front read LOVE BLOSSOM FARM.

She glanced at her watch. Billy's competition would be starting any minute now.

"I'll be back for the judging," she assured Coralynne as she headed through the open flap of the tent.

Shelby hurried toward the stable, an old weathered

structure that had served the county fair for generations. Just beyond was the riding ring, which was surrounded by bleachers, and a makeshift platform where the announcer would stand and where the winner would receive their ribbon.

"Excuse me." Shelby inched her way past the other spectators' knees toward an empty seat in the middle of the row.

She sat down carefully, conscious of the splintered wood beneath her bare legs. She had arrived just in the nick of time—the announcer was blowing his whistle and the first contestant was leading her reluctant mare into the ring.

Billy and his horse were in the wings awaiting their turn. Shelby bit her lip as she watched the horse prance and buck. Billy had been thrown during a lesson a couple of months ago and had broken his arm. Shelby was still trying to figure out how she was going to pay the doctor bills. She had medical insurance for catastrophic emergencies, but apparently broken arms didn't fall into that category.

The young girl led her horse around several strategically placed barrels, then trotted down the home stretch toward the finish line.

And then it was Billy's turn. Shelby wasn't sure what she was more frightened of—Billy falling off his horse and getting hurt again or Billy being disappointed at making a poor showing in the contest.

Shelby needn't have worried—Billy handled his horse like a seasoned pro, deftly leading the American quarter horse around the barrels and then flying down the open stretch to the finish line.

She could tell by the smile on Billy's face that he was pleased with his performance.

Even though it was September the sun was still warm, and Shelby used the bottom of her T-shirt to blot the perspiration gathering on her forehead. It was the time of year when you needed a sweatshirt in the morning but could be putting on your bathing suit for a swim by afternoon.

Finally all of the contestants had had their turn. A hush settled over the crowd as the announcer climbed the stairs to the platform draped in red, white, and blue bunting. He tapped the microphone a couple of times, jumping back as it emitted a loud screech that bounced around the makeshift arena.

Shelby found herself digging her nails into the palms of her hands and forced herself to relax and take a deep breath. It didn't matter if Billy won or not—he had acquitted himself well, and that's what counted.

After some brief tinkering by a thin fellow with thick black glasses, the microphone behaved and the judge began announcing the winners.

"First place goes to Darcy Meadows," he said with a flourish.

Shelby noticed the disappointed frown that crossed Billy's face before his look again became one of anticipation as the judge prepared to announce second place.

"And the second place winner is . . . Billy McDonald."

Shelby let out a whoop at the sound of Billy's name.

"One of yours?" the red-haired woman next to Shelby asked.

"Yes." Shelby grinned, trying not to burst with pride.

"Congratulations."

"Thanks."

Shelby barely heard the names of the other winners—she couldn't wait to give Billy a big hug even though she knew from experience that that would embarrass him.

Shelby scooted past the bare knees of the spectators between her and the end of the row of bleachers, murmuring *excuse me* as she went. She reached the end and jumped to the ground.

She rushed over to where Billy was retrieving a bottle of water from a large cooler.

"I'm so proud of you," Shelby said as soon as she was in earshot of her son. She gave him a big hug and kissed him on the forehead.

Billy squirmed like a worm on a fishhook but Shelby didn't care—she wanted to enjoy this moment of glory with her second born.

"Billy sure did great," Jim Harris said as he approached Shelby.

Jim was Billy's riding instructor. He was a thin but wiry man with sinews that looked like steel cables running through his arms. He had a cowboy hat pushed back on his head and was wearing well-worn and very dusty leather cowboy boots. No jodhpurs and gleaming riding boots for him. He viewed riding as a means of getting around a farm.

He cracked his gum along with a big smile. "Next year you're going to take the blue ribbon, right, Billy?"

Billy nodded shyly, fingering his red one.

"You've got a fine young man here," Jim said, slapping Billy on the back.

"Thanks," Shelby said, choking back tears. If only Bill was here to see how splendidly Billy was growing up.

She quickly wiped her eyes and thanked Jim.

After Billy had had the chance to splash some water on his face—all he was willing to do by way of cleaning up—it was time for the food contest. He had his ribbon pinned to the front of his overalls, and Shelby could have sworn he was walking with his chest puffed out, he was so proud.

Dear Reader, while it would be nice to win a prize for my jams and jellies, it's not as important as Billy winning a ribbon—and a red ribbon to boot!

They headed across the field toward the tents. The odor of manure got stronger, and they heard the mooing of cows and bleating of goats coming from the barn.

"Can we get a goat, Mom? Please?" Billy said staring wistfully after the barn.

"I don't think a goat would be a good idea. We'd have to be sure to keep it out of the lettuce patch and the herb garden."

"Aww, Mom," Billy said when they were interrupted.

"You've won something, I see." Jake Taylor strode up alongside them and pointed at Billy's ribbon.

Shelby always thought Jake looked like he was right out of a romance novel—tall, dark, handsome, and rugged with a charming smile and perfect manners. Shelby rented him the pasture alongside Love Blossom Farm for his cows, and he, in turn, kept her supplied with plenty of fresh milk.

Billy looked like he was going to explode with pride. He told Jake all about the competition as they walked— about how the horse didn't want to maneuver around that last barrel and how for a fearful moment, when he'd lost his stirrup, he thought he was going to slip off. The entire time he stared at Jake with adoring eyes.

"Are you going to try your hand at some of the games?" Shelby asked.

Jake shook his head. "No, I'm here in my capacity as a member of Lovett's volunteer fire department. We're doing a demonstration on using the Jaws of Life. The mayor donated an old black Volvo station wagon for us to use. It should be quite something—I hope you can come."

"I will."

Shelby willed herself not to blush. Jake always made her feel like a tongue-tied schoolgirl.

Jake took off at a lope toward the other end of the fair while Shelby and Billy continued toward the tent where a hand-lettered sign affixed to the side read *FOOD CONTEST.*

"There you are, dear," Coralynne said in her singsong voice as Shelby entered the tent. "We're about ready to start, aren't we, Eleanor?"

A crowd of women had gathered under the tent, many with anxious expressions as they hovered near their own pies, cakes, or jars of preserves.

Judges were seated behind a folding table covered with a white cloth and festooned with bunting along the front. Daniel Mather, a widower and the fairly new rector of St. Andrews Church, was nervously running the tablecloth through his fingers.

Isabel Stone, who was wearing way too much perfume and was overdressed for a county fair, was next to Daniel with Mrs. Willoughby, the secretary at St. Andrews, on her other side. St. Andrews was certainly well represented.

Mrs. Willoughby gazed longingly at the lineup of pies and cakes ready to be sampled, her plump sausage fingers drumming against the table.

Coralynne was acting as master of ceremonies and was

obviously relishing every minute in her exalted role. She was oozing with self-importance, which Shelby could see was getting on Mrs. Willoughby's already frazzled nerves.

Billy had wandered off and was sniffing the pies set out on the table.

"Please, please," Coralynne shrilled. "Don't go near the pies, young man."

Billy shrugged and moved away. He sank to the ground as gracefully as a ballet dancer, plucked a piece of grass, and stuck it in his mouth.

A woman came to stand next to Shelby. She was tall and big-boned and was plain to the point of being nondescript, with mousy brown hair and rounded shoulders. She was kneading her mannish hands as if they were slabs of dough.

"Do you have a pie in the contest?" Shelby asked.

"Yes, the rhubarb." She pointed to a pie that a young girl in cutoffs and a red bandanna was carrying to the judges' table.

"I don't think we've ever met." Shelby extended a hand in an attempt to defuse the tension. "Shelby McDonald."

"Tonya Perry." The woman smiled.

"You go to St. Andrews, don't you? I think I've seen you at the Sunday service."

Tonya nodded. "Yes. Back pew, left side."

Shelby smiled. While no one had assigned seats at the church services, people tended to choose the same general location or even the same pew, over and over again.

The judges were now ready to sample the first pie. Shelby thought she saw Daniel smile in Tonya's direction.

Mrs. Willoughby closed her eyes as she savored her bite.

"I think Mrs. Willoughby likes it," Shelby whispered.

"I hope so."

The judges were wiping their lips with napkins, preparing to sample a blueberry pie. Then it was on to a frothy-looking lemon meringue.

"That's Jenny Hubbard's famous lemon meringue," Tonya whispered to Shelby. "She's won the contest for the last five years."

"I've got my fingers crossed for you," Shelby said.

They both watched as Isabel Stone raised a dainty bite of pie to her lips.

As she chewed, a strange expression came over her face. It quickly morphed into a look of panic as she clutched her throat, gasping for air, before being seized by a violent fit of sneezing.

Mrs. Willoughby stood up so abruptly, her chair fell over backward. "Someone go get help!" She flapped her arms around. "Someone needs to get help."

3

Dear Reader,

I've heard of pies or cakes not quite turning out, but I've never heard of one knocking a person to their knees before. Although the time I got the bright idea to dye a cake green—I was only twelve years old at the time—it sure did turn people off. Of course the thing was also as heavy as a doorstop. That's why you have to be extra careful when you measure your flour. If your recipe calls for sifted flour, sift it right into your measuring cup and level it off. Your cake will come out as light as a feather.

Reverend Mather took over in his calm, unflappable way. He rolled up a tablecloth and put it under Isabel's feet in case she had merely fainted. She was obviously breathing and making small noises of distress, but no one could get a word out of her. And no one could figure out what exactly was wrong, either.

Jenny Hubbard, a tall, thin woman with rounded shoulders that made her look like a question mark from the side, hovered nearby, wringing her hands and protesting that there was nothing wrong with her pie.

"No one has said it's your pie that's at fault," Reverend Mather said soothingly, putting a hand on Jenny's back and steering her away from the scene.

The rest of the audience—mostly women—crowded around Isabel, staring at her as if she was a sideshow in the circus. Daniel rather gently urged them to move back and give her some air.

News of the incident had traveled like wildfire through the fairgrounds, and soon all the members of the Lovett volunteer fire department had arrived at a trot with two of them bumping a gurney over the uneven terrain as they ran.

They were wearing their black boots and overalls over county fair T-shirts.

By now Isabel seemed to be coming around. She was moaning and tossing and turning as they hoisted her onto the gurney. Coralynne hovered over her, wringing her pudgy hands and making mewling noises.

"Isabel," she said when Isabel's eyes opened.

They were red and tearing furiously. She tried to speak but the effort sent her into new gales of sneezing.

The firemen put their heads together with Coralynne and Mrs. Willoughby and decided that the safest course of action was to take Isabel to the hospital for evaluation. An ambulance was already stationed by the riding ring in case of accidents, and one of the firemen summoned it via walkie-talkie.

The ambulance had barely come to a halt before two paramedics jumped out and quickly loaded Isabel into the back. They all stood and watched as it drove away, slowly at first but then gaining speed.

The firemen trickled away one by one and went back to preparing for their show with the Jaws of Life.

Shelby was about to turn away when Tonya clutched her arm. "I wonder what happened." Her gray eyes were troubled.

"I don't know. An allergy, maybe?"

Coralynne and Mrs. Willoughby joined them.

"Well, I never!" Coralynne exclaimed, her many chins quivering in agitation. "I wonder what happened."

"That's what we were saying," Shelby said. "We thought perhaps she has an allergy of some sort. Maybe to one of the ingredients in the pie? I've heard of people getting a rash from lemon."

Mrs. Willoughby shook her head and her precariously pinned bun wobbled threateningly. "We've never had anything like this happen in the history of the county fair. We've been holding the fair here in Lovett since 1945. I was only a toddler at the time, but there are pictures of me standing with my mommy and daddy by the Ferris wheel." She pulled a handkerchief from the sleeve of her dress and wiped her face. "And certainly nothing like this has ever happened before."

"Mom."

Shelby became aware of Billy tugging on her shirt.

"Can we go now? They're going to demonstrate the Jaws of Life, and Jake's going to do it."

Shelby glanced at her watch. "There's time yet. I want to see who wins the pie contest, okay?"

"All right," Billy grumbled, kicking at the ground with the toe of his sneaker.

Shelby turned to Coralynne. "Will you continue the contest?"

"I suppose we shall. The crowd is still here." She gestured toward the group of women waiting expectantly.

Mrs. Willoughby took her seat again as the girl with the red bandanna retrieved the next pie. The judges looked nervous as she presented each of them with a small piece. Mrs. Willoughby took a tentative bite, and her face cleared when she realized there was nothing wrong with the pie. She took another bite and then another.

Daniel sampled a tiny bit of his piece and pushed the rest away.

And then it was on to the next pie. They tasted apple pies, banana cream pies, blueberry pies, and finally Tonya's rhubarb pie.

"The judges will need a few moments to decide on the winner," Coralynne announced as Daniel and Mrs. Willoughby put their heads together.

The contestants fidgeted as the minutes ticked by. Finally, Daniel and Mrs. Willoughby looked up and motioned to Coralynne.

They spoke briefly, and then Coralynne turned to address the crowd.

"We have a winner," she crowed excitedly.

A hush fell over the crowd.

Coralynne continued to pause dramatically until someone in the back yelled, "Tell us, already."

Coralynne shot them a disapproving look.

"And the winner is . . ." She licked her lips and took a

deep breath. "And the winner is Tonya Perry and her rhubarb pie."

Everyone clapped politely as Coralynne scanned the crowd.

"Tonya, please step up to get your award." Coralynne held up a blue ribbon.

There was a rustling sound as everyone turned around to see if they could spot Tonya.

Coralynne waited a few more moments before acknowledging that Tonya was obviously not going to come forward.

ıııııııııııııııııııııı

Billy tugged on Shelby's arm. "Can we go now? I want to try the games. Please?"

"Okay." Shelby allowed Billy to pull her toward the heart of the fair.

They passed one booth where a large stuffed woolly mammoth was dangling from a hook—the grand prize if you managed to get three Ping-Pong balls in the cups of water placed on a counter several feet away.

"Mom, can I try that, please?" Billy pointed to the stuffed toy. "I want to win that. I can do it. I know I can."

Shelby had her doubts, but she dug in her pocket for a dollar and handed it to Billy.

None of his balls landed in a cup. He turned to Shelby, crestfallen.

"Can I try again, Mom? Can I?"

"I don't think so, Billy. The game is very hard. I doubt anyone is going to win that stuffed animal. Besides, the Jaws of Life demonstration will be starting soon. Don't you want to see it?"

Billy's face cleared. "Yes! Let's go."

An excited crowd had already gathered along the fence surrounding a dented and rusted Volvo station wagon. The black paint was scratched in some places and completely gone in others. The front was deformed by a huge dent to the driver's-side door, and it was easy to imagine the dummy propped in the front seat being trapped.

Members of Lovett's volunteer rescue squad were also on the scene, lending an extra fillip of reality to the proceedings. The ambulance should have been there, too, but had been used to transport Isabel Stone to the hospital. Earl Bylsma, whom Shelby knew from St. Andrews, was setting up a gurney, its crisscrossed legs unfolding and making it look like a crane stretching after a nap.

The crowd continued to swell as they waited for the start of the demonstration. Shelby glanced toward the tent they had just left, wondering if they'd gotten to the jams and jellies yet. She would have to miss the announcement of the winner. But it was worth it to see the excitement on Billy's face. Especially when Jake came by and ruffled his hair.

"How are you doing, sport?"

Billy beamed with pleasure when he noticed the envious looks from some of the other boys being shot in his direction. Shelby thought he grew at least an inch right then.

The crowd was noisy and it was hard to hear. Billy tugged on Shelby's shirt again and she bent down so she could listen.

"Is that a real person in there?" he asked, pointing to the car.

"No, that's a dummy. It's not real, but it's supposed to look real."

By now the firemen had donned their coats and hats and were in full regalia.

Dear Reader, I must admit that Jake looks very attractive in his fireman's getup. And terribly virile. But I shouldn't be thinking about that right now, should I?

It appeared as if Jake was going to be the one to wield the Jaws of Life. Shelby was glad she and Billy had snagged a spot in the front row. She pushed him in closer so he could see better.

It was hard to imagine that anything could cut through the incredibly heavy steel of a car, but Jake was about to do just that.

He held up one of the huge pieces of equipment that had been arranged next to the car. Shelby thought it looked like a lobster claw from a horror movie.

"This is a cutter. It can cut through the metal of a car as easily as your can opener cuts through a tin can. It exerts 12,358 pounds of cutting force at the blade center."

The sound of the crowd drawing in its breath was audible.

Jake put down the cutter and picked up another piece of equipment. "This is a spreader. It can tear into a vehicle with greater force than we could ever achieve without it." He smiled at the crowd. "Both pieces are powered by a hydraulic system."

He laid that piece of equipment on the ground as well and picked up a third one. "This"—he held it up so the crowd could see—"is a ram. We can use this to push up the dashboard of a car to help to extricate the victim."

Billy began fidgeting. He was anxious for the demonstration to start.

"As you can imagine," Jake continued, "this equipment

is expensive. The Lovett Fire Department is hoping to purchase another set, so if you can throw some money into the hat, we'd appreciate it." He pointed to where one of the firemen was holding out his hat. "This equipment has saved many lives on the road, but it's come in handy for certain farm accidents as well."

That got everyone's attention, and several people pulled out their wallets.

Jake must have become aware of the restlessness of the children in the crowd. He grinned. "I'm sure you're all anxious for the demonstration to begin."

He started up the cutter and picked a strategic part on the car. He began cutting, and slowly the unwieldy-looking contraption bit through the metal of the car, as if it were child's play. Jake put the cutter down and picked up the spreader. He used that to pry open a hole in the side of the car.

He stopped briefly. "If this were a real accident, there's a good chance the dashboard and steering wheel would have been pushed forward, trapping our poor victim. We would then use the ram to push it out of the way."

Jake once again wielded the spreader, slowly enlarging the gap in the car.

"Cool!" Billy exclaimed as he watched the procedure.

By now Jake's face was shiny with perspiration. He shoved his hat back on his head and reached into the hole he'd cut in the side of the car. Earl Bylsma was standing by with his gurney at the ready.

Jake grabbed the dummy by the shoulders and began to pull it out of the car. A strange look came over his face but was quickly replaced by one of calm determination.

The dummy slithered the rest of the way out and Jake placed it carefully on the ground.

Something was wrong. Shelby sensed it but didn't know what it was. Her instinct was to rush Billy away from the scene, but he was too enthralled to be moved that easily.

Jake took off his hat and knelt next to the dummy. He appeared to be feeling for a pulse. It was then that Shelby noticed the thin trickle of blood that was flowing away from the dummy.

Jake motioned for Earl to join him. Earl glanced toward the dummy, and even from a distance Shelby could see how white his face had become.

He dropped to his knees, put his hands on the dummy's chest, and began chest compressions.

The crowd was stunned into silence except for a large woman in a flower-printed top and matching capris who began to scream.

"It's not a dummy." She pointed toward where Earl and Jake were kneeling. "That's a real body." And she screamed again.

4

Dear Reader,

There were certainly some surprises at the county fair. Not the least of which was the ending of Jenny Hubbard's five-year winning streak with her famous lemon meringue pie. After what had happened to Isabel Stone, the other judges declined to taste it.

Tonya Perry took home the blue ribbon for her rhubarb pie in what everyone is calling a stunning upset. Please don't think I'm bragging, but my jams and jellies came in first, and I now have a blue ribbon to my credit.

And Billy has his red ribbon, which he proudly pinned to the bulletin board in the kitchen.

Of course the most surprising event of all was finding that the dummy in the station wagon being used for the Jaws of Life demonstration wasn't a dummy at all . . . but a real body.

The firemen quickly formed a cordon around the body that had been pulled from the wreckage of the Volvo. Earl grabbed a sheet off the gurney and with obvious reverence draped it over the corpse.

Several of the firemen tried to get the crowd to disperse, but they were reluctant to move for fear of missing out on something interesting. Shelby could imagine this would be the talk of the town at dinner tonight and for many weeks beyond.

She shielded Billy as best she could, but he was determined not to miss anything.

"Is that a real body, Mom? Is it?"

"It looks like it," Shelby said, putting a hand on his shoulders and squeezing. "It's terribly sad. I think we should move away and let the authorities do their job."

"But then we'll miss all the good stuff," Billy protested.

Right then Shelby felt a tap on her shoulder and turned around to see Matt standing behind her. She couldn't control the sigh of relief that escaped her.

"Hey, Billy, how about you come with me? I need to collect some traffic cones from the field where the tractor pull was held. Think you can drive the truck in a straight line for me?"

"You bet! Can I go, Mom? Can I?"

"He'll be fine," Matt mouthed at Shelby.

"Okay. But be careful. Please!"

Billy took off without a backward glance, for which Shelby was very grateful.

It only took minutes, but it seemed like forever before the police arrived—two uniformed officers who quickly began stringing up crime scene tape.

A familiar face suddenly appeared in the group crowded around the body and Shelby felt her spirits lift. Without thinking she began walking toward the figure in the Tigers baseball cap and worn jeans.

Frank was a hair taller and a little older than his brother, Bill McDonald, had been, but his appearance never failed to give Shelby a jolt. It was like seeing Bill come back to life, and it always made her heart beat a little faster.

Frank looked up when he saw Shelby coming, and despite the solemnity of the occasion, he couldn't help giving her a big grin.

Shelby hovered in the background, admiring the way Frank, as the lead—and only—detective on the Lovett police force, took charge of the situation. Shelby knew she should collect Billy and leave but instead she stood and watched as Frank chatted with each of the firemen in turn.

He spoke briefly to one of the uniformed officers, then walked over toward where Shelby was standing.

He looked Shelby up and down, a small frown puckering the skin between his eyebrows.

"Are you okay?"

"Yes."

"And Billy?"

"He seems okay. Matt came along and took him away shortly after they pulled the body from the car."

Frank nodded toward the car. "It's Zeke Barnstable. Do you know him?"

"He has the farm down the road from Love Blossom. He gives us corn every summer."

"Can you tell me what happened? I can't get a coherent story out of anyone else."

Shelby explained about the demonstration and everyone's horror when the dummy turned out to be a real body.

"We're waiting for the ME—we'll know more when she gets here."

"Do you think it was . . . ?"

"Murder?" Frank shrugged. "We'll find out."

<hr style="width: 30%; margin: auto;" />

Frank had told Shelby to go on home and that he would stop by later. She didn't know why, but that thought was comforting.

Billy was tired and dirty and smelled like the barnyard when they got back to Love Blossom Farm. He'd had a hot dog, a corn dog, cotton candy, a pretzel, and some funnel cake. Shelby hoped he wasn't going to be sick, but so far he seemed to have been blessed with a cast-iron stomach. After a brief argument she managed to convince him to get in the tub. Amelia had stayed behind at the fair with a friend whose mother promised to bring her home after the fireworks.

Shelby felt at loose ends. The scene at the fair had upset her more than she realized. Bitsy and Jenkins were anxious to go out, so she opened the back door and stood on the steps. The air was cooling as the sun dipped in the sky. Shelby gazed out over the farm and felt some sense of peace return. There was the faint scent of thyme and rosemary in the air from her herb garden, along with the ever-present aroma of manure from Jake's farm next door.

Finally, she went back inside and retrieved her jumbled knitting from the basket by the living room sofa. The ladies in the knitting group she'd joined had convinced her not to give up, but Shelby suspected it was hopeless no matter how hard they tried to help her. She held up the needles and gazed in dismay at the tangled mess hanging from them. There were holes where there shouldn't have been any, places where the stitches were too loose, and places where they were too tight. Shelby shoved the whole thing back in the basket and went out to the kitchen.

The sound of splashing from the tub upstairs had ceased and moments later Billy appeared in the kitchen with his damp hair smoothed down. He was wearing a pair of pajamas that were clearly too small. He was growing so fast, Shelby thought. Before she knew it both he and Amelia would be out of the house and on their own. She made a promise to herself to cherish every moment between now and then.

She kissed Billy good night and listened as he climbed the stairs to his room. She was about to settle down in front of the television when the front doorbell rang.

Frank was leaning against the doorpost when she opened the door.

"Hello." His voice was raspy and he sagged from weariness.

"Come in." Shelby swept an arm toward the living room. "Would you like something to drink?"

"Would coffee be too much trouble?" He sighed. "My day isn't over yet." He scrubbed a hand over the stubble on his chin.

"I'll put some on."

He followed Shelby out to the kitchen, turned one of the kitchen chairs around, and straddled it. He watched as she spooned coffee into the coffeemaker, filled the carafe with water, and then added it to the machine. The machine gurgled to life shortly after Shelby pushed the ON button.

She turned around and leaned against the counter.

Frank looked around the kitchen. "A person could feel at home here." He gave an embarrassed half smile. "I mean, compared to my place. The few pictures I have are still stacked against the wall and the furniture is pretty much where the movers put it down."

He glanced at Shelby's laptop, which was sitting open on the kitchen table. "Are you still writing that blog or whatever it's called? Doreen—she's our new department secretary—says she reads it all the time."

"I enjoy it, and it brings in some money," Shelby said. She saw the stack of bills on the counter out of the corner of her eye and sighed. "Of course Billy would have to break his arm."

"I'd be more than happy to help—"

"No, that's fine. I'm managing."

The coffee machine had gone silent, and Shelby was grateful for the excuse to turn around so Frank couldn't see her face. She brushed at the tears that had collected in the corners of her eyes and retrieved two mugs from the cabinet. She filled them and handed one to Frank.

"I can't thank you enough for this." He took a gulp and closed his eyes. "Murder is always hard to digest," he said finally. "It's not something you ever get used to."

"Murder?"

Frank groaned and rubbed his eyes. "There was a sizable dent in the back of Zeke's head."

"Could he have fallen?"

"According to the ME . . . no. Besides, someone had to have hauled the body over to that car and then shoved it inside."

Shelby suddenly felt very tired. She pulled out a chair and sat down.

"Did you know Zeke at all?" Frank turned the chair back around and rested his elbows on the table.

He suddenly seemed terribly close, and Shelby leaned as far back in her chair as she could.

"I didn't know Zeke—not really. He was quiet. Some people thought he was standoffish, but I think he might have been shy."

"He seems to have been a bit of a loner. We haven't found anyone who knew him very well."

"That's often the way with farmers—they're out in the field from sunup to sundown. There's not a lot of time for socializing, except maybe for church on Sunday."

Frank cracked a grin. "Makes my job sound like a piece of cake."

Shelby pushed her empty coffee cup away. "I doubt that."

Frank stretched his arms overhead. He looked at his watch. "I'd better get going. There are a few more things I've got to do before I can call it a day." He reached out and touched Shelby's hand. "I wanted to make sure you were okay."

Shelby felt heat rush into her face.

Frank pushed back his chair, scraping it across the floor. He stood up.

"If you need anything, call me, okay? I promised Bill I would take care of you and the kids, and I meant it."

||||||||||||||||||||||||||

Shelby felt unsettled by Frank's visit. She forced herself to sit down and turn on the television. Bitsy and Jenkins took this as their cue to curl up on the sofa for a nap, grunting and snorting as they got into a comfortable position.

Shelby was flipping through the channels when the front door opened and then slammed shut so forcefully, the pictures on the wall rattled.

"Amelia?" Shelby jumped up from her seat as footsteps stomped down the hall.

"What's the matter?" Shelby asked when she caught sight of her daughter. Amelia's eyes were red and her face was streaked with tears.

Amelia balled her fists at her side. "My life is over," she yelled at Shelby.

"What happened?" Shelby said calmly. Amelia looked fine—clearly this wasn't a life-or-death situation. There was no blood or signs of blunt trauma.

"It's over between me and Ned," Amelia said on a sob.

Dear Reader, over? Amelia is too young to date—at least in my opinion—and so far her relationship with Ned has consisted of declaring their undying love for each other and passing notes in class. (Miss Fischer, Amelia's English teacher, called me to complain about that. Amelia is right—she's a dinosaur who's forgotten what it's like to be young.)

Shelby was suddenly overcome with fatigue—all that

had happened at the fair, and now this—and she longed for the comfort of her bed. But Amelia needed her.

"What happened?" She shooed the dogs off the sofa, sat down, and patted the seat next to her.

Amelia sank into the sofa cushions and crossed her arms over her chest. She stuck out her chin and glared at Shelby. "My life is over—I'm not kidding."

"You still haven't told me what happened. Did you and Ned have a fight?"

"No. That's the thing." She turned to Shelby. "It's all your fault. If you would let me date this wouldn't have happened."

"What happened?" Shelby said for what felt like the millionth time, exasperation creeping into her voice.

"I saw Ned—at the fair."

Shelby nodded encouragingly. "And?"

"He was holding hands with Katelyn. He even won her a stuffed animal." Amelia buried her head in Shelby's shoulder. "I thought she was my friend." She hiccoughed.

"I'm sorry. I know that hurts." Shelby patted her on the back. "Did I ever tell you about Hayley Robbins?"

Shelby felt Amelia's head moving back and forth against her shoulder.

"We were starting high school and she had just moved to Lovett with her family. We had homeroom together and quickly became friends. People used to joke that we were twins because we did everything together." Shelby paused, surprised at the emotions the memory still stirred. "Then I caught her trying to kiss your father at one of our school dances. She'd lured him into an empty classroom."

Amelia raised her head a couple of inches. "What happened?"

"Nothing, really. Your father told her to get lost, and we were no longer friends."

Amelia pushed away from Shelby and jumped up from the couch. "That's because Dad loved you. Nobody loves me!"

5

Dear Reader,

It's September, which means winter is around the corner—it tends to come early to our part of the world. More than a few times, the children have gone trick-or-treating in the snow! On a farm, fall is the time to prepare for winter. We try to live off of what we grow as much as possible, sometimes trading with other farmers for things we don't produce ourselves. And to get us through the long winter months, we can fruits and vegetables from our summer crops.

Home canning is not as hard as a lot of people think, and it's such a pleasure to open a jar of beets or peppers that you put up yourself. I've always admired pioneer women, and this makes me feel a teeny bit like one of them, although I know their life was much harder than mine is.

"Billy, stop dawdling or you're going to be late."

Shelby looked at her son with exasperation. He claimed to have brushed his hair but it hadn't done much to tame the cowlick that sprang from his crown like the bright red comb on their rooster Jack Sparrow's head.

Billy was slumped over a bowl of cereal, picking out the raisins—which he claimed he didn't like although Shelby could have sworn he'd liked them last week—and lining them up on the table alongside his place mat.

"You're going to miss the bus if you don't hurry," Shelby said.

Billy looked up. "I'm not taking the bus. Jake said he'd drive me to school. He has to go into town anyway, he said."

"What? You didn't tell me."

Billy shrugged and fished out another raisin that was floating in the milk in his cereal bowl.

Shelby cringed with embarrassment. "I hope you didn't ask him for a ride."

Jake was always ready to lend a hand when needed, but she certainly didn't want the children begging for favors from him.

A brisk knock at the back door made her jump. She saw Jake's outline through the lace curtain on the window and ran a hand through her hair, wishing she'd taken the time to brush out the tangled curls.

Jake didn't wait for an answer but cracked open the door and stuck his head around the edge. "Okay if I come in?"

Dear Reader, I really wanted to say, "No, wait! Let

*me go brush my hair, dab on some lipstick, and change
out of my baggy old jeans and this sweatshirt with the
stretched-out neck."*

"Please." Shelby grabbed the knob and pulled the door
open the rest of the way.

Shelby's kitchen wasn't huge, but Jake made it seem
even smaller than usual with his height and his broad
shoulders.

"Almost ready, bud?" He ruffled Billy's hair, making
his cowlick even more pronounced.

Billy pushed his cereal bowl away and jumped up.
"Let's go," he said breathlessly.

"Halloo," a voice called from the front hall. "Anybody
home?"

"In the kitchen, Bert."

Bert Parker bustled into the room, her stick-thin figure
bristling with energy. Her given name was Roberta but
no one ever called her by her full name. Her husband had
been named Ernie and she had taken a never-ending delight in introducing the two of them as Bert and Ernie.

Bert had been a fixture at Love Blossom Farm ever
since Shelby could remember. She helped out wherever
it was necessary, whether it was weeding the herb garden
or minding the kids.

Bert stopped short when she saw Jake leaning against
the counter.

"Hello, Jake." She gave him a slow smile and looked
from him to Shelby and back again. She glanced at the
clock over the sink. "Billy, I passed the school bus about
a quarter of a mile down the road. You'd better hurry or
you'll miss it."

"Come on, partner." Jake put an arm around Billy's shoulders. "The truck is out back."

Billy grabbed his backpack from a hook by the back door and was about to follow Jake when Amelia flew into the room.

Jake stopped and turned to Amelia. "I'm taking Billy to school. Do you want to ride with us?"

"Sure."

Billy looked momentarily disappointed, then shrugged. "Bye, Mom," he called over his shoulder just before the door shut behind him.

As soon as the door had fully closed, Bert turned to Shelby and raised her eyebrows.

"What?" Shelby said.

"I didn't say anything," Bert said, grabbing an apron from the hook next to the stove and tying it around her waist. "If you don't want to tell me about it, that's fine."

"It's not what you think," Shelby insisted.

Bert turned to her with her hands on her hips. "Now, missy. First off, you have no idea what I'm thinking, and second, so what? So what if Jake spent the night?"

"He didn't," Shelby protested.

"Would it be so terrible if he had?"

"I'm . . . I'm not ready for that yet. It's only been a couple of—"

"Years. It's been years now, Shelby. You have to start living again."

"I am," Shelby said. She felt her cheeks flush. "But it wouldn't be right . . . not with the children here. What would they think?"

"They can stay at my place anytime you want. It would

be fun. We can order a pizza, and I've promised to teach them how to play poker."

Shelby opened her mouth and then closed it again. The less said, the sooner she could get Bert off this topic.

Bert opened a cupboard door, pulled out a large pot, and clanged it down on the stove.

"It's time we made that apple butter you've been wanting to try. Those apples aren't going to keep forever, you know."

Shelby breathed a sigh of relief at the change of subject.

"The apples are out on the front porch. I'll go get them."

When she returned with the bushel basket, Bert was lining up a dozen Mason jars on the counter.

Shelby put the basket on the kitchen table, and Bert stuck a hand in and pulled out an apple. She squeezed it and sniffed it.

"Good stuff," she said finally. "The Tedfords grow some fine Cortlands." She grabbed several and put them on the counter. "We'd better get to peeling these," she said to Shelby, "or we'll be here all day."

Shelby hid a smile. Bert's bark was always worse than her bite and hid a heart as soft as melting ice cream.

Shelby retrieved two paring knives from her knife block and handed one to Bert.

"I imagine you and the kids went to the fair yesterday," Bert said, tossing some peeled and cut-up apple chunks into the pot on the stove. "I was going to go but I had a touch of lumbago and thought I'd better not. Even though Doc Fitzgibbons insists there's no such thing as lumbago." Bert snorted. "Little does he know. I told him, 'Just wait till you get it.' Young whippersnapper," Bert said under her breath.

"Do you want to sit down?" Shelby asked in concern. "If your back is hurting—"

"Good heavens, don't you start, too. It was only a bit of a pain, nothing to get all worked up over. I'm perfectly fine today, so no need to treat me like I have one foot in the grave."

Bert grabbed another apple and began examining it for bad spots. "So, tell me about the fair. How did Billy make out in the riding competition?"

"He won a red ribbon." Shelby couldn't keep the pride out of her voice.

Bert put her hands on her hips. "No kidding!" She shook her head. "Too bad his father wasn't there to see it. He'd be as proud as punch."

Shelby looked down. "I know."

"I didn't mean to go upsetting you," Bert said. "Tell me about your jams and jellies."

Shelby felt her face flush. "I took the blue ribbon."

"I knew it," Bert said, slapping her knee. "Good for you." Bert picked up the apple and began peeling it. "I heard there was quite a to-do at the fair yesterday. Something about Zeke Barnstable turning up dead."

Shelby paused with the paring knife in her hand. "It was awful. His body ended up in that old car the fire department was using for the Jaws of Life demonstration."

Bert gestured to the apple in Shelby's hand. "You want to get these peeled and in the pot before they turn brown."

Shelby took the hint and finished peeling the apple.

"Why Zeke Barnstable? I wonder." Bert scooped up her apple chunks and tossed them into the pot. "He never did anyone any harm so far as I can tell. Kept to himself, too. Not one to gossip or stick his nose in other people's business. He used to be good friends with Jim Harris, Billy's riding instructor—they spent every Thursday night at the Dixie Bar and Grill over on the highway just outside of town, having a couple of beers and playing pool. My neighbor waits tables there a couple of days a week and said she hasn't seen the two of them together in ages."

"Maybe they had a falling-out?" Shelby picked up the last apple and began to peel it.

"Could be." Bert reached for the canister of sugar on the counter. She popped a piece of apple into her mouth and chewed. "Two cups of sugar ought to do it. These apples are plenty sweet already. We all have our little rituals, I suppose," Bert said, spitting out an apple seed. "Jim and Zeke going to the Dixie every Thursday. Zeke's wife, Brenda, and her gal friends spending every Friday night there catching up with one another. Same day Jim and his brother, Sid, would go for a couple of drinks and a round of pool."

Bert scooped sugar from the canister and added it to the pot on the stove.

"What else do you need?" Shelby asked, wiping her hands on her apron.

"I usually add cinnamon, cloves, and allspice to mine."

"Sounds good." Shelby opened a cupboard and retrieved the spices. "What else?"

"A cup of apple cider and a splash of lemon juice."

Shelby opened the fridge, pulled out the bottle of apple cider, and plucked a lemon from the bowl of fruit on the kitchen table.

Bert put the lemon on the cutting board and cut it in

half. "He sure was a creature of habit, was Zeke, even more than the rest of us," she said as she worked a wooden reamer into one of the lemon halves. "Sundays it was church at St. Andrews—third pew from the front, over to the left of the altar. Mondays you knew you would see him at the Lovett General Store getting his provisions for the week. Same things in his basket every time. Then Thursdays with his buddy Jim, but, like I said, he and Jim haven't been out together in ages."

"Does Zeke have any family?" Shelby thought it sounded like a terribly lonely existence and she felt sorry for him.

"He has a sister by the name of Rebecca. She left Lovett a long time ago—I think it might have even been before she graduated high school. Then she suddenly appeared again. Gave no explanation for her absence as far as I've ever heard. She works at the Lovett Feed Store, and they rent her the apartment above it." Bert wiped her hands on a paper towel. "Then there was the wife, of course."

Bert handed Shelby the jars of spices, and Shelby put them away in the cupboard.

"You'd better fill a big pan with some water and get it boiling," Bert said, frowning. "We need to sterilize the jars if you plan on keeping the apple butter through the winter."

"Okay." Shelby squatted down and pulled the large pot she used for canning from the cupboard. "Tell me about Zeke's wife," Shelby said as she turned on the hot water tap and held the pot under it. "I had no idea he was married."

"He's not," Bert said, running a hand through her short

gray hair. "At least, not anymore. The missus disappeared three years ago. There was quite the to-do about it."

Shelby turned the tap off and swiveled around to face Bert. "I'm surprised I don't remember that."

"I'm not." Bert gave the pot on the stove a stir. "You had your hands full at the time."

Shelby realized with a shock that that was when she'd been recently widowed. No wonder she didn't remember hearing about Zeke's wife disappearing. She didn't remember much from those days—only that they seemed endless and she didn't think she would ever get through them.

"Did his wife ever turn up?"

"Nope. There were some who thought she'd run away—got tired of the predictability of her life: church on Sundays, dinner at the diner on the occasional Saturday, and pizza and beer with her gal friends every Friday night at the Dixie. Plus working part-time at the Laundromat and spending the rest of her day working on the farm. Some people might want more out of life than that."

Bert peered into the simmering pot of apples again. Fragrant steam was beginning to fill the kitchen. "These are coming along nicely. Is that water boiling yet?"

"Yes."

"Better put the jars in, then. The apple butter won't take much longer."

Shelby carefully inserted the Mason jars into the boiling water.

"So, people thought she ran away? We got corn from Zeke every summer but I never had a real conversation with him. He was always in a hurry." Shelby levered the last jar into the pot. "She doesn't sound like the type to run off like that—a farmer's wife."

"Appearances can be deceiving, but the police agreed with you and suspected foul play. Naturally Zeke was suspect number one. It sure took a toll on the poor man. He's not been the same since."

"Was anything ever proven?"

"Nope. And that's what makes it worse." Bert turned off the gas under the apples. "The stink of suspicion lingered around the man like the smell of a skunk lingers in the air long after it's sprayed."

"What do you think? Do you think Zeke had anything to do with his wife's disappearance?"

Bert pursed her lips and paused, a hand on her chin. "Let's just say that still waters run deep, as the saying goes."

Dear Reader,

My kitchen is now redolent of the scent of apple butter, and it's heavenly. Bert and I canned most of it for the winter, but I did keep a small jar in the fridge to have on toast for breakfast.

When I finish writing this, I've got to get out to the garden. I want to pick some green peppers. Did you know that green and red peppers are from the same plant? The difference is that the red ones have been left on the vine to fully ripen, which is when they turn red.

And our potato plants are blooming. Flowers on top mean potatoes underneath! I'm going to pick some for our suppers now but I won't harvest the rest until I'm ready to store them for the winter. You need to keep your potatoes in a cool, dark place—light will turn them green.

I absolutely love potatoes no matter how they're prepared. Don't you? Fried, boiled, mashed—it doesn't matter!

Bert is certainly a fountain of information. She's lived in Lovett all her life and knows almost everybody. That was interesting news about Zeke's wife—it must have been hard on the poor man not knowing where his wife disappeared to and then being suspected of doing her harm on top of it.

Shelby knelt on the ground and dug her spading fork into the rich earth alongside one of the potato plants. She gently lifted the plant and carefully removed the potatoes she wanted. She brushed off the dirt and tossed them into her basket. She was only picking what she needed for the next couple of days.

She carefully replaced the plant and tamped down the earth. There wouldn't be a hard frost for a couple more weeks, so she could leave the rest of the potatoes and harvest them right before she planned to store them for the winter.

The dogs had followed Shelby outside. Jenkins was busy digging a hole with more efficiency than a Bobcat, his paws moving so fast, they were a blur. Clods of earth flew out behind him. Bitsy was lumbering about attempting to catch a large fly that was making lazy circles around her head.

Farming was dirty work, but Shelby hardly ever noticed the dirt under her fingernails or the mud caked on the knees of her jeans until it was time to leave Love Blossom Farm for church or to go to the store. Today she'd offered to help out at St. Andrews stuffing envelopes for the annual appeal. Mrs. Willoughby, the church secretary, had strong-armed several women into volunteering for the project.

Dear Reader, I guess this means I need to take a shower and change my clothes?

Once in the shower, Shelby relished the feel of the hot water on her overworked muscles, and she was tempted to linger, but the water quickly turned tepid, reminding her that her water heater only put out a finite amount of hot water.

Shelby toweled off and went into the bedroom to stare at the meager contents of her closet. She might not have been able to do *fashionable* but she could at least achieve *clean*. She grabbed her denim skirt and hesitated, her hand hovering over the hanger with her white blouse—it needed ironing after it was washed and Shelby was very nearly allergic to ironing.

In the end she decided on a white no-iron T-shirt that she could easily wash, snatch out of the dryer, smooth out, and put back in her drawer.

Shelby heard the rise and fall of feminine voices as soon as she neared the church hall. The chatter reached a crescendo when she pushed open the door to the large room that functioned as an auditorium, a place to hold the annual pancake supper, a venue for coffee and doughnuts after the Sunday service, and an exercise room where Miss Dalyrimple held weekly yoga classes for seniors.

The sexton had set up a long table in the center of the room with a row of folding chairs on either side. Boxes of envelopes and stacks of letters were neatly lined up down the center.

"There you are, dear," Mrs. Willoughby said when she looked up and spied Shelby standing by the door. "Come in, come in. Please take a seat—it's time we got started. They'll be needing the room later this afternoon for the monthly Mothers Coffee."

Shelby slipped into a vacant seat between Coralynne and Margie Dale, who worked part-time behind the counter at the Lovett General Store and with whom Shelby had a nodding acquaintance.

"So, Mrs. Willoughby wrangled you, too," Margie said, leaning close to Shelby.

She was a tiny woman who looked like she'd been left out in the sun too long—her skin was rough and wrinkled and resembled the dried-up bed of a river.

"Mrs. Willoughby takes no prisoners," Shelby whispered back.

"Now that everyone is here"—Mrs. Willoughby paused dramatically, her hands clasped in front of her ample chest—"I will explain how things are going to work. We're going to have a sort of production line. Person number one will take a letter." She picked one up and waved it around. "Their job will be to fold the letter." She folded the letter in thirds and held it up. "Like this. You will then pass it to the next person, who will insert it into an envelope and then remove the protective strip on the flap and seal it."

Mrs. Willoughby picked up an envelope and tried to insert the letter, but it kept getting caught at the edge. Shelby had to put a hand to her mouth to hide the smile she couldn't quell.

Mrs. Willoughby finally managed to insert the letter into the envelope, and she waved it in the air again. "Next—the label." She peeled a label from one of the printed sheets stacked on the table. "You will affix the label. Always being careful to center it properly." She once again held the envelope up for everyone to see. "The final step will be adding the postage stamp, which will be the job of the last person in the line."

Everyone began to talk at once, and Mrs. Willoughby cleared her throat forcefully. "We will rotate positions every fifteen minutes so that no one has the chance to get bored. That's when slipups happen."

Margie rolled her eyes. "Says who?" she whispered to Shelby. "You'd think we were on the factory line at General Motors."

Shelby half expected Mrs. Willoughby to blow a whistle to indicate they should start but she settled for clapping her hands and trilling *let's begin*.

Mrs. Willoughby, Shelby noticed, hadn't assigned a task to herself but was acting as a sort of quality control manager, inspecting each envelope before placing it into a large bin.

Conversation swirled around Shelby as she stuffed letters into envelopes and sealed them, and she was only half listening when Mrs. Willoughby's voice rose above the rest.

"That was quite something at the pie contest at the fair on Sunday, wasn't it?" She looked at the group assembled around the table. "I don't imagine anything like that has ever happened before."

"How is Isabel? Have you heard?" Coralynne turned toward Mrs. Willoughby, momentarily forgetting the letter in her hands, thereby slowing down the entire production line.

Mrs. Willoughby waved at her to continue with the task at hand. "Reverend Mather had a call from the hospital. Isabel is fine. She was released shortly after she was brought in."

"I wonder what caused that terrible reaction. Was it an allergy?" Coralynne absentmindedly fiddled with the piece of paper in her hand.

Mrs. Willoughby gave her a stern look, and Coralynne put the letter down and smoothed it out carefully.

"You won't believe it," Mrs. Willoughby said.

She paused until everyone around the table was nearly quivering with anticipation.

"Jenny Hubbard's lemon meringue pie had been doctored."

A collective gasp rose from the women around the table.

"What do you mean—doctored?" Betty Duffy asked. She had tightly permed gray hair and clear blue eyes.

"Doctored," Mrs. Willoughby repeated with relish.

"With what?" Margie asked with a trace of irritation in her voice.

"Pepper," Mrs. Willoughby pronounced with a flourish. "The pie was laced with pepper."

"Who would do such a thing!" Coralynne said, her face flushing with excitement. "What I wonder," she said in a sly voice, "is whether or not Jenny Hubbard had a reason to dislike Isabel." She looked at the others gathered around the table as if seeking affirmation.

"But who's to say that Daniel wouldn't have taken the first bite? Or you, Mrs. Willoughby?" Shelby pointed out.

"Yes," Margie said. "Did Jenny have some reason to dislike you?" She looked pointedly at Mrs. Willoughby.

Mrs. Willoughby dropped the envelope she was holding and had to bend down to get it. The unaccustomed exercise caused her face to turn red and her breath to come in audible gasps.

"It seems more likely that someone wanted Jenny Hubbard to lose the pie contest this year," Shelby said, sealing her envelope and passing it to Margie for a label.

"I think you're right," Coralynne declared, and Mrs. Willoughby gave her a displeased look. "The pies were sitting out on the table for at least half an hour. It wouldn't have been difficult for someone to come along and dump some pepper onto Jenny's lemon meringue."

"I hadn't thought of that," Mrs. Willoughby conceded. "But who? Who would do such a thing?"

"Someone who wanted to win the contest themselves," Betty said in her soft voice.

"Who did win the competition? I wasn't there," Margie said, sticking a label on the envelope Shelby had handed her.

"Tonya Perry," Mrs. Willoughby said. "With her rhubarb pie."

Margie shuddered. "I can't stand rhubarb. My mother used to make rhubarb pie all the time. She would tell me it was cherry, but as soon as I took a bite, I knew what it was."

"Don't you think it odd that Tonya wasn't there to get her ribbon when the prizes were handed out?" Coralynne asked no one in particular.

"Very peculiar, if you ask me," Mrs. Willoughby said.

"I don't like to jump to conclusions—" Coralynne began before Mrs. Willoughby interrupted her.

"Maybe Tonya was the one who added the pepper to

Jenny's pie. She might have been determined to win the contest this year."

"It wouldn't surprise me," Margie said. "Given her behavior lately."

"I know." Mrs. Willoughby blew out a gust of air, causing her tightly curled bangs to quiver. "I blame Daniel, too, you know."

Shelby felt like she was in a play where everyone knew the lines except her.

"What does Reverend Mather have to do with it?"

Mrs. Willoughby and Coralynne exchanged a conspiratorial look.

"Daniel and Tonya have been . . . stepping out, as we used to call it."

Shelby was confused. "Daniel is widowed, and Tonya isn't married, so—"

"It's not seemly." Mrs. Willoughby's mouth snapped shut like a steel trap. "Not with Prudence barely in her grave."

"It's been a few months," Shelby protested.

Dear Reader, that's quite rich of me, don't you think? Given that I haven't let myself date yet even though it's been a few years now.

"Still," Mrs. Willoughby said as if that was that.

"But Daniel's not the sort who thrives as a bachelor," Coralynne put in. "He needs a woman to run the house and help out with parish duties."

"When I was growing up, our rector was a bachelor," Margie said. "And he managed just fine."

"Daniel's not the sort to manage on his own," Coralynne insisted. "I help out with the cleaning and cooking and such, and I can see how lost the poor man is . . .

wandering around the rectory in that old cardigan of his. I asked him to give it to me so I could mend it, but he wouldn't part with it. He has holes in his socks, too, no doubt."

"I don't know." Mrs. Willoughby shook her head.

The expression on her face made it clear she *did*, indeed, know. And she obviously didn't approve.

"So, it seems likely that Tonya is the one who ruined Jenny's lemon meringue pie," Margie said.

"It stands to reason, doesn't it?" Mrs. Willoughby said.

7

Dear Reader,

As the Bible verse reminds us, "To everything there is a season," and that couldn't be more true than on a farm. I've been working hard getting the gardens ready for the cooler-weather vegetables—working our home-made compost into the soil, removing any straggling plants whose season is over, and planting carrots, broccoli, cauliflower, radishes, and Brussels sprouts. Even if Billy refuses to go near Brussels sprouts. I've found chopping them and cooking them in butter and some bacon fat makes them more than palatable—they're actually quite delicious.

Those are the vegetables whose flavors are enhanced by cooler weather—even the slightest nip of a frost can bring out the best in them.

The house seemed so empty when Shelby got home despite the vociferous greeting she received from Jenkins and Bitsy. The two dogs wore themselves out jumping on her, wriggling against her legs, and wagging their tails. Both were now stretched out in a sunbeam, panting, their pink tongues stretched long and thin.

It always took Shelby a couple of weeks to get used to having the house to herself when the children went back to school. She missed the television blaring cartoons, Billy's shouts as he played with his cars and trucks, even Amelia's music seeping through the floor from upstairs.

Shelby's stomach growled and her thoughts turned toward food. She went into the kitchen, tied on her apron, and opened the refrigerator. There was some homemade Greek yogurt and a bit of roast chicken left over from another night. Neither appealed to her at the moment. She opened the produce drawer, but it was nearly empty. There were half a dozen large brown eggs she'd collected the day before from the Rhode Island Reds she kept out back by the barn. And a few pieces of bacon, but the thought of fried eggs and bacon didn't appeal, either.

Suddenly she had an idea. She went out the back door to the garden, where she picked a handful of leaves from a head of butter lettuce and carried them inside cupped in the bottom of her apron.

She would fry the bacon and cut it into lardoons for her salad. She would then make a dressing with the bacon fat, olive oil, and a dash of balsamic vinegar. And on top of the salad, like the cherry on top of an ice cream sundae, she'd carefully slip a poached egg.

The first bite convinced Shelby she was onto something. She quickly scribbled down the steps she'd taken to make the salad—she would share the recipe on her blog tomorrow.

She was chasing the last bit of lettuce around on her plate when the front doorbell rang. Shelby wiped her hands on her napkin and went to see who it was.

"Howdy." Her best friend, Kelly Thacker, was standing on the doorstep.

She smelled of horse, barnyard, and manure and there were bits of hay stuck in her tumble of auburn curls. Kelly was the local vet. She dealt mostly with farm animals but once a week she held a clinic for household pets.

"I was over at the Mingledorfs' farm, and I thought I would stop in," she said as she wiped her boots on Shelby's doormat. "Old Mr. Mingledorf was convinced that his cow was pregnant, so I did an exam and felt—" She stopped short at the look on Shelby's face.

Kelly loved sharing tales of her veterinary cases, but Shelby had finally convinced her to leave out some of the more delicate details.

"Anyway, the cow is pregnant and that made Mr. Mingledorf quite happy." Kelly dug some dirt out from under a fingernail. "He was all in a tizzy about Zeke Barnstable. Apparently he's known him since he was a kid, and he said he was practically a saint. As Mr. Mingledorf put it, 'there was no cause for him to go and get himself murdered.' As if poor Zeke had done it on purpose to upset him."

"I have to confess, I've had the same thought," Shelby said. "He was practically a recluse, from what I understand. Why would someone want to kill him? And who?" She took her dish to the sink, rinsed it, and put it in the dishwasher.

"I can tell you who," Kelly said. "Ryan Archer, for instance."

Shelby took a seat at the table again. "Who is Ryan Archer? I don't think I've ever heard of him."

"No reason you should have," Kelly said, fiddling with a pen Shelby had left on the kitchen table. "He's not someone who would pop up on your radar—he's younger than we are but older than Billy and Amelia."

"What's his connection with Zeke?"

"Zeke caught Ryan defacing a gravestone in the cemetery. Worse luck, it was Zeke's wife's grave, although everybody knows she's not really buried there. But he insisted on the headstone even though she hadn't been missing long enough to be declared dead."

"I can imagine that would have made Zeke want to kill this Ryan. But why would Ryan want to kill Zeke?"

"Zeke reported him even though Ryan begged him not to. He even said he would pay for the damage."

"What happened to him?"

"Ryan? He spent a month in jail and all the money he was saving to buy a car went to pay for cleaning the headstone and toward the hefty fine that had been levied against him."

Shelby looked at her friend in amazement. "How do you know all this?"

"Ryan's younger brother is a friend of my younger brother, Jacob," Kelly said. "Although Ryan's a couple of years older than him."

"He doesn't sound like someone you'd want your younger brother hanging out with."

Kelly rolled her eyes. "Jacob's a good kid. And he and Ryan aren't buddy buddies. A bunch of guys go around in a pack, like wolves, and Ryan sometimes hangs around the fringes."

Shelby grabbed a basket of peas off the counter and retrieved a bowl from the cupboard. She put the bowl in her lap and the basket on the table and began shelling the peas. They tumbled into the bowl, pinging like miniature green marbles.

"How's Seth?"

Seth was Kelly's fiancé and the local family doctor.

Kelly groaned. "Seth is fine, but his mother . . ."

Shelby reached for another pea pod. "What is Mrs. Gregson up to now?"

"What isn't she up to?" Kelly sighed. "It's about the wedding. She fails to understand that it's our wedding— we're paying for it, so we get to make the plans."

"Does she have ideas of her own?"

"Does she ever! She wants a formal sit-down affair with men in black tie and women in ball gowns. And those fiddly covers on the chairs, with the big bows in back. And a string quartet and huge centerpieces so that no one can see across the table. What doesn't she want?"

"Obviously you and Seth have different ideas."

Kelly held out her hands. "You know me, Shelby. I'm not that sort and frankly neither is Seth. Half the time I've got straw in my hair." Her hand went to her head reflexively and she shook loose a piece of hay, which she stuck in the corner of her mouth.

"I can't picture myself all done up in the gowns she's been showing me—huge tulle skirts, embellished with beads, crystals, and precious stones." She snorted. "I'd probably trip and rip my dress on the way to the altar."

"How do you picture your wedding?" Shelby popped three peas out of the pod she was holding.

Kelly's brows lowered over her eyes. "I haven't given it much thought. I've been too busy being horrified by Mrs. Gregson's suggestions." She crossed her arms over her chest. Suddenly she giggled. "Don't laugh but I imagine wearing my cowboy boots under my dress—a comfortable dress that I can hike up and dance in. And simple food like fried chicken or chicken-fried steaks with plenty of mashed potatoes and green beans cooked in bacon fat."

"So far it sounds great."

"And square dancing." Kelly's eyes were alight now. "And a make-your-own sundae bar with a whole bunch of homemade pies."

"Sounds perfect," Shelby said, sniffing back a tear.

Dear Reader, my wedding with Wild Bill had been much like that. How in love we'd been! We'd naively assumed we would be together forever.

"Where would you hold it?"

Kelly's shoulders slumped. "I don't know. Somehow the function room at the Comfort Inn out on the highway doesn't quite do it for me."

An idea was forming in Shelby's mind. *Why not?*

"Why not have it here at Love Blossom Farm?"

Kelly bolted upright in her chair. "Are you serious?"

"Absolutely. We could hold it in the barn. I've been planning on installing some electrical wiring anyway. And we can have a wooden dance floor brought in."

Now Kelly's eyes were shining. "That would be wonderful! I can picture it," she said, her gaze turning dreamy.

"But what would Mrs. Gregson say?"

Kelly lifted her chin. "I don't care what the old dragon

wants. If Seth likes the idea, and I like the idea, then that's what we'll do."

She jumped up and gave Shelby a hug, which nearly sent the peas in her bowl scattering to the four corners of the room.

"I can't thank you enough. It will be such fun! Seth and I would like to be married sooner rather than later—if we hope to start a family we've got to get a move on—and this way we won't have to deal with venues that insist you book three years in advance."

Kelly plopped down in her chair again. "I do hope Seth likes the idea."

8

||||||||||||||||||||||||||||

Dear Reader,

I love the idea of hosting Kelly's wedding here at the farm. I do hope Seth agrees with our plan. I have a feeling that even Mrs. Gregson would end up having fun. Who can resist square dancing?

And pies, and mashed potatoes, and fried chicken . . . Speaking of fried chicken—if you decide to make it, you'll want a bird that weighs no more than three and a half pounds. And after you coat it with flour the second time, let it rest on a rack for about twenty minutes. It needs to rest again after you've cooked it—set your oven to 250 degrees and let the chicken wait while you prepare the sides. And please, whatever you do, don't drain your fried chicken pieces on paper towels! That's how you get a soggy crust.

Speaking of sides—my favorites are vegetables straight from the garden dressed up with a little butter and a sprinkle of herbs.

The house seemed especially empty when Kelly left. Shelby smiled. Her friend had enough energy and vitality for several people.

Shelby was dusting the living room—a chore she'd neglected for far too long and she didn't want Bert taking her to task for it—when the doorbell rang. Bitsy and Jenkins, who had been sleeping peacefully moments before, occasionally opening an eye to see what Shelby was doing, bolted to their feet and made a beeline for the front door, scrunching the throw rugs under their paws as they ran.

Two visitors in one day—that was unusual. Bert would simply walk in, so it wasn't her. Shelby thought nothing of opening the door to a stranger—crime was rare in Lovett. *Except for the murder,* she thought, pausing with her hand on the doorknob.

In the end she yanked the door open to find a UPS deliveryman standing on the step with a large cardboard box next to him and a bored expression on his face.

His expression changed quickly to one of alarm as Bitsy and Jenkins arrived to check him out.

Shelby noticed beads of sweat forming on his forehead and took pity on him. She whistled and called the dogs to order—sort of. At least they stopped jumping on the poor man's leg.

"Don't worry. They're perfectly harmless," Shelby said although he clearly didn't believe her.

He quickly glanced down at his clipboard, obviously anxious to be on his way. "Ms. McDonald?"

"Yes."

"This here's for you." He nudged the box with his foot.

"Can you bring it inside?" Shelby asked as she tried to read the address label.

"Sure thing."

He picked the box up and, keeping an eye on the dogs, muscled it into Shelby's living room.

"If you'll sign here?" He handed her the clipboard.

Shelby scribbled her name, trying to remember what on earth she had ordered that was coming in such a large package. She handed the deliveryman the clipboard, showed him to the door, and shut it behind him.

By now she was dying of curiosity. She turned the box around so she could read the label. The return address was somewhere in Des Moines, Iowa, and the company was called Armor Cookware.

Now she remembered! Their marketing department had asked her to become a spokesperson for their new line of cookware. It was quite a feather in her cap, really. Her blog was obviously hitting the big time. And she was going to be paid. The thought of Billy's hospital bill crossed her mind. The money was definitely going to come in handy.

Of course, she'd insisted on trying out the new pots and pans before agreeing to the deal. Her reputation was at stake here—her readers trusted her and they trusted her opinion. She couldn't let them down.

Shelby sighed. She hadn't realized they would be sending quite so much. But she could always donate the merchandise when she was done.

She only hoped she liked the company's product.

Because if she didn't, she would have to turn the offer down.

|||||||||||||||||||||||||||

Shelby thought about what Kelly had told her as she vacuumed the living room and foyer—about Ryan Archer. So, Zeke did have at least one enemy after all. She could imagine that Ryan had been very angry with Zeke—a month in the county jail must not have been particularly pleasant for such a young man. And then a fine on top of that. But would Ryan have wanted to compound the crime by resorting to murder?

It was possible. Shelby had lived long enough to learn that anything was possible. Fortunately it wasn't her problem—she would leave the police work to Frank.

Shelby was wrapping the cord around the vacuum cleaner when the back door opened and slammed shut again.

"Mom, I'm home," Billy called from the kitchen. "And I'm hungry."

Shelby smiled. Lately Billy was always hungry. She suspected he would soon have another growth spurt.

He was standing in front of the refrigerator with the door open when she walked into the kitchen. Her first instinct was to give him a hug, but she knew better than to even try. Hugs were now reserved for special occasions such as birthdays and Christmas. Her baby was growing up and it made her more than a little sad.

She made Billy a peanut butter and jelly sandwich, which he wolfed down while barely taking a breath.

Dear Reader, it was my prizewinning jelly. Is it okay

if I glow a little? I'm still excited about my blue ribbon. I hope I never get too jaded to be thrilled by something like that.

Billy disappeared upstairs and Shelby heard the door to his room close. Very shortly afterward the back door opened and slammed shut again with even more vigor than when Billy had arrived home.

Amelia. Shelby turned around to say hello to her daughter—hugs were entirely out of the question as far as Amelia was concerned as well—when she stopped short. Amelia's face was red and tear streaked.

Amelia pulled a tissue from her pocket and blew her nose.

"Is something wrong?" Shelby ventured as delicately as possible.

"No." Amelia gave a huge sniff followed by a hiccough.

"Something is wrong," Shelby insisted.

Amelia flung herself into her mother's arms, astonishing Shelby to no end.

"Mr. Campbell accused me of cheating," Amelia said, her voice rising to a wail.

"What?"

Amelia burrowed farther into Shelby's shoulder. "I didn't cheat. I didn't."

Shelby put out a hand and tentatively stroked Amelia's hair. "I know you didn't. You would never do that. Mr. Campbell is mistaken."

"She copied from my paper."

"Who is *she*?" Shelby continued to stroke Amelia's hair, surprised her daughter hadn't made a peep of protest about this unaccustomed intimacy.

"Brittany Morse."

"You have to tell Mr. Campbell what you've told me. He needs to know who's really at fault. He won't be doing Brittany Morse any favors by letting her get away with cheating."

"I can't," Amelia wailed. "I just can't."

"Of course you can."

Amelia shook her head back and forth, rubbing her face against Shelby's shoulder. "You don't understand."

Shelby tried to hide the sigh that was her automatic reaction to that statement. It was always *you don't understand*. As if she, herself, had never been young but was born a married mother with two children.

"Why can't you tell Mr. Campbell that you didn't cheat—that it was the other way around? This Brittany copied off of your paper."

"Do you know who Brittany Morse is?" Amelia pulled her head away from Shelby's shoulder and stared at her mother with an incredulous look on her face.

"Brittany Morse is, like, the most popular girl in our class . . . in the whole school!"

"What does that have to—"

"No one will ever talk to me again if I tell on her. I'll have to eat lunch all by myself or, worse yet, sit with nerds like Leslie Dowdle." Amelia gave a sob. "It's not fair!"

Dear Reader, Amelia is right—it's not fair that she should become an outcast because Brittany Morse is so popular. I suppose you think I should persuade her to talk to her teacher, but I know from experience that she's never going to listen to me no matter what I say.

꜏꜏꜏꜏꜏꜏꜏꜏꜏꜏꜏꜏꜏꜏꜏꜏

Shelby was working on another blog entry when she looked up at the clock. Almost dinnertime. She'd better get something started before Billy and Amelia came slinking downstairs, like ravenous lions, to pillage the refrigerator and cupboards of the small amount of junk food Shelby allowed in the house.

Dinner was going to be simple tonight—breaded and baked pork chops, scalloped potatoes, and a vegetable. She thought for a moment. Broccoli would be good—sautéed in some olive oil with a hint of garlic.

Her broccoli crop was still going strong. She had enough for their own use and plenty left over to take to the farmers' market.

Shelby paused and listened—it was quiet up above. Amelia and Billy knew she expected them to be getting a start on their homework.

She opened the back door and stepped outside. Jenkins and Bitsy were right on her heels. Jenkins immediately charged under a bush—no doubt on the scent of some small creature that had already burrowed its way to safety.

Bitsy amused herself by chasing a monarch butterfly that easily eluded her and disappeared into a tree.

The breeze had picked up, and Shelby noticed the old wooden swing that hung by ropes from the apple tree just beyond the garden was moving back and forth as if pushed by an invisible hand. Her grandfather had rigged up that swing before she was even born. Her father had been the first to use it, she'd played on it herself, and then her children had taken it over.

On an impulse, Shelby went over to the swing and sat on it. The wooden board that served as a seat was bleached almost white by the sun and the rough edges had been smoothed down over the years.

She pushed off and gently swung to and fro. She gave another push and went a little higher, then pumped her legs until she really got going. Her hair blew in the wind and she relished that feeling in her stomach when the swing dropped—much like the sensation she enjoyed on a roller coaster.

Shelby was so engrossed in what she was doing, she didn't hear Jake approach. She was unaware of his presence until he put a hand against her back and gave her a push that sent her flying higher than ever.

She squealed with delight and let the sensation wipe out all her thoughts, cares, and worries. Suddenly a memory wriggled into her mind—Bill pushing her on this very same swing, then helping her off and wrapping his arms around her and lowering his lips toward hers.

Shelby put her feet down and dragged them in the hollow that had formed beneath the swing until she came to a halt. She twisted around and gave Jake an apologetic smile.

She was taken aback. He seemed different tonight—his characteristic electric energy had been drained out of him and he looked white and strained.

He gave Shelby a tight smile. "I wanted to bring over some milk and thought I'd better make sure this was a good time. Then I saw you on the swing and . . ." He shrugged apologetically.

"Yes, that's fine," Shelby stammered, not sure how to ease the suddenly awkward moment. She hesitated. "Is everything okay?" She slipped off the swing and turned to face Jake.

"Not really. I'm sure it won't amount to anything, but it's disconcerting being suspected of murder by the police. I have to say that's a first."

"What? Why on earth would they suspect you? That's ridiculous. Did you even know Zeke?"

Jake traced a circle in the dirt with the toe of his boot. "His land abuts my pasture, so sure, I knew him."

"And just because you're neighbors, the police think you killed him?"

"Not exactly. Do you remember the incident at the pie contest?"

Shelby nodded. "Yes. I was there."

"The whole squad went running over to the tent when they got the emergency call. Except me. I'd forgotten some gear in my car and I went to get it. There were already more than enough people to handle the situation. They didn't need me."

"Did anyone see you at your car?"

Jake gave a brief laugh. "Let's hope so." He kicked at the dirt. "Because if anyone tells the police about the fight between me and Zeke, I'm done for."

Shelby felt herself go still. "A fight?"

"Zeke thought the runoff from my fields had tainted his well water." Jake looked down at his feet. "And I accused him of stealing one of my cows. There are plenty of people unscrupulous enough to buy a cow at a good price even if it has someone else's brand on it."

"Does anyone know you two had this fight?"

"It's possible. Zeke might have told someone."

"From what everyone has said, Zeke pretty much kept to himself."

"You could be right. I *hope* you're right."

Jake looked at Shelby and gave a forced smile. "I'm sorry. I don't mean to sound so negative."

Jake was looking over Shelby's shoulder, toward her house, when the expression on his face suddenly changed and he froze.

Shelby spun around to see Frank standing outside her mudroom door. With his baseball cap tilted low over his face and his arms crossed over his chest, his resemblance to his brother was startling. Shelby almost took a step toward the house before realizing it wasn't Bill.

Jake was scowling. "I'd better go. I'll bring the milk around tomorrow, okay?"

"Sure."

Jake walked away, his steps speeding up until he was almost trotting as he neared the fence separating Love Blossom Farm from his pasture.

Shelby hurried toward where Frank was standing, his arms still crossed in front of him.

"Mind if we go inside?" he said when Shelby reached him.

He held the door as Shelby walked ahead of him through the mudroom and into the kitchen.

"Would you like a cold drink? I have iced tea, lemonade . . ." Shelby opened the refrigerator. "And a bottle of beer." She grabbed it by the neck and pulled it out.

Frank smiled and held out his hand. "Just what the doctor ordered," he said as he twisted the top off and took a long drink.

He wiped the back of his hand across his mouth. "I needed that."

Shelby poured herself a glass of iced tea and took the seat opposite Frank.

"The divorce is final," he said after a long pause. "Today. It's over."

"I'm sorry," Shelby said.

Frank shook his head. "Don't be. At first it was what Nancy wanted, but I've had time to think, and I've realized that things weren't working out and were probably never going to work out." He took another sip of his beer and put the bottle down on the table. "We gave it a shot, and that's that."

He leaned his chair back and balanced on two legs.

"I'm sorry" was all Shelby could think to say.

"Like I've told you, there's only one woman I've ever really been in love with."

Frank looked at Shelby so intently that she had to turn away.

"I need to start dinner. The kids will be getting hungry."

Frank let his chair drop back into place. He jerked his head toward the mudroom door. "You might want to stay clear of that fellow next door."

"Jake? Why?"

"We don't have much to go on yet, but there's a chance he was involved in Zeke Barnstable's murder."

Shelby had thought Jake was exaggerating the police's interest in him, but apparently not.

"I don't believe it."

"Do me a favor, would you?" Frank smiled. "I promised my brother I'd look out for you and the kids." He drained the last of his beer. "Steer clear of him until we

know more, okay? We already know he had the means—
we just don't know what his motive might have been."

*Dear Reader, it was one of those moments when ev-
erything goes still, sounds are amplified, and you can
hear your own heart beating.*

Shelby knew what Jake's motive might have been. She
couldn't imagine Jake . . . or anyone . . . murdering over
a stolen cow, but stranger things had happened.

She knew she ought to tell Frank about Jake and Zeke,
but she was positive Jake didn't have anything to do with
Zeke's death, so that would only be sending Frank on a
wild-goose chase.

Wouldn't it?

9

Dear Reader,

We've had a barn owl living in the corner of our barn for quite some time. The children named him Elvis. Don't ask me why. Maybe it's his soulful dark eyes in that white face. We don't catch too many glimpses of him, but we can hear his screeching cry at night as he hunts for rodents and other small creatures. Elvis's call used to scare the children when they were little, but they are used to it now.

Patches, our calico, once got too near the spot where Elvis had built his nest and Elvis let out an angry hiss that had Patches flying out of the barn with comical speed. Patches now steers a wide berth around that corner.

Elvis's night vision is excellent—certainly better than that of old Mrs. Wolfenbarger, who thought her mailbox was a stalker and called the police. But his hearing far surpasses even his vision and is what enables him to catch mice and other animals even when they are hiding in dense grasses. And get this—he swallows his prey whole. Yes, I agree, that is quite disgusting when you think about it. Come to think of it, that's kind of how Billy eats—I'm always having to remind him to chew his food!

It was still dark when Shelby opened the back door and headed toward the barn, although the sky to the east was lightening.

The barn door squeaked loudly as she opened it and Shelby cringed. She knew there was no one to wake out here—goodness knew the chickens were already up, pawing the ground, waiting for their morning meal. Nonetheless, Shelby made a mental note to take the oil can to the door as soon as possible.

Jack Sparrow, Love Blossom Farm's elderly rooster, strutted around and around in a circle as if he was trying to corral the chickens into some form of order. For the most part they ignored him, all their attention focused on Shelby and the metal pail over the crook of her arm.

She threw seed in a wide arc and watched as the chickens pecked at their breakfast. The morning was quiet and the air had a coolness and freshness that the sun would chase away as the day wore on.

Shelby finished with the chickens and headed back toward the house. She made another mental note to stop at the Lovett Feed Store soon—her stock of feed for the chickens was getting low. She passed the herb garden and noticed some weeds poking out between the stalks of rosemary and clumps of thyme. She stopped, knelt down, and began pulling them out. There was something about the task that was inherently very soothing, Shelby thought, and the more you did, the more you wanted to do.

She was tempted to linger even longer, but she knew she'd better be getting back to make sure the children were up and getting ready for school. The sky was already considerably lighter than it had been when Shelby left the house.

Amelia was sitting at the kitchen table, eating a piece of apple pie left over from the night before. Shelby raised her eyebrows and opened her mouth but then shut it. There were more important battles ahead to be fought— Amelia wouldn't develop scurvy or malnutrition from one breakfast of pie.

Billy was nowhere to be seen . . . or heard.

"Where's your brother?" Shelby asked as she measured coffee grounds into the coffeemaker.

Amelia shrugged, picked up her phone, and began punching keys. Shelby gritted her teeth. The phone had been a present from her parents, and while she liked being able to track Amelia down when necessary, her daughter's constant obsession with it was driving her crazy.

She was at the foot of the stairs, calling for Billy, when the front door opened and Bert walked in, carrying the newspaper under her arm.

Bert jerked a thumb over her shoulder. "Saw the school bus go by. Looks like Billy missed it if you're only just calling him now."

Dear Reader, this is the kind of thing that makes me

feel like a terrible mother. Looks like I'll be driving Billy to school.

Shelby heard the water go on in the upstairs bathroom. Maybe Billy was up after all. She hoped he'd hurry—they still might make it on time for the first bell.

"I don't know what the world is coming to," Bert said as she slapped the newspaper down on the kitchen table.

"I assume you're talking about the murder at the fair?"

"Well, that, too, but I was thinking about yesterday. I stopped by the Lovett General Store to pick up a couple of pork chops and some oil for my sewing machine. I parked my car in back like I normally do, and when I came out, there was a dent in the passenger-side door. It looked like somebody might have opened their own door too fast, and they hit mine. But no note!" Bert threw her hands up in the air. "Nothing. Heck, they had to know I was still in the store. There were only half a dozen cars in the lot. How hard would it be to track down the owner of the car you'd just dinged?"

"That's awful," Shelby said, grabbing a bowl from the cupboard and filling it with cereal.

"People today have no moral scruples at all." Bert gestured toward the newspaper. "You've only got to read the front page of the paper to see that."

"Morning," Billy mumbled as he walked into the kitchen and sat down at the table.

Shelby pushed the bowl of cereal in front of him and handed him the milk.

"I'm going to have to take you to school today. Bert says you've missed the bus."

"That's okay," Billy said, spooning up a large portion of cereal. "Jake said he could take me anytime."

"You can't keep bothering Jake. He has work to do."

"I already called him and he said it was okay."

Bert looked at Shelby and raised an eyebrow.

"Don't you start," Shelby said to Bert as she turned her back.

Billy was taking the last bite of his breakfast when there was a honk from the driveway.

"Gotta go. Bye, Mom. Bye, Bert." He swiped his napkin across his mouth and dashed toward the door, slamming it behind him.

Shelby gave Bert a look that said, *Don't you dare say anything.*

Bert shrugged and reached for the apron on the hook by the back door.

"I already told you what I think. Whether you listen or not is up to you." Bert put her hands on her hips. "How about we get to putting up that pepper relish you wanted to try selling at the general store?"

Shelby was more than happy to get out the supplies she needed—celery seed, sugar, mustard seeds, turmeric, tarragon—and avoid any further discussion of her next-door neighbor and her relationship with him—or lack thereof.

Shelby was chopping the peppers while Bert measured out the vinegar and herbs and spices when Amelia dashed into the kitchen.

"Do you want something to eat?" Shelby said.

"Can't. I'm going to be late." Amelia grabbed an apple out of the bowl on the kitchen table. "Bye, Mom. Bye, Bert."

She blew her mother a quick kiss as she bolted from the kitchen.

Shelby was startled. That was the most affection Amelia

had shown her since she entered her preteen years. Maybe the phase was almost over?

"Have you ever heard of a kid named Ryan Archer?" she asked Bert.

Bert paused with the jar of mustard seeds in her hand. "Archer? That would be Dick Archer's son. Why?"

Shelby tried to sound as casual as possible. "Oh, Kelly mentioned that he was caught defacing the headstones in the cemetery."

"Yes. And it was Zeke Barnstable who caught him and turned him in." Bert turned to face Shelby with her hands on her hips. "Do I need to remind you of what happened the last time you decided to meddle in a murder case?" Bert grunted. "You nearly got yourself killed, remember?"

"I know. I'm curious, that's all."

"Ryan Archer is an odd duck. Not surprising, given his family. His mother was Amish but ran off with his father when she was only sixteen. She came from Centreville, down in St. Joseph County. As you can imagine, she was shunned by the rest of the family, and here Dick Archer was an only child with rather elderly parents. No relatives to speak of." Bert measured out a teaspoon of mustard seeds. "Dick Archer is a little odd, too. Some people say it's because of the horses he works with all the time and that one of them must have kicked him in the head, although I don't know that there's any truth to that."

"Why do you say Ryan's an odd duck?" Shelby dumped her pepper chunks into a pot and added the ingredients Bert had measured out for her.

"Basically he's a good kid, but then all of a sudden he'll go off and do something wild like defacing those headstones or breaking old Mrs. Wilson's window."

"But you don't think he's capable of murder?" Shelby asked as she adjusted the flame under the peppers.

Bert hesitated. "It's quite a leap from defacing gravestones to murder . . . but you never know, do you?"

"I guess not." Shelby selected a wooden spoon from the jar on her counter and stirred the peppers again. The fragrant steam rising from the pot was making her hungry, and she realized that she hadn't eaten anything yet.

"Is that a new pot?" Bert pointed toward the stove. She was wiping down the kitchen table and putting Amelia's plate and Billy's bowl in the dishwasher.

"Yes." Shelby stared at the pot. "It's a new line of cookware I've been asked to endorse on my blog."

Bert whistled. "Well, aren't we going big-time?"

Shelby grinned. "You got that right." Then her expression sobered. "Goodness knows the money will come in handy, what with the bills for Billy's arm. Then there'll be the Snow Ball at Amelia's school in December, and she'll want a new dress. We'll have to go down to Grand Rapids to shop at that mall there. Hopefully we'll find something she approves of on sale."

Bert snorted. "In my day, we wore what our mama sewed for us."

"Not anymore," Shelby said, opening the refrigerator. "It's all about keeping up with the Joneses. Are you hungry?"

"I could go for a little something."

Shelby pulled out a container of fresh milk that came from Jake's cows. "I made some granola yesterday. How does that sound?"

"Good. I'll get the place mats."

Shelby put the container of homemade granola on the table.

Dear Reader, you can make granola in your slow cooker. Did you know that? I used very little sugar and only a dash of maple syrup, so it's quite healthy. I'll post the recipe soon, I promise.

The pot on the stove had started to boil, and Shelby went to turn down the gas to a reasonable simmer. She gave the contents a stir and then stopped in horror. She pulled the spoon out of the pot and held it up.

"What's the matter?" Bert said.

Shelby shook her head and gave the contents another stir. Once again she removed the spoon and looked at it. She turned around to face Bert.

"Something's wrong. What is it? Did I measure out too much vinegar?"

"No, it's not that. Look." Shelby held the wooden spoon toward Bert.

"What's that?" Bert pointed toward some metallic-colored flakes mixed in with the peppers.

"It's the coating from the pot." Shelby dropped the wooden spoon on the counter. "The lining of the cookware is coming off."

Bert frowned. "That's not good."

"No, it isn't." Shelby plopped into a seat at the table and put her head in her hands. "What am I going to do?" She looked up at Bert. "I've already cashed the check for the endorsement." Shelby groaned. "I can't recommend this cookware on my blog. My readers trust me to tell them the truth."

"Maybe it's a fluke and it's only the one pot that's defective. I would wait to see how the others hold up before you decide."

"Good idea," Shelby said although she sincerely

doubted whether the other pots and pans would turn out to be any better.

|||||||||||||||||||||||||||

Shelby tried to put the murder out of her mind and take Bert's advice to leave the detective work to the police, but she couldn't help being curious.

Dear Reader, you would want to know the truth, wouldn't you? Especially if a friend of yours was being targeted as the prime suspect?

Shelby was on her way to the Lovett General Store to pick up a few things she needed. She tried to make do as much as possible with what she could grow on the farm but that wasn't always practical, of course. She couldn't provide her own meat, for instance, and Amelia was certainly not going to wear dresses made out of flour sacks like farmers' wives did in the old days.

Shelby passed the drive that led to the Tedfords' apple orchard. A crude wooden structure had been set up to serve as a farm stand where they were selling bushels of apples and Mrs. Tedford's homemade pies.

Seeing the pies made Shelby think of the pie contest at the county fair. Mrs. Willoughby was convinced that Tonya was the one who had put the pepper in Jenny Hubbard's lemon meringue pie. It was obvious to jump to the conclusion that it had been done to keep Jenny from winning the blue ribbon. But what if it had been done to create a diversion?

All the volunteer firemen had come running when Mrs. Willoughby called for help—*except for Jake,* a small voice in Shelby's head whispered. The car where Zeke's body was found was left unattended—had that been the real purpose behind the pepper stunt?

If that was the case, it couldn't have been Tonya who doctored the pie—what motive could she possibly have for murdering Zeke?

Shelby was still pondering that question as she pulled into the parking lot behind the Lovett General Store.

Matt Hudson was behind the counter, as usual. Shelby often wondered if he ever took a day off. He greeted her with a big smile that caused his eyes to crinkle at the corners.

"I'm sorry I never got to buy you that ice cream I'd promised you. When word spread about finding Zeke's body, a lot of people decided to leave, and they needed help directing traffic."

Shelby shivered at the image that came to mind. "I wish Billy hadn't had to see that."

"Fortunately kids are resilient."

"Frank said he was hit on the head."

"Yes." Matt straightened a display of mints next to the cash register. "I was there when they found the weapon later on."

"What was it?"

"Some kind of hammer. Dangerous-looking thing. I don't suppose there will be any fingerprints on it. Killers are too educated today to make a novice mistake like that."

"Unless it was a spur-of-the-moment act. Zeke had an argument with someone, and they grabbed the nearest thing to hand and conked him on the head."

"They did a pretty clever job of hiding the weapon, although I don't know why they didn't take it with them and toss it in a lake or river."

"I guess our killer wasn't that smart after all." Shelby pulled her shopping list out of her purse. "Where did they find the hammer?"

"You won't believe it. The Lovett police force isn't very large, so you can imagine it took quite some time. They searched for hours. And then some kid found it in one of the gondolas on the Ferris wheel." Matt leaned his elbows on the counter. "Pretty clever of the killer, if you ask me."

"How awful for that poor child."

Matt smiled. "I don't know. I imagine all his friends are going to be jealous that they weren't the ones to find the murder weapon."

Shelby thought of Billy and realized that Matt was probably right. He would be too young to fully understand the situation but would certainly glory in all the attention.

Matt fiddled with a pack of gum, turning it over and over in his hands. He cleared his throat.

"Margie ought to be here in . . ." Matt looked at his watch. "Ten minutes. Time enough for you to do your shopping, and then I can duck out for a few minutes and take you for a cup of coffee at the lovely Lovett Diner."

Shelby looked up from her shopping list. "Coffee? The diner?" She felt panicky. "I don't know. I have to—"

"Hey, if you don't want to, that's fine." Matt put the pack of gum back in the display rack. "It's only a cup of coffee. Not a commitment."

"Next time, okay?" Shelby said in desperation. That would give her time to think. And to get used to the idea of going out with someone.

Dear Reader, I can hear Bert's voice in my head telling me I need to move on. And I will, I promise. Just not today.

10

Dear Reader,

Did you know that a fresh egg will sink to the bottom of a bowl of water, an egg that is a couple of weeks old will stand on its end in the water, and a very old egg will float to the surface?

And if you're planning on cooking some eggs sunny-side up? A fresh yolk will stand up while an older one will flatten out. Ever crack open an egg and find a double yolker? Double- or triple-yolk eggs are usually found in young pullets around 20 to 28 weeks old. The probability of finding a multiyolk egg is estimated at 1 in 1000 overall but with a young pullet the odds are better—1 in 100. Some people say they're good luck, but I couldn't attest to that! I do know I like the yolk so it's a bonus when I crack an egg open and find two yolks inside.

Shelby was filthy. She was in the garden attacking the dirt with a hoe as if it was the enemy. If she worked hard enough and sweated enough, perhaps she could quiet the thoughts that went through her mind like a filmstrip. Her conversation with Matt had unsettled her. She felt bad for turning down his invitation for coffee—heck, it wasn't as if he was asking her to move in with him—and she was disturbed by the fact that Frank's face kept coming to mind. She pushed the unwelcome thoughts as far away as she could and raised the hoe over her head again. She was preparing to plant some mesclun, spinach, and mâche—crops that would grow in the cooler weather of a Michigan September.

Shelby was kneeling in the dirt, carefully nestling the delicate plants in the aerated soil, when the cell phone in her pocket vibrated. She pulled off her gloves and yanked it out. A call during the day was unusual—she always worried that something had happened to one of the children at school.

Fortunately it was Kelly on the other end of the line asking Shelby if she could meet for a quick bite for lunch at the diner. She wanted to hammer out some more wedding details before she talked to Seth about the possibility of holding the reception in Shelby's barn.

Shelby felt guilty agreeing—she'd turned Matt down on the pretense of having a lot of work to do. Which she did. But what woman could ever resist talking about weddings?

Shelby finished the row she had been planting and returned the hoe to the barn. She glanced down at herself. There was no way she could leave the farm looking the way she did. A shower was certainly in order.

Shelby was surprised that the water in the shower didn't turn to mud, considering the amount of dirt she'd tracked inside with her. She'd long ago given up on keep ing the inside of the farmhouse as spick-and-span as the places you saw pictured in magazines. She was all about comfort, and if that included a little bit of clean dirt—so what? Because Shelby truly believed in the concept of clean dirt—earth from the garden was definitely clean dirt. Dirt picked up on your shoes from walking city streets or through parking lots or from the unwashed tile floor in the bathroom at the bus station was dirty dirt.

Fortunately Kelly's idea of dressing was grabbing the nearest pair of jeans and yanking a clean T-shirt out of the laundry basket, so Shelby didn't have to worry about how she looked. She pulled her damp hair back in a ponytail, fished a cleanish pair of jeans from her closet along with a plaid cotton shirt, and deemed herself ready for anything the Lovett Diner could dish up.

::::::::::::::::::::::::::::

Kelly had offered to pick Shelby up since she would be passing Love Blossom Farm on her way back from a veterinary call. Shelby was more than happy to accept since it would save on gas. The needle on her car's fuel gauge was a little too close to the *E* for comfort, but she was trying to get by for as long as possible.

A friendly toot on the horn announced Kelly's arrival. Shelby picked up her purse and headed toward the front door. Bitsy and Jenkins were sprawled on the sofa, sound asleep. Jenkins twitched in his sleep and his paws moved as if he was on the trail of a particularly juicy rodent. Shelby looked at their muddy paws and cringed. But as

Bert always said, you could have a nice house or you could have children and pets. And there was no question which one Shelby favored.

Kelly was standing outside her truck, leaning against the side. She was wearing jeans and a black T-shirt with *Go-Pro Dog Chow* in white letters across the front. As Shelby got closer she noticed the faint aroma of manure, but fortunately, that was a scent that didn't bother her at all—it was synonymous with home and Love Blossom Farm.

Shelby opened the passenger door of Kelly's truck.

"Here, let me get that out of the way."

Kelly pulled a large black canvas bag off the seat and took it around to the back of the truck. She slipped into the driver's seat.

"I don't know about you, but I'm ready for some food," Kelly said as she started the car.

The parking lot of the diner was filled with pickups and two tractor-trailers that took up four spaces at the end when Shelby and Kelly arrived. They managed to grab a booth in the back. A pair of truckers was sitting at the counter, wolfing down the diner's famous biscuits and gravy. They didn't talk to each other, but Shelby got the impression that they knew they were kindred spirits.

A handful of Lovett denizens was scattered among the booths, clad in dungarees, denim overalls, and plaid shirts, their hands rough and callused from hard work. Heavy white mugs filled with coffee were at their elbows and full plates of sliced turkey with gravy on toast or chicken potpies sat in front of them.

Shelby and Kelly each ordered iced tea and a chicken salad sandwich, then settled back in their seats to gossip and chat.

The waitress whizzed by their table and plunked down two glasses of iced tea. Kelly took a long gulp of hers. "I've been dying of thirst. It was so hot out at the Meyerlings' farm. I usually carry a couple of bottles of water in the truck, but I forgot to grab some this morning."

Kelly took another long gulp of her drink, nearly draining the glass. "I had to vaccinate a number of the Meyerlings' cows—don't want them getting IBR."

"What on earth is that?" Shelby asked, glad that she wasn't in the business of raising cattle.

"*IBR* is short for *infectious bovine rhinotracheitis*, also known as red nose."

"That's certainly a little easier to pronounce."

"It's a highly contagious respiratory infection. The nose and muzzle often become inflamed, which is how it got the nickname of red nose." Kelly leaned back in her seat as the waitress slid a plate in front of her. "Anyway, I'm sure you don't want to hear about that."

Dear Reader, what's that saying? Truer words were never spoken.

Shelby put her napkin in her lap and took a bite of her sandwich.

"I really want to tell Seth about our wedding idea, but I'm afraid he's going to shoot it down, and I'll be disappointed."

"I think Seth would do anything you wanted. He's crazy in love with you. Seriously," Shelby added when she saw the doubtful look on Kelly's face.

They continued discussing the wedding as they finished their sandwiches.

"So, you don't think having those portable toilets is

going to put people off?" Kelly asked as she pushed her plate away.

"No, not at all. For weddings they make special white ones with mirrors, hand sanitizers, lights—the works."

"That doesn't sound too bad. Although I'm sure Mrs. Gregson will turn her nose up at them."

"She's welcome to use the powder room in the house if that makes you feel any better."

Kelly was about to answer when her cell phone rang. She mouthed *sorry* at Shelby and put the phone to her ear.

"Have you listened to his gut?" Kelly asked after listening briefly. "Okay, I'll be right out."

She clicked off the call and replaced the phone in her pocket.

"I'm sorry." Kelly looked at Shelby. "It was Jim Harris. One of his horses has colic. Colic isn't necessarily serious, but I don't like the sound of this. There can be a twist in the bowel that requires immediate attention. If that's the case, there's no time to waste." Kelly frowned. "I'll drop you off at home and then head out to the Harrises'."

"I'll come with you," Shelby said decisively.

Kelly breathed out a sigh that sounded like relief. "Thanks. It's probably only ordinary gassy colic, but I'd hate to see someone lose a horse because I was wrong."

||||||||||||||||||||||

It was hot on the ride out to the Harrises' stables. They had the windows rolled down and the scent of newly mown grass mingled with hay drifted into the cab of the truck.

Kelly glanced at Shelby and sighed. "Jim Harris still owes me for my last visit out to the stables. I'm letting it slide because he's always been good for it. He seems to have hit some hard times lately."

Shelby knew Kelly wasn't the first person to extend credit to someone who was momentarily down on their luck. People ran a tab at the Lovett General Store, which they paid off when their crop came in. The pediatrician who treated Amelia and Billy the time they both came down with bronchitis let Shelby pay the bill in installments. Even the plumber and the electrician were known to accept payment for a bill in produce, fresh eggs, or milk.

The smell of horse became stronger as they turned into the drive leading to the Harrises' stables. They passed a modest but tidy white house with red geraniums in planters and an American flag hanging from a flagpole out front. The drive wound around the house toward the stables in back.

Kelly stopped the truck in the small graveled parking area in front of the stable. A van was already parked there. It was an unusual-looking vehicle. The side was lifted up to reveal a large amount of equipment that Shelby didn't recognize.

Kelly must have noticed her puzzled look.

"That's the farrier's van. He brings his shop with him when he makes a call."

Jim Harris came around the side of the stable and walked toward Kelly's truck. He looked worried—his brow furrowed and his mouth clenched in a thin, straight line.

"I'll wait here," Shelby said as Kelly opened her door. "You go on ahead."

"Okay." Kelly jumped out of the truck and walked over to where Harris was waiting for her.

Shelby sat for a moment, but it was hot inside the truck. There was a large shade tree off to the side of the drive with a weathered-looking picnic table underneath that seemed very inviting.

As Shelby got out of the truck she noticed the writing on the back of the farrier's van. It read ARCHER'S FARRIER SERVICE.

The shade under the tree and the soft breeze felt heavenly after the stuffiness of the truck. Shelby sat on the bench in front of the picnic table and stretched out her legs. She had a million things to take care of on the farm, but it felt good to be resting and doing nothing for a change. She wasn't going to allow herself to feel guilty about it.

Shelby closed her eyes and was almost drifting off when the sound of voices caught her attention. A man wearing a canvas apron with various tools sticking out of the pockets was walking toward the farrier's van.

A woman was with him. Shelby recognized her as Mrs. Harris. They'd never met but Shelby had seen her around the house when she brought Billy for his riding lessons. She was as thin and wiry as her husband, with faded blond hair cut short.

Their voices carried over to where Shelby was sitting.

"I can't imagine what's become of my hammer," the farrier said to Mrs. Harris.

Shelby supposed he was Mr. Archer, the owner of the van. She wondered if he was a relative of Ryan Archer, or maybe even his father.

"It's not like me to lose a tool or a piece of equipment," Archer said. "A place for everything and everything in its place, I always say."

"I imagine you'll have to come back," Mrs. Harris said.

Archer shook his head. "Nah, I'll call my boy and get him to bring me another hammer. I have a spare back in the shop."

He pulled out his cell phone and punched in some numbers. He turned his back to Shelby, and she couldn't hear what he was saying.

Archer disappeared back into the stable, and Mrs. Harris walked off toward the house. Shelby closed her eyes and was once again drifting off when the throb of rock music woke her. A car was speeding down the drive with the windows open and the radio blaring.

Ryan Archer? she wondered.

The car came to a sudden halt, gravel spitting out from under its tires. Shelby doubted that Ryan had been driving so fast because he was anxious to fulfill his father's request.

Ryan opened his door and ambled toward the stables, the hammer in his hand by his side.

Shelby gave herself a shake and stood up. If she sat under the tree any longer she would fall asleep for sure. She wandered over toward Ryan's car. It was a second-hand car or possibly even third- or fourth-hand. A good portion of the left front fender had been eaten away by rust and huge swaths of paint were scraped off.

The interior wasn't in any better shape. The driver's seat was covered with a towel and the upholstery on the passenger seat was frayed with holes where the foam showed through.

In the passenger seat was a stuffed animal—a woolly mammoth just like the one Billy had hoped to win at the county fair.

So Ryan had been to the fair. Had he taken that opportunity to get back at Zeke for turning him in?

Shelby heard the crunch of gravel and looked up to see Ryan walking toward her. His head was down and his bangs flopped onto his forehead. They looked like they could have used a trim, and his skin was pockmarked as if he'd had acne when he was younger.

"Hi," Shelby said.

Ryan looked up and scowled.

Not the most personable kid on the planet, Shelby thought. She gestured toward the stuffed animal in his car.

"I see you've been to the county fair. My son really wanted to win one of those woolly mammoths."

"I didn't go," Ryan mumbled.

He wasn't personable and he was definitely a man of few words, Shelby thought.

"Oh," she said. "I've never seen a stuffed animal like that anywhere else. Did you buy it somewhere? I'd like to get one for my son for his birthday." She crossed her fingers behind her back.

Ryan shook his head. "Nah, I found it."

He walked around Shelby and got into the car. As soon as the engine turned over, he cranked up the radio and shot down the drive.

11

Dear Reader,

Kale is a vegetable that does well in cooler temperatures. Lacinato, or dinosaur kale, can even be harvested after a snowfall. Other varieties can handle a light frost. The young leaves are tender and perfect for a salad but the older leaves can be tough and bitter. But not if you massage them! I know that sounds weird, but it works. Remove the stems and chop the leaves, add some salt and olive oil, and massage the leaves between your fingers for a couple of minutes. They will turn silky and sweet.

Billy still won't eat it, but I love it that way. Kale is packed full of nutrients in every bite. You can also use the greens in soups or, baked or sautéed in olive oil, as a side dish.

Kale chips are the latest craze and so easy to make! You might even fool your kids into eating them. Drizzle torn pieces of kale with olive oil, sprinkle with salt, and bake for ten to fifteen minutes, then enjoy!

Kelly had just dropped Shelby off at home when she remembered she needed to stop at the Lovett Feed Store for more feed for the chickens. She'd have to trust that she could make the trip on the gas fumes left in the car. Her old pickup truck was in need of fuel as well and Shelby usually only used it for trips to the farmers' market.

Events had turned out well at the Harrises' stables. Kelly had been a bit alarmist in suspecting the horse had a twisted bowel—it turned out to be ordinary colic, soon cured with a dose of mineral oil.

Seeing Ryan Archer with that toy woolly mammoth had been a bonus, Shelby thought. Now she knew he had both motive and opportunity. He claimed not to have been at the fair, but it was easy enough to lie about it and the stuffed animal proved it.

He certainly had more motive than Tonya Perry. Most likely the pepper had been sprinkled on Jenny Hubbard's lemon meringue pie to eliminate her from the competition and not to create a diversion for the murderer.

Shelby sighed with relief when she pulled into the parking lot of the feed store. The needle on her gas gauge was quivering over the *E*, and she was counting on the fact that there was usually a little more gas in the tank than was indicated by the gauge.

The feed store was unusually quiet, with dust motes dancing in the beam of sunlight coming through one of the small windows on the side. A young man in a canvas apron approached Shelby and asked if she needed help. She gave him her order and he grabbed a nearby handcart and went off in search of the bags of feed she was looking for.

Shelby went to the front counter to pay. The clerk at the cash register had lank brown hair in need of washing and nails that were bitten to the quick. Shelby glanced at her name tag and saw it read REBECCA. This must be Zeke's sister.

"Whatcha got?" the woman asked Shelby.

"Two fifty-pound bags of Blue Seal chicken feed."

The woman punched some numbers into the register. "That'll be thirty-six dollars and eighty one cents."

Shelby dug her wallet out of her purse. She hesitated for a moment.

"You're Zeke Barnstable's sister, aren't you?"

The woman eyed Shelby suspiciously. "Yes."

"I'm very sorry for your loss."

Rebecca snorted. "Some loss," she said bitterly.

Shelby looked at her quizzically.

Rebecca shrugged. "My brother and I weren't close, you know? Still, I can't believe someone finally took him out."

She accepted the money Shelby held out toward her, put it in the cash register drawer, then ripped off the receipt that was ejected from the machine like a tongue. She handed it to Shelby.

"Zeke always did believe in an eye for an eye and a tooth for a tooth. There are many around here who still think he murdered Brenda, his wife." She pushed a piece of hair off her face and tucked it behind her ear. "Do you know Tonya Perry?"

"Sort of."

"Her and Brenda were good friends. Almost like sisters—did everything together. She's made no secret of the fact that justice wasn't done. If she had her way, they'd lock Zeke up and throw away the key."

"But why would Zeke kill his wife? Did they fight?"

Rebecca leaned her elbows on the counter. "Not really. Zeke could be jealous—not that there was much to be jealous of. How many men could Brenda meet working part-time at the Laundromat or sitting in her living room watching *Dancing with the Stars*? She loved that show. Never missed an episode."

One of the store managers appeared around the end of an aisle and Rebecca pushed off from the counter and moved back slightly. "Besides, Zeke took her disappearance hard. Of course no one can tell whether that's because he loved Brenda or because he missed having someone cook his meals and wash his clothes. That's what they all want, isn't it?"

Shelby didn't comment—she just smiled.

"But Tonya took it even harder than my brother."

The manager had disappeared down another aisle, and Rebecca leaned over the counter again. "I heard Tonya threaten to kill Zeke."

||||||||||||||||||||||||||

Shelby crossed her fingers, started up her car, and pulled out of the feed store parking lot. She'd certainly gleaned some interesting information. Not only did Tonya have a reason to kill Zeke; she'd actually been heard threatening to do just that. Shelby thought back to the pie contest at the fair where she'd first met Tonya. Tonya was a big woman who looked strong enough to hit Zeke over the head with a hammer and drag him into that old Volvo the firemen were using for their demonstration.

Had she been trying to cast suspicion on Jake by putting the body in the car? She probably knew about the animosity between Jake and Zeke from Brenda. She hadn't struck Shelby as being that clever or devious, but as the old saying went, you shouldn't judge a book by its cover.

On the other hand, Ryan Archer had lied about being at the fair. Why do that unless he was trying to cover up his guilt?

As Shelby pulled into the driveway she decided that she was glad she wasn't responsible for solving the case.

She was opening her trunk when a pickup truck pulled into the driveway behind her.

It was Frank. She wondered if there had been a break in the case.

She waited beside her car as Frank approached, his loping walk so like his brother's that grief momentarily washed over Shelby.

Frank pulled off his baseball cap. "Looks like you just got back. Been shopping?"

"Yes, but nothing very exciting—two bags of feed for the chickens."

"There's nothing very exciting to buy around here," Frank said, "unless you consider buying a new snow shovel exciting." He gestured toward Shelby's open trunk. "You're going to need some help with those."

Normally Shelby would have muscled the bags out of the car, inch by inch, and into a waiting wheelbarrow. It was a process that usually left her a panting, sweaty mess, so she was more than happy to let Frank do it for her.

"Wheelbarrow in the barn?"

"Yes."

"I'll take care of these, and then I'll be back."

The dogs were waiting by the back door when Shelby opened it. She crouched down and let them lick her face while she rubbed their heads. She could always depend on a warm welcome from Jenkins and Bitsy.

She washed her hands and opened the refrigerator. She got out a pitcher of lemonade and put it on the table along with some glasses.

Dear Reader, I'm rather nervous about what Frank has to tell me. Because I hope he doesn't still think that Jake is responsible for Zeke's death.

The door to the mudroom opened and Frank walked in. He pulled off his baseball cap and ran a hand over his head. Shelby noticed that his hair was thinning a bit in front. Would that have happened to Bill, too, if he'd lived?

"That sun sure is hot," Frank said, turning a kitchen chair around and straddling it. He pointed at the pitcher of lemonade. "Is some of that for me?'

"Help yourself." Shelby pushed a glass toward him.

Frank filled his glass, downed half of it in one gulp, and wiped his hand across his mouth.

"A couple of people have had their cars broken into in the parking lot of the Dixie Bar and Grill. It doesn't make sense—there's not much to steal out of most of the cars you'd find parked there. A radio, maybe. A handful of spare change left on the console? Heck, most people around here don't even have a functioning air conditioner." He picked up his glass and drained the other half of the lemonade.

Shelby pushed the pitcher toward Frank.

"And this murder case has me running around in

circles." He leaned his elbows on the back of the chair. "You know . . ."

Frank paused, not looking at Shelby. He picked at some loose paint that was chipping off the top of the chair.

"I don't . . . trust myself with this case." Frank ran a hand along the back of his neck and looked up at Shelby.

"Why? You've got plenty of experience. It's not your first murder case."

Frank shook his head. "It's not that."

Shelby waited patiently while Frank continued to scrape at the loose paint with his thumbnail.

"It's an odd case," Frank said finally. "There's not much evidence to go on. But what we do have points to your neighbor Jake Taylor. We now know he had a motive—Zeke blamed him for contaminating his well and was threatening to go to the Department of Health and Human Services to report him. By all accounts they had a humdinger of a fight over it."

"But if they had a fight"—Shelby was thinking fast—"then wouldn't Jake, or Zeke for that matter, have been more likely to duke it out right then and there?"

Frank dropped his head into his hands and groaned. "I don't know," he mumbled between his fingers. "You're probably right." He looked at Shelby over the tips of his fingers. "It's because of you."

"Me?" Shelby pointed to herself in confusion.

Frank gripped the top of the chair until his knuckles turned white. "I know that Jake has his eye on you."

Shelby started to protest but Frank held up a hand.

"It's quite obvious." He scowled.

"But what does that have to do—"

"It's like this." Frank looked down at the table. "I *want*

him to be the killer. And I think that's coloring my judgment. I've never let something like this get in the way of my judgment before."

"So why now?" Shelby took a sip of her lemonade—her mouth had gone dry.

"Because I told Bill I'd take care of you." He shook his head abruptly and got up so suddenly, the chair scraped across the floor.

Shelby stood up as well.

"That's a lie," Frank said, looking earnestly at Shelby. "It's because I'm jealous."

Frank took a step forward and put his hands on Shelby's shoulders. She held her breath and, without even realizing it, closed her eyes. She sensed him lowering his head.

Dear Reader, what was I thinking? Of course I'm attracted to Frank—he looks so much like Bill. But I don't know him. Not like I knew Bill. It's an illusion. A mirage or a magic trick. I can't do this.

Shelby turned her head and moved away, quickly putting some distance between herself and Frank. He looked at her for so long she began to feel uncomfortable, but then he grabbed his cap and tugged it back on his head.

"I'm sorry. My fault—I was out of line."

Frank's expression was grim, and Shelby's first reaction was to reach out and comfort him, but she knew she couldn't do that. Things had gone far enough.

She accompanied him to the door and watched as he walked to his truck. He turned, gave her a brief wave, got in the driver's seat, and shot down the driveway, spewing bits of gravel as he went.

12

||||||||||||||||||||||||||||||

Dear Reader,

I tried that cookware I told you about again. I felt it deserved a second chance—heck, sometimes we all deserve a second chance, right? Well, I'm afraid it failed again.

With the nights getting chillier now that we're into September, I had a craving for some soup. Specifically split pea soup. Did you know that split peas are actually split? There's a natural dividing line in the peas and splitting them helps them cook faster. They are full of protein and almost no fat and are very inexpensive!

I like to add some sausage to my soup. The general store has a selection of locally made sausage that is fabulous. It gives the soup all the flavor you could want.

I know what you're thinking—your kids wouldn't eat split pea soup. Mine love it, but then they're used to eating what's on hand rather than what's on the shelves at the grocery store.

Shelby rinsed the dinner dishes and stacked them on the counter. She'd have to put them in the dishwasher later. She hated leaving them like that, but she had to get Amelia and Billy to choir practice.

She went to the foot of the stairs and yelled, "Amelia, Billy! Time to go."

Amelia had a lovely voice and enjoyed singing in the choir but she hated having to go to practice.

"Amelia," Shelby called again, and this time she heard Amelia's bedroom door open.

Amelia stood at the top of the stairs, her lips drawn together into a pout.

"Don't even bother to argue with me," Shelby said, pointing toward the door. "We've got to go."

Amelia's sigh was audible all the way down the stairs. She brushed past Shelby, grabbed her fleece from the closet, and tied it around her waist.

Dear Reader, at least I don't have to remind her that it will be colder when she comes out of practice and she'll freeze to death in those cutoffs she insists on wearing.

Shelby, Billy, and Amelia piled into the car and Shelby began the drive to St. Andrews, which was just down the road from St. Mary Magdalene, the Catholic church. On Sundays, church bells could be heard pealing at the end of the service at St. Andrews at eleven o'clock and again at noon at St. Mary's.

Billy, who was relegated to the backseat whenever Amelia was in the car, somehow managed to kick the back of Amelia's seat even though he was securely buckled into his seat belt. *His legs must be getting longer,* Shelby thought with a pang of sadness. Her little boy wasn't going to stay little forever.

The two immediately began bickering and Shelby was relieved when they reached the church and she pulled into the parking lot. A handful of cars was already there. She glanced at the clock on her dashboard—it was surely a miracle but they were five minutes early. She breathed a sigh of relief.

Amelia got out of the car and headed for the choir room without saying a word.

Shelby watched her go. When was this period of adolescence going to be over?

Billy trooped behind Amelia, stopping to kick at a loose stone that was beside the path that led to the back door of the church hall.

The air felt close and stuffy as they climbed the creaking stairs to the second floor, where choir practice was being held. Amelia's group was practicing in the room at the very end of the hallway whose ancient flowered carpet was faded and stained from its many decades of service.

It had taken some time, but Shelby had talked Billy into—*okay, dear reader, I forced him*—joining the youth choir at the beginning of the year. He had a voice like a bullfrog but so did half the other boys and this way he was occupied with his group while Amelia was occupied with hers.

Shelby usually took advantage of the time to read—there was always a paperback tucked into her purse—or to chat with any of the other parents who hung around waiting for their kids. Farming could sometimes be a lonely existence and she enjoyed the opportunity for some adult company.

That thought gave her pause—maybe Bert was right and she needed to think about dating again. Maybe she needed to get more active socially. She couldn't imagine inviting another couple for dinner when the chair across from her would remain empty and she'd be forced into the role of third wheel.

Shelby was still shaken by Frank's visit. She had almost let him kiss her. What had come over her? She leaned against the wall and watched the people milling about in the hallway. The choirmaster was standing at the open door of the choir room, checking for stragglers, and the youth choir director was rounding up a couple of reluctant participants and herding them into the room with the finesse of a sheepdog.

Shelby looked up to find Mrs. Willoughby bearing down on her like a freight train run amok. She had skinny legs and a large belly that made her look like Humpty-Dumpty on stilts.

"There you are," she said to Shelby as if Shelby had purposely been hiding from her and not standing out in the open in full view of everyone. "I wanted to talk to you about the Christmas bazaar." Her face was flushed from her trot down the hallway and the tip of her sharp nose was red. "I do hope Love Blossom Farm will be taking a table again this year."

"Of course we will."

Mrs. Willoughby had a clipboard tucked under her arm. She pulled it out and flipped through the pages that were attached to it.

"Can't see a thing anymore without these." She picked her glasses up off her bosom, where they'd been resting peacefully at the end of a chain, and slipped them on.

"I'll mark you down as a *yes*, then?" She looked at Shelby questioningly, as if Shelby might have changed her mind in that brief interval.

"Definitely a *yes*."

"You'll be doing your jams and jellies and one of those lovely bay leaf wreathes to auction off?"

"Yes."

Mrs. Willoughby made another check mark on her paper, tucked her clipboard back under her arm, and let her glasses fall back onto her bosom. "Splendid!" She beamed at Shelby.

Perfume—the scent of gardenias and tuberose, Shelby thought—wafted in their direction. Shelby turned to see Isabel Stone coming down the hall. She looked as if she'd recovered well from the incident at the county fair. She was wearing a long skirt in the ankle-length style Shelby knew had become popular thanks to the circulars in the Sunday newspaper, with a slim-fitting sleeveless black turtleneck and suede booties. It took a long time for changes in fashion to trickle down to Lovett, but Isabel had always been ahead of the curve.

Shelby spotted Tonya Perry coming out of Daniel's office. So maybe the rumors about her and the pastor were true, she thought. In sharp contrast to Isabel, Tonya was wearing a pair of denim capri pants and an ill fitting, stretched-out plain white T-shirt.

Isabel had set her cap for Daniel when he'd first arrived as rector of St. Andrews, but Tonya, with her comfortable sandals and unpolished toenails, seemed a far more suitable match for him and much more likely to take to life as the rector's wife.

Shelby could tell by her posture that Isabel had noticed

Tonya. Her back stiffened and her shoulders went rigid. She began to walk toward Tonya, slowly at first, then gathering speed like a hurricane picks up force as it travels over the water.

Shelby watched as the unsuspecting Tonya continued her journey down the hall until the two women were finally abreast of each other.

"You," Isabel said loudly enough that everyone gathered in the hallway of the church hall turned to look.

Tonya stopped midstride with a look of horror on her face.

"Did you think that attempting to poison me at the county fair was going to pave the way for you to get your clutches on Daniel?"

Tonya's face shut down.

Isabel's face, on the other hand, was mottled red.

"I don't know what you mean," Tonya said, her eyes narrowing. "I think you'd better explain it."

"You put the pepper on that piece of lemon meringue pie, didn't you?" Isabel pointed a finger at Tonya.

"Me?"

"Don't deny it."

"But how would I . . . Why would I . . . ?"

Isabel waved a hand, dismissing Tonya's protests. "That little stunt also won you first prize in the contest, didn't it?"

Tonya's expression went from one of astonishment to one of white-hot anger. She opened her mouth but no words came out—she was obviously too furious to speak. Instead she lashed out, giving Isabel a shove that sent her rocking back on her stiletto heels.

"You pushed me!" Isabel exclaimed in disbelief.

"And I'll do it again if you don't stop spreading rumors about me."

Meanwhile, Mrs. Willoughby must have become aware of the altercation, because she was moving toward Tonya and Isabel at the speed of lightning.

"Ladies, please. Please remember where you are."

Mrs. Willoughby attempted to get between Tonya and Isabel but met with very little success. It would have taken a much thinner person to insinuate herself into the gap between the two women, who were now standing practically nose to nose.

"Is everything okay? I heard a noise. . . ."

Daniel, who had come out of his office, stuttered to a halt at the sight of Tonya and Isabel. He was slightly disheveled looking—his shirt could have used a touch-up with an iron and he was overdue for a haircut. It did seem as if he needed someone to look after him, Shelby thought.

"Mrs. Stone," he said, putting a hand on Isabel's bare arm. He withdrew it as quickly as if he'd touched a live wire. "You know what it says in the Bible about casting stones." He stopped abruptly and rubbed his chin. "Although perhaps that isn't totally apt in this case."

"You led me on," Isabel said through gritted teeth, her lips clenched and white.

"I did no such thing," Daniel protested. "I haven't treated you any differently than any of my other parishioners."

Tonya, meanwhile, looked as if she was gearing up for round two.

And Daniel looked as surprised, flustered, and flattered

as any man of modest looks and means would while enjoying the unprecedented experience of being fought over by two women.

iiiiiiiiiiiiiiiiiiiiiiiiii

"Have you talked to Seth about the wedding?"

"Yes," Kelly said, rocking her chair back and forth, one leg tucked under her, a glass of iced tea in her hand.

She and Shelby were sitting on Shelby's darkened front porch, listening to the chirping of the crickets and watching the stars twinkle in the black sky. Shelby had pulled on a sweatshirt and Kelly was wearing a fleece over her usual T-shirt and jeans.

Kelly stopped rocking and turned to face Shelby. "He loves the idea."

Shelby couldn't see her friend's face all that clearly but she could tell by the warmth in Kelly's voice that she was smiling.

"I'm so glad for you. What about his mother? Has he told her?"

Kelly snorted. "Not likely. Seth is totally in command when he's in his office seeing patients or at the hospital supervising the new residents, but he reverts back to a little boy in short pants when he's around his mother. He won't say *boo* to her."

Shelby laughed. "Someone has to tell her. Unless you plan to wait until she receives the invitation."

"I'm afraid that's going to be me," Kelly said. "Besides, I'm the bride, right? The bride is the one who plans the wedding. I'm sorry my mother isn't here to—"

She broke off and Shelby thought she caught the sound of tears in Kelly's voice. Kelly's mother had died while

Kelly was in college, and while she was close to her father, a girl missed her mother at a time like this.

"Would you like a refill on your iced tea?" Shelby asked, thinking it would give Kelly time to collect herself.

"Sounds great."

Kelly handed Shelby her glass.

Shelby pushed open the screen door with her hip and went inside.

Billy was sitting on the floor in front of the television watching a rerun of *The Brady Bunch* when Shelby walked through the living room, and the faint strains of some current hit song drifted down the stairs from Amelia's room. Jenkins and Bitsy were sprawled on the sofa, their pink tongues lolling as they dozed.

Shelby glanced into the sink as she headed toward the refrigerator. The night's dinner plates and the ruined pot stared back at her reproachfully. She silently promised to get to them as soon as Kelly left.

"Here you are." Shelby handed Kelly her glass as she resumed her seat in the rocking chair.

She waited while Kelly took a sip of her drink.

"I'm in something of a pickle," Shelby said.

"Mmmhhmm?" Kelly mumbled.

"The shipment of cookware arrived from the company that's asked me to promote it on my blog. The first pan I used was a disaster—the nonstick coating flaked off. I thought perhaps it was simply a matter of my getting a defective piece. I'm sure that happens from time to time. Tonight I decided to give the cookware a second chance, and I tried another one of the pots. The same thing happened—it ruined my whole batch of pea soup."

"Are you going to send them back?"

"That's the thing." Shelby bit her lower lip. "They've already paid me for the endorsement. It would mean sending the money back as well."

"Oh, I see."

"I don't know what to do."

There was a rustling sound and Shelby was aware of Kelly turning around in her chair to face her.

"Shelby McDonald, I haven't known you this long to not be absolutely certain of what you're going to do. You'd never be able to live with yourself if you promoted those pots and pans on your blog, knowing that they're shoddy merchandise. You know you're going to send them back."

Shelby rocked back and forth in her chair, hoping the rhythm would soothe her.

"Of course you're right. I don't know why I'm even wasting time thinking about it. I wouldn't be able to live with myself if I didn't."

"Well, that's one problem solved, then." Kelly laughed.

"I wish this murder case were as easily solved."

Shelby told Kelly about what had happened at church that night.

"What I wouldn't give to have seen that," Kelly squealed. "What a sight! Our self-effacing pastor being fought over by two women." Kelly paused. "Do you think Tonya was the one who put the pepper on that pie, ruining poor Jenny Hubbard's chances of winning the contest?"

"I don't know," Shelby admitted. "I would have said it seemed out of character from the very little I've seen of Tonya. But after tonight—I'm not so sure. I wonder, however, whether it was done to skew the contest or to create a diversion—which it certainly managed to do."

"If it was meant to create a diversion, and Tonya was

the one who did it, then that would make Tonya a suspect in Zeke's murder." Kelly started rocking again. "And what reason would she have for killing him?"

"Apparently she blamed Zeke for his wife's death."

"It would help if we knew more about Tonya. I don't know much about her. Do you?" Kelly slurped up the last of her iced tea.

"No. I've seen her in church and that's about all. The first time I ever spoke to her was at the county fair."

"She brings her cat to the clinic for its shots. I know she moved here from Allenvale. She said her grandmother died and left Tonya her house here in Lovett. She said it was too good to pass up."

"Does she have a job?"

"She works at the car wash back in Allenvale. At least she used to. I took the truck there once. It was covered in mud and I was too bone-tired to wash it myself." Kelly turned around in her chair and hung her long legs over the arm.

They rocked in silence for a moment. Shelby was tempted to tell Kelly about her encounter with Frank but for some reason she was hesitant.

Maybe it was because she felt ashamed by the incident—although she hadn't done anything wrong. Or had she?

If she hadn't, then why was she feeling so guilty about it?

She needed to move on—from Bill's ghost and from the feelings Frank stirred in her.

She decided that the next time—if—Matt asked her out, she would say yes.

13

Dear Reader,

Some of you have asked about the bay leaf wreath I am making for the St. Andrews Christmas bazaar auction. Unfortunately, I can't grow enough bay leaves to make a number of them—the trees don't winter in Michigan, so I have to keep the plants small enough to bring inside when the weather turns cold. In a warm climate, the trees can grow to thirty feet tall!

Bay leaves are thought to have numerous medicinal properties, such as being antiseptic, antiviral, and antioxidant. They are also full of vitamins.

The Greeks and Romans believed that the bay leaf symbolized wisdom, peace, and protection. I don't know about you, but I could certainly do with all three of those.

Making the wreath takes quite a long time, but I'm
happy to do it for St. Andrews. I'm afraid I can't put very
much in the collection plate on Sundays—sometimes
not much more than a handful of coins—so this is my
way of contributing. The wreath usually fetches an astonishing sum of money at the Christmas bazaar's silent
auction.

Shelby finished typing her blog entry and looked at the
clock on the kitchen wall. Almost bedtime. She yawned
and stretched her arms overhead. The house was quiet—
the children asleep upstairs and both dogs curled up under
the table at her feet.

She checked her e-mail and answered a couple of mes-
sages, spent a few minutes posting an update on her pro-
fessional Facebook page and trolling through her personal
feed. She came upon a post courtesy of the Lovett County
Fair—a picture of the tractor pull. She clicked on it and
went to the county's Facebook page.

There were dozens of pictures from the fair—she even
discovered one of Billy accepting his red ribbon in the
horse competition. She clicked SHARE and posted that
one to her own timeline.

She scrolled a little further and came upon a picture of
Mrs. Willoughby announcing the winner of the pie con-
test. The caption read, Tonya Perry wins the annual Lovett
County Fair pie competition with her rhubarb pie.

Shelby's eye strayed to the comments underneath the
picture. Most congratulated Tonya on her win but one
was different. Very different. Shelby's eyebrows rose as
she read it.

You've never been a winner, Tonya Perry, because you're
a loser. You said it was an accident but everyone knows
it wasn't. I hope you get what you deserve. And soon.

What on earth did that mean? Shelby wondered. Someone obviously had it in for Tonya. And what did they
mean by *you said it was an accident*?

The commenter's profile picture was not of themself
but of a tuxedo cat, and the person's name was B. J. Price.
Man or woman? Probably female, Shelby decided based
on the picture of the cat.

She clicked on the name and was taken to B. J. Price's
page. Her timeline was filled with more pictures of cats,
cartoons, and links to recipes. Shelby was pleased to see
a link to her own blog, The Farmer's Daughter, and her
recipe for meat loaf.

She skimmed the About section and discovered that
B. J. Price worked at a hair salon in Allenvale—the Hair
Boutique. Shelby's hand unconsciously went to her own
tangle of curls.

It was high time she had a haircut, wasn't it?

||||||||||||||||||||||||

Shelby felt guilty as she left for Allenvale the next morning. She had plenty of chores to keep her busy on the
farm—there was really no need to go gallivanting off to
Allenvale for a couple of hours. The specter of Jake being
charged with murder drove her on, though, and soon she
was passing the WELCOME TO ALLENVALE sign.

Allenvale was bigger than Lovett, with a main street
lined with mom-and-pop shops. The Hair Boutique was

sandwiched between a hardware store and a butcher advertising locally made venison sausages.

Shelby had called first thing in the morning to request an appointment with B. J. Price for a trim. The shop was empty when Shelby arrived. A woman with dyed blond hair in an elaborate updo was leaning on the reception desk, idly turning the pages of a fashion magazine. She looked up when Shelby entered.

Life had left its mark on her face, which was pinched and hard, with eyebrows plucked thin and a carefully outlined mouth. She glanced up as Shelby walked toward the desk.

"I have an appointment with B. J. Price."

"That would be me." B. J. slapped closed the magazine she'd been reading. "This way."

She led Shelby over to a row of three sinks. "What are we doing today?"

"A trim?"

"Okay."

After a quick and efficient shampoo, B. J. took Shelby over to one of the salon's three stations. Pictures of children around Billy's age were tucked into the frame of the mirror.

"Are those yours?" Shelby asked.

B. J.'s face relaxed. "Yes." She pointed a long French-manicured nail at a photo of three dark-haired children.

"That's Alexa—she's ten. And that's her brother, Garth, who's eight, and Garth's twin, Madison."

"A lovely family."

"Thanks."

B. J. began pulling a comb through Shelby's hair.

She frowned. "Your ends are awfully split. How about

we take a good inch off? You'll still have plenty of length."

"Sounds fine to me."

B. J. sectioned Shelby's hair and put the upper layer in clips.

"I haven't seen you in here before, have I?" B. J. made the first few snips, the hair clippings falling onto Shelby's shoulders. "You from Allenvale?"

"No, Lovett, actually."

B. J. stopped scissoring abruptly. "Did you hear about the murder?"

"Yes, I did." Shelby decided not to say anything about actually having been at the fair when it happened.

"Things like that don't normally happen around here." B. J. reached for a spray bottle of water and spritzed Shelby's hair. "And the woman that won the pie contest, Tonya Perry, used to live here in Allenvale. We were in high school together."

"Really?" Shelby managed to look reasonably surprised, but B. J. was concentrating on trimming the back of Shelby's hair and probably wasn't even looking.

"Tonya and I used to be friends until—" B. J. put her head down and appeared to be concentrating on cutting the sides of Shelby's hair.

"Did something happen?" Shelby asked gently.

B. J. put her scissors down on the counter and looked at Shelby's reflection in the mirror.

"Tonya and I were friends but I was best friends with Emily. Emily was real smart—not like me. I went to vocational school to become a hairdresser, but Emily was going to go to college—she was that smart."

B. J. picked up her scissors again and continued trimming Shelby's hair.

"Emily won a scholarship and all. Her family didn't have much money, so college seemed like nothing more than a dream to her even though all the teachers and her guidance counselor were begging her to apply. But winning that scholarship made it look like her dream had a chance of becoming a reality."

Shelby made a comforting noise, not wanting to say anything that might stem the flow of B. J.'s reminiscences.

"John Allen—he's the owner of a plant here in Allenvale that makes some kind of plastic molds; don't ask me what they're used for—but his family founded Allenvale back in the 1920s. They made a ton of money. He wanted to give back to the community so he created this scholarship for a worthy graduating senior from Allenvale High. And that's what Emily won."

Shelby was beginning to wonder if this story had anything to do with Tonya, and if so, did it have any bearing on Zeke's murder? Was she wasting her time here?

"But then Emily died."

Shelby sat up a little straighter in her chair. She hadn't expected that.

"Emily died?"

B. J. nodded. "Everyone said it was an accident but I don't believe that for one single minute."

"Why not? How did Emily die?"

"She and Tonya went swimming. There's this lake—it's not much more than a pond, really. It used to be a quarry back in the old days. Emily was a good swimmer—she was on the swim team at Allenvale High and she worked as a lifeguard during the summer. But somehow she managed to drown."

"Oh."

"I can tell you don't believe it, either," B. J. said, pulling open a drawer and removing a blow-dryer. "Tonya said Emily must have hit her head or something, because she dove into the water and never came back up again. Tonya said she tried to save her but the water was too murky for her to be able to see. She said she couldn't find Emily." B. J. turned Shelby's chair around and looked her in the eyes. "With Emily dead that scholarship ended up going to Tonya instead. Don't you think that's just a little suspicious?"

<hr>

Shelby left the Hair Boutique with her hair neat and trimmed and in very becoming soft waves. She thought of taking a selfie—her hair would never look like this again, certainly not after she'd spent a couple of hours weeding in the garden—but that seemed way too indulgent. She'd leave the selfies for reality television stars and teenage girls.

Shelby had asked B. J. if she knew where Tonya had gone to college and B. J. had said Tonya had been accepted at Allen State University. That meant she'd have been able to live at home and save on room-and-board fees.

B. J. didn't know if Tonya had graduated or even what she'd majored in. She'd lost track of Tonya after high school. B. J. had never been able to get over the feeling that Tonya had had something to do with her best friend Emily's death.

Obviously Tonya had done well in school if she'd been

in second place for that scholarship, Shelby thought as she drove back to Lovett. She wondered how Tonya had ended up working in a dead-end job in a car wash if she'd been such a promising student.

Shelby had enjoyed school herself, but in the end a degree in political science hadn't opened a great number of career doors, and while she'd enjoyed working in Chicago before coming back to the farm, she hadn't exactly given up a spot in the corner office to do so.

And she loved what she was doing. Her life was full—her children, her friends, family, and animals, her church and the beauty that was Love Blossom Farm.

The only thing missing was . . . a mate. She pushed the thought from her mind as she pulled into the driveway of the farm. No time to think about that now—she had to get ready for the farmers' market.

The farmers' market was winding down, given that it was almost halfway through September, but Shelby still had crops to sell: herbs, lettuce, leeks, kale, peppers, spinach, and zucchini—if everyone hadn't already had their fill of zucchini. She'd passed a farm stand on her way back to Lovett that had a sign out that read FREE ZUCCHINI—HELP YOURSELF. The vegetable was hardy, easy to grow, and usually abundant by the end of the summer.

Bert's car was in the driveway when Shelby arrived back at the farm. She noticed the dent in the fender as she pulled up alongside it. She wondered if Bert had ever found out who had caused it.

"Well, would you look at that?" Bert said when Shelby walked in the back door.

She twirled a hand over her head to indicate Shelby's new

hairdo. Bert was standing at the counter, putting together bunches of herbs—basil, thyme, sage, and chives—for Shelby to sell at the farmers' market.

Shelby was embarrassed by the attention—she rarely gave more than a passing thought to her appearance. As far as she was concerned, the only thing that counted was cleanliness.

"You must have a hot date tonight," Bert said, tying a piece of string around a bundle of chives.

"Yes. A hot date with my favorite television show."

"That's a shame. You look wonderful. You should go out somewhere and show off."

"Where? The Dixie Bar and Grill?"

Bert snorted. There's a nice Italian place over in Allenvale."

"Lucia's?"

Bert nodded.

"You're forgetting one thing," Shelby said, opening the refrigerator and pulling out a pitcher of lemonade.

"What's that?"

"I don't have anyone to go with."

"Ask one of those boyfriends of yours."

This time Shelby was the one who snorted. "What boyfriends?"

"Those two lovesick puppies who are always mooning over you."

"Don't you think it would be awfully forward of me to ask them out? I've always been told that a lady waits to be asked out." Shelby retrieved a glass from the cupboard and poured herself some lemonade.

"Not according to that feminist—what's her name? Gloria something?"

Shelby plucked a handful of herbs from the basket on the counter and began dividing them into bundles. They were both silent for a moment.

"I heard that your brother-in-law's divorce is final," Bert said.

Shelby froze with a piece of string halfway around a batch of sage. Was Bert's remark simply a random thought that had crossed her mind at that particular moment or did she mean for it to be part of their conversation about boyfriends?

Shelby didn't know. And she was pretty sure she didn't want to know, either.

14

Dear Reader,

If there isn't a farmers' market near you, have you ever considered joining a CSA? A CSA, or Community Supported Agriculture, guarantees you receive fruits and vegetables at their peak of freshness.

A CSA will introduce you to new varieties of produce you might not have thought of trying before. My children will eat almost anything that comes off a tree or a vine or out of the ground because we've grown it ourselves. Your children might react the same to a box of produce from "your" farm. And you will be putting the very freshest ingredients on the table for your family to enjoy.

Shelby's was the last truck to pull onto the empty field on the left just before Lovett Diner. Most of the farmers already had their stalls set up—Shelby was late.

She quickly backed her truck into the spot behind her allotted space and began setting up her stall. She had a canopy she normally placed over it to keep the worst of the sun off of her, but this time she didn't want to make the extra effort. She began unloading her crates of vegetables and fresh herbs, and it wasn't long before she was drenched in perspiration even though the temperature hovered around a very comfortable seventy-eight degrees.

Her first customers appeared before she even finished getting her stall ready.

Shelby brushed her hair out of her eyes, conscious of the fact that her sleek waves and curls were quickly becoming transformed into their usual uncontrolled jumble by the humidity. She spent a moment regretting her lost hairdo, pulled off the elastic tie she wore around her wrist, and swept her hair into some semblance of a ponytail.

She looked up and smiled at the woman approaching her stall. Shelby recognized her from the pie contest at the county fair. It was Jenny Hubbard, who usually took first place and a blue ribbon but whose pie had been laced with pepper this time. Shelby didn't know her well—most of Shelby's limited social life revolved around St. Andrews, and Jenny was a member of St. Mary Magdalene's down the street.

Jenny returned Shelby's smile. She had white hair and the weathered skin of someone who spent a lot of time outdoors. She was wearing a visor that shaded her eyes and had a green recyclable shopping bag slung over her arm.

"Can I help you? It's Jenny, isn't it?"

Jenny glowed at being recognized. "I see you have a few red peppers left. I'll take four of those. I'm making stuffed peppers for dinner tonight." She tapped her bag. "I have some lovely spinach to fold into the mixture of ground beef and rice."

"That sounds delicious," Shelby said, realizing she was getting hungry herself.

She placed the peppers in a paper bag and handed them to Jenny.

"Although I must say," Jenny said with a quiver to her chin, "the very word *pepper* makes me want to scream."

"I'm sorry about what happened at the county fair. Have they discovered who did it?"

Jenny shook her head. "No. At least not that I've heard. I suppose *que sera, sera*, as they say. I have a whole drawer full of blue ribbons. Perhaps it was time for someone else to win." She clenched her fists. "If only it hadn't been that Tonya Perry."

Shelby raised an eyebrow but didn't say anything.

"Frankly I don't think they have to look any further than Tonya to find the culprit. It's just the sort of thing she would do."

"What do you mean?"

Jenny put down her shopping, pulled a tissue from her purse, and wiped it across the back of her neck.

"It reminds me of what happened to my daughter," she said cryptically.

"Your daughter?"

Jenny nodded and tucked the tissue back into her purse. "It was when the two of them were in college. At Allen University. Tracy is the first member of our family to graduate from college." Jenny puffed out her chest, making her look like a bird with ruffled feathers.

"What happened . . . with your daughter and Tonya, I mean?"

"Our Tracy is very artistic. She's a graphic designer at an advertising firm in Grand Rapids. She's being considered for the position of creative director, if you can imagine."

Shelby bit her tongue and tried to be patient. She hoped no customers would approach and put Jenny off her tale.

"She did other kinds of art when she was in college— sculpture, painting, watercolors. But you can't make a living doing that, now, can you?" Jenny took the soggy tissue from her purse and ran it along the back of her neck again. "So she took some courses in graphic design." She tapped her head with her index finger. "Our Tracy is a smart girl. Always thinking."

Dear Reader, I have no idea what on earth all this has to do with Tonya Perry, but I suppose I shall have to listen if I want to find out.

"Tracy entered an art competition at school. There was a prize—a cash prize." She rubbed her fingers together. "Everyone agreed that Tracy was going to win."

"Did Tonya have a piece in this competition as well?" Shelby asked, suddenly suspecting where this was going.

"Yes, she did. Hideous thing—it looked like something a kindergartner might have done, all splashes of color thrown willy-nilly at a canvas. Now, our Tracy's piece was something else, a magnificent scene of the Presque Isle Lighthouse—the new one, not the old one— all done in quilting. Took her months to complete it."

Jenny paused for breath, her face flushed and glistening with perspiration.

"What happened?" Shelby asked although her mind was racing ahead, drawing its own conclusions.

"A fire. That's what happened. Completely destroyed Tracy's piece. All that hard work gone up in flames. She was devastated." Jenny took a long, shuddering breath. "Of course the university art gallery was badly damaged as well. As you can imagine they did an investigation but never figured out who set the fire."

"But it was arson?"

"According to the report in the newspaper. It said police found evidence that Tracy's quilt had been doused with kerosene before it was set on fire."

Jenny raised her chin as if that said it all.

"Why do you think Tonya—"

"She was always jealous of my Tracy. They were in high school together. Tonya never liked being in second place. Like when they cast the school play—they were doing *The Music Man.* I always did like that show. Tracy got the part of Marian and Tonya ended up in the chorus. I think she built up a lot of resentment—like a pressure cooker builds up steam. Do you know what I mean?"

"So, nothing was ever proven?"

"Nah. I imagine the police had bigger fish to fry. But Tonya left college soon after and that says something, don't you think?"

"Yes, certainly."

"So it wouldn't surprise me at all if it was Tonya who put pepper on my pie so she could win that contest. Like I said, she always wanted to be the best."

Jenny paid for her purchases and with a nod at Shelby moved on, heading toward the parking lot.

Dear Reader, that is certainly food for thought, don't

you think? But the fact that Tonya might have set fire to Tracy Hubbard's art piece and might have doctored Jenny's pie doesn't necessarily make her a murderer.

||||||||||||||||||||||||

Shelby had just finished serving her last customer when Matt came along. Shelby felt slightly awkward—she hoped she hadn't hurt Matt's feelings by refusing to have coffee with him.

"Let me give you a hand," Matt said as Shelby began filling crates with the produce that hadn't sold. Fortunately there wasn't much left.

"Thanks."

Shelby wished Matt had come by earlier—while her fancy new hairdo was still intact.

Matt carried the filled crate to Shelby's pickup while she collected the empty ones, took them to the truck, and stowed them in the back. Together, she and Matt quickly folded the tablecloth Shelby used to dress up her old pockmarked table. Matt then collapsed the table, and with it tucked in beside the crates, there was nothing more to do.

Matt leaned against the rear fender of the truck and fixed his gaze on Shelby.

"Want to grab an iced tea or something else cold to drink at the diner? And I don't know about you, but I haven't had any lunch and my stomach is grumbling in complaint." He held up a finger before Shelby could answer. "If you say no, I'm going to keep asking you until you change your mind, so you might as well make it easy on both of us and say yes now."

Shelby laughed. "Okay. Yes. I'd love to."

"Meet you there in a couple of minutes, then." Matt turned and headed toward his own truck.

Shelby's truck bounced and shimmied as she drove across the bumpy field to the main road. She held the steering wheel with one hand and with the other she tried to capture the loose hairs flying around her face. She wished she'd at least brought a compact and some lipstick with her. But then Matt had already seen her looking the way she did, so what did it matter?

Matt had secured a corner booth by the time Shelby got to the diner. It wasn't crowded—it was past noon, the time when the diner was busy with the lunchtime crowd.

Shelby slid into the seat opposite Matt. His smile seemed strained and there were lines of fatigue around his eyes.

"You look tired."

Matt spun his spoon around and around on the table, turning it with his finger.

"I guess I am. It's always . . . hard at this time of year."

Matt had been working in lower Manhattan during the attacks on September 11. His memories had eventually driven him out of New York City to Michigan, where he bought the Lovett General Store and settled into country life.

He stilled the spinning spoon with his hand, looked up, and smiled at Shelby.

"Enough of that. I'm here with you and that's all that matters."

Shelby felt her heart lurch at Matt's words. She took a deep breath and reminded herself that she didn't want to be alone forever with only her memories to keep her company.

"I guess I'd better decide what I want," Matt said, reaching for the plastic-coated menus that were tucked between the napkin dispenser and the salt and pepper shakers.

He handed one to Shelby.

Shelby's hunger had abated somewhat—or perhaps she didn't notice it, sitting here with Matt. She opened her menu although she already knew what she wanted. The diner's menu hadn't changed in all the years Shelby had been going there. Everyone in Lovett had their favorite dish whether it was meat loaf and mashed potatoes, turkey with gravy, or their mile-high club sandwich.

Shelby chose the chicken salad sandwich, which was made with chicken, mayonnaise, and nothing else. The diner didn't go in for what the chef called *furbelows* in their chicken salad—chopped pecans, raisins, dried cranberries; if you wanted fancy fare like that, you had to go farther afield than the Lovett Diner.

Matt ordered a hamburger, medium rare. The waitress frowned at him, her pencil hesitating over her pad until Matt repeated *medium rare*.

He laughed as the waitress moved away from their table. "I guess the diner still isn't used to what I'm sure they call my *city ways*."

"People around here do tend to go in for their meat cooked well-done."

Matt folded his hands on the table. "Has there been any more news about poor Zeke's murder?"

Everyone knew Frank was Shelby's brother-in-law and everyone assumed he shared confidential police information with his family.

Shelby told Matt what she'd learned about Tonya

Perry—how she'd been suspected of her friend Emily's death and how Jenny Hubbard blamed her for the fire at the Allen University art gallery.

Matt whistled, and the waitress spun around sharply. He mouthed *sorry* at her and turned back to Shelby. "Tonya shops at the store like everyone else in town, but I don't really know her. I must say, though, that news surprises me."

"Me, too," Shelby admitted. "And to think she's become involved with our rector. Although I suppose we have to remember—innocent until proven guilty."

"That's right." Matt leaned back as the waitress slid his hamburger in front of him with a disapproving toss of her head. "If what you've told me is true though, it does mean that Tonya is capable of anything—including murdering Zeke to avenge her friend Brenda's death."

Shelby nodded as she picked up her chicken salad sandwich. "I don't think we can rule her out."

They finished their lunch, and Matt insisted on paying for Shelby's chicken sandwich, refusing to listen to her protests. They walked outside and stopped at the front door of the diner.

"Thanks for having lunch with me." Matt touched Shelby's arm. "Maybe next time we can make it dinner somewhere nice—like Lucia's?"

Shelby nodded her head mutely.

Dear reader, what am I getting myself into here?

Matt leaned toward Shelby and kissed her on the cheek, then turned and headed toward his van.

Shelby walked back to her truck in a daze. The spot where Matt had kissed her cheek tingled all the way home.

15

Dear Reader,

Did you know that Michigan is the second largest producer of carrots in the United States? Carrots are harvested between July and November, giving them a long season, which is a boon to farmers and those of us who feed our families with what we grow.

Most people don't realize that not all carrots are orange! There are varieties called Black Knight (sadly it's on the bitter side), Atomic Red, and Purple Haze.

Roasting carrots brings out their delicious sweetness. Toss cut-up carrots with olive oil, salt, and pepper, spread on a baking sheet, and roast at four hundred degrees for around twenty minutes.

Tonight I'm making a carrot cake for Bert's birthday. Although it's not a traditional birthday cake, it's her favorite. I'm hoping Amelia will be willing to help me. Baking provides wonderful mother-daughter bonding time . . . assuming your teen is willing.

"Well, don't you look like the cat that swallowed the canary?" Bert said when Shelby walked in the door of her kitchen.

Bert had a basket of fresh eggs on the counter and was placing them in cardboard cartons that had LOVE BLOSSOM FARM stamped on the top.

"Quite a bumper crop from the hens this week." She gestured toward the basket of eggs. "They must be happy."

Shelby laughed. "I guess I must be doing something right."

Even though Shelby had grown up on Love Blossom Farm and knew every inch of it by heart, she sometimes still worried about whether she was doing everything correctly. People in Lovett used to say that Shelby's father was so charming that the hens laid twice as many eggs for him, and that no one could beat her mother's apple pie. Sometimes Shelby was afraid she'd never measure up.

"What have you been up to?" Bert turned around to face Shelby, her hands on her narrow hips.

Shelby sighed. She thought the subject had been successfully changed, but apparently not.

Bert shook a finger at her. "And don't say *nothing*, because it's obviously something."

Shelby knew better than to try to argue. "I had lunch with Matt Hudson—he owns the general store."

"I know perfectly well who Matt Hudson is," Bert said, wagging her finger at Shelby again. "Don't forget I'd already lived here a whole lifetime before you were even born."

Shelby breathed a sigh of relief when she heard the screen door to the mudroom slam.

"I'm hungry," Billy said as he tossed his backpack on the kitchen table.

"How was school?" Shelby said as she swept Billy's backpack off the table and onto a kitchen chair. She shuddered to think of all the places Billy had probably set it down and the germs that must be lurking on the bottom.

"Okay."

"What did you do today?" Bert asked, closing the last of the egg cartons.

"Nothing."

"That must have been exciting," Bert said with a twinkle in her eye.

She looked at Shelby and they both shrugged.

"You have your riding lesson this afternoon," Shelby said.

"But I told you—I'm hungry."

"I'll make you a sandwich, but we have to make it quick, okay?"

‖‖‖‖‖‖‖‖‖‖‖‖‖‖‖‖‖‖‖

Billy walked out to the car, carrying the last quarter of his peanut butter and jelly sandwich. Shelby had long ago given up worrying about crumbs or spills in the car. What did it matter, when a tear in the upholstery of the front passenger seat had been mended with black electrical tape?

Shelby turned down Jim Harris's drive and followed it around the house, where the American flag was whipping in the breeze that had picked up since that morning. She followed the drive toward the stables around back.

Jim Harris was leaning against the fence that encircled the paddock, his hat pushed back on his head, his arms folded across his chest. His face had sagged into defeated-looking lines.

Shelby was surprised. Jim usually greeted them with a smile and a warm welcome. Shelby supposed everyone could have an off day. Perhaps he wasn't feeling well.

He motioned to Billy to come with him and the two of them disappeared inside the stable.

Shelby stood by the fence, waiting. She always felt so proud seeing Billy controlling one of Jim's enormous horses. She heard one of them snort loudly, and Billy came out the stable door riding Blackjack. He was a big horse with a mind of his own. Jim didn't let just anyone ride him. Shelby felt herself glowing with pride.

Billy began going around and around the ring—a trot, then a canter, then back to a trot.

The sun was still hot and soon Shelby felt rivulets of perspiration running down her sides.

The weathered picnic table under the shade tree looked very inviting, so she took a seat and pulled a pad and pen out of her purse. She would work on her next blog post. She was so engrossed in what she was doing that she didn't notice someone approaching until she caught a glimpse of movement out of the corner of her eye.

She turned to see Jim Harris's wife coming toward her. Shelby had seen her around the farm, but they'd never actually met.

"I'm Dawn." The woman held out a rough and callused hand when she reached Shelby.

"Shelby McDonald." Shelby gestured toward the ring,

where Billy was cantering and churning up dust. "That's my son."

Dawn shaded her eyes with one hand and looked over to the paddock. "He's going to make a fine horseman one day." She dropped her hand and smiled at Shelby.

"Thanks."

"I came down to see how Jim was doing," Dawn said, taking a seat opposite Shelby. "Today's a hard day for him."

"Oh?" Shelby put down her pen and leaned her elbows on the picnic table.

"It's the anniversary of his brother Sid's death." She shook her head. "Such a shame, really."

"I heard he was . . . in an accident."

"I guess you could call it that. Mowed down by someone who was in a dang hurry to get where they were going. They never even stopped." She wiped a tear from her eye. "Sid was a good guy even though he had his problems." She mimed drinking from a glass.

"And they never found the person who did it?"

"That's the worst of it," Dawn said. "It's haunted Jim ever since. For the longest time he couldn't put it out of his mind, but now—"

Dawn broke off when she realized Jim was right behind them. The ring was empty—Billy must have taken the horse back into the stable.

"Sid's death was a crime," Jim thundered, slamming his fist into the palm of his other hand. "The worst thing is that justice wasn't done." He looked at Dawn.

"Maybe karma will catch up with whoever—" Shelby began, but Jim stopped her.

"I believe in an eye for an eye and a tooth for a tooth,

like it says in the Bible," Jim said loudly, sounding like a preacher in church.

Shelby shrank in her seat. She'd never seen Jim so upset before. He'd always struck her as easygoing and laid-back.

Shelby noticed Dawn raise her eyebrow at her husband. He dropped his hands to his side and slowly opened his clenched fists.

"Sorry." He gave Shelby a sheepish look. "It still rankles, especially on the anniversary of the day it happened."

He smiled at Shelby, turned on his heel, and walked off.

"Don't pay any attention to him," Dawn said, putting her hand on Shelby's. "He'll be back to normal tomorrow or the day after. It happens every year."

Shelby nodded and smiled, but inside she was quite shaken. She was glad when Billy appeared in the open door of the stable and they were able to head back to the farm.

||||||||||||||||||||||||||

Amelia was home when Shelby got there. She was sitting at the kitchen table opposite Bert, and there was a bowl of popcorn between them. It was made from some of the small crop of corn Shelby had planted this year—the Tom Thumb variety, which grew quickly and didn't need a lot of space. Popped in a pan with some olive oil, it was tender and delicious.

"Don't eat too much of that," Shelby warned Amelia. "I'll be cooking dinner soon."

"I'm starving," Amelia said with her mouth full of corn.

Shelby reached into the bowl and helped herself to a handful. She leaned against the counter and munched it one piece at a time.

"By the way, did you ever talk to Mr. Campbell about that girl copying from your paper? What was her name— Brittany?"

Amelia shook her head and her long blond hair whipped back and forth. "I told you, Mom, I can't."

"Of course you can. It's not fair that Brittany is doing this to you."

Bert was looking back and forth between them as if she was watching a tennis match.

"Justice is awfully elusive sometimes," Bert said, reaching into the bowl for more popcorn.

She pushed her chair away from the table and stood up. "I'd better shove off. Poker is at my house tonight." She rubbed her hands together. "I'm feeling lucky."

"I hope you win," Shelby called after her as Bert slipped out the front door.

"So do I," Bert called over her shoulder.

Shelby faced Amelia and wet her lips. Why was she so scared of asking her own daughter to help her? "Would you help me bake a cake after dinner? It's Bert's birthday tomorrow, and I'd like to surprise her with a carrot cake—it's her favorite."

Amelia scrunched up her nose. "Some of my friends are going to have a bonfire tonight. Mrs. Quinn said she'd help us make s'mores."

Shelby hesitated. She knew the Quinns from church. Mrs. Quinn was on the grounds committee, and Marcia was in the choir with Amelia. Still, she didn't like Amelia going out so late—especially on a school night. And who knew who else would be there? Maybe boys?

"I don't know. . . ."

"Mom," Amelia said, drawing out the word so that it

became multiple syllables and not just the one. "It's *fine*. Mr. and Mrs. Quinn will be there. Nothing is going to happen."

Shelby sighed. She knew this was only one of the many battles ahead of her during the coming years. She had to pick and choose carefully.

"I suppose it's all right. But get your homework done first, okay?"

Amelia's face lit up. "Thanks, Mom. I won't be late, I promise."

"Do you need me to drive you?"

Amelia shook her head. "Viola's going. Her mother said she'd pick me up."

Her eyes slid away from Shelby's. Shelby felt a frisson of alarm but decided she was imagining things. As Amelia had pointed out to her many times—she would be just *fine*.

Still, as Shelby cleaned up the dinner dishes and began measuring flour for Bert's carrot cake, she couldn't shake the sense of uneasiness that hovered over her like a persistent cloud.

16

Dear Reader,

Bonfires are a popular activity here in Michigan pretty much year-round. Even summer nights get cool enough that the heat from a fire actually feels good. Instead of standing around in someone's overdecorated living room with a fancy cocktail, we prefer to be outside, watching the sun leave a fiery path in the sky as it plummets toward the earth, and warming our hands in front of the blaze from someone's fire pit.

Bill and I spent many evenings cuddled together in front of the roaring flames. Believe me, it's more romantic than going out to dinner at a fancy restaurant . . . tucked into a sleeping bag watching the sparks light up the sky . . .

Shelby stopped typing suddenly. A montage of images and sensations went through her mind: cuddling together with Bill, his hands warm on her body . . . passionate kisses hotter than any fire—what had she been thinking, letting Amelia go to this bonfire?

There was nothing she could do about it now. Showing up at the Quinns' would embarrass Amelia—she knew it would be a long time before Amelia forgave her if she did that. Besides, she was probably being ridiculous.

Shelby decided she needed to take her mind off the endless loop it was on, and making Bert's cake was the perfect way to do it. She measured flour, sugar, and baking powder. She grated carrots. She stirred and stirred until the batter was silken and smooth.

She was pouring it into cake pans when the front door opened so abruptly, it ricocheted off the wall and slammed shut again.

Shelby put down her spatula, wiped her hands on her apron, and hurried toward the foyer.

Amelia threw herself into Shelby's arms. Her face was streaked with tears, and bits of leaves and twigs were caught in her hair.

Shelby held her tight, rocking back and forth and murmuring *there, there* like she used to when Amelia was a baby.

Finally, Amelia's sobs abated until all that was left was a case of the hiccoughs.

She looked up at Shelby with red-rimmed eyes and swiped a hand across her nose, which had started to run.

"You have to come. We don't know what to do. It's horrible."

"Where's Mrs. Quinn? Who drove you home?" Shelby was confused.

"Chip. He's waiting outside. I said you would know what to do."

Dear Reader, that's very flattering but I'm too alarmed at the moment to appreciate it.

Amelia began tugging on Shelby's sleeve.

"Wait. Where are we going?"

"To the field behind Zeke Barnstable's farm."

"What were you doing there?"

Amelia just shook her head and tugged harder on Shelby's arm.

"Chip is waiting."

"I don't know who Chip is, but I can assure you, we're not riding with him. We'll take my car."

Shelby was startled when Amelia didn't argue.

"I have to get Billy. I don't want to leave him here alone."

"No!" Amelia said. "You can't take Billy there. Can't he stay home by himself this once?"

Shelby stopped at the foot of the stairs. "Billy," she yelled. "I have to go out for a minute. Will you be okay?"

Billy's blond head popped over the bannister. "Sure, Mom. I told you, I'm old enough to stay by myself. Everyone does it."

Shelby rather reluctantly followed Amelia out to the car. Her hands were shaking as she inserted the key in the ignition. She had no idea what had happened or what she was going to find. Surely if there had been an accident of some sort, the kids would have had the smarts to call 9-1-1.

A light drizzle had started falling and Shelby switched on the windshield wipers. She usually found their rhythmic *whoosh, whoosh* across the window soothing, but not tonight.

She followed the pinpricks of red that were the tail-lights of Chip's car through the falling dusk.

"Who is Chip?" Shelby asked.

"Some boy."

"I gathered that. Do you know him from school?"

"Yes. He's a junior."

Shelby opened her mouth to say something but snapped it shut. This wasn't the right time to discuss it. Amelia was clearly in distress and didn't need to hear a lecture.

The rain picked up in intensity as they neared Zeke's farm. Shelby switched the windshield wipers to a higher speed and turned on the rear-window defogger. The windows were steaming up, and with the interior of the car darkened, she felt claustrophobic.

"You still haven't told me what you were doing at Zeke's farm," Shelby said, her fingers tense on the steering wheel.

"The Quinns wouldn't let us have a bonfire. Mrs. Quinn had a migraine and Mr. Quinn said we would be too noisy, and besides, the smoke would bother her."

"You said Viola's mother was picking you up from our house. I'm guessing she didn't."

Amelia shook her head and her hair swished back and forth against the back of the seat.

So Chip must have driven her, Shelby thought. No point in worrying about it now—they'd obviously made it safely.

Dear Reader, have you ever taken too big a bite of something and then couldn't swallow it? That's how I feel right now.

Shelby glanced at Amelia out of the corner of her eye

and saw that she was biting her nails—something she had stopped doing two years ago.

Chip's car turned onto the dirt road that ran past Zeke's farm and Shelby followed him. The road was rutted and she had to take it slowly. As the needle on the speedometer dropped, her heart rate sped up. She couldn't imagine what she was going to find. And Amelia was still unable to tell her.

They passed Zeke's plain white farmhouse. The front porch listed to the right, and the siding was weathered and badly in need of painting. One of the upper windows was crisscrossed with tape meant to mend a long, jagged crack.

"Where are we going?" Shelby asked as Chip continued down the road.

Amelia pointed out the window. "To those trees behind the cornfield."

The dirt road ended at the edge of the small group of trees. Shelby came to a stop behind Chip's car and got out. It was still raining—although not heavily—and she wished she'd thought to bring her slicker with her. She glanced at Amelia in her sodden T-shirt and shorts—she must have been freezing.

Chip went ahead of them, cracking twigs underfoot and rustling the leaves that had already started to dry and turn color. Shelby and Amelia followed behind.

Shelby was surprised when Amelia grabbed her hand and held it like she used to when she was a little girl.

Chip pushed aside a sinewy branch that was in their path, and it whipped back, slapping Amelia in the face.

She let out a cry, and her hand flew to her face.

"Are you okay?" Shelby asked in hushed tones. She didn't know why she was whispering.

By now they had reached the center of the cluster of trees. A cloud floated in front of the moon and the shadows created by the trees intensified the darkness. Shelby felt the ground with her feet and held an arm out in front of her as she walked, much like a blind person might negotiate unfamiliar terrain.

They were in a small clearing. Two girls and a boy were huddled together on a rotting log. They were soaked through from the rain, their faces ashen. A girl with long hair plastered to the back of her wet T-shirt jumped up when Shelby and Amelia approached.

"You won't tell, will you, Mrs. McDonald?" she said. Her teeth were chattering.

Shelby recognized her from one of Amelia's birthday parties. Hannah, she thought her name was. She was a pretty girl, but right now her face was creased with concern, and she looked frightened out of her mind.

"What's going on? What's happened?" Shelby looked at the white, frightened faces that surrounded her. "Someone needs to tell me what is going on," she said with a heavy feeling of dread.

The boy jumped to his feet. He was wearing a sports jersey with the number twenty-five on it and sagging jeans with holes in the knees.

"It's like this. Chip and I began digging a pit for our bonfire." He jerked his head toward where Hannah and the other girl were standing close together, holding on to each other. "Hannah and Lauren started collecting rocks so we could circle them around the pit."

He stifled what sounded to Shelby like a sob, and then lifted his chin and swiped a shaking hand across his eyes.

"Then we found it."

"Found what?" Shelby asked.

"Come and see for yourself," the boy said, gesturing toward the rough circle dug into the ground.

Shelby edged closer. She was bracing herself for what she would find in the hole. A dead animal of some sort, maybe? She peered into the shallow pit. Even in the near dark she could tell what it was. And it wasn't an animal.

She put a hand over her mouth and staggered backward.

17

||||||||||||||||||||||||||||||||

Dear Reader,

Did you ever have one of those moments when things appear to be going in slow motion? And you're seeing everything through a fog so that lines are blurred and edges softened? That's what was happening to me. They say it's your brain's way of protecting you from a terrible shock. I think that's true. And I couldn't be more grateful for it.

Shelby dug her cell phone from the pocket of her shorts with shaking hands. It took her three tries to punch in the numbers 9-1-1.

The dispatcher answered on the first ring, and Shelby explained the situation. She was proud that her voice barely trembled as she recounted the scene.

The woman listened patiently and asked the occasional question. It was obvious she was as shocked by the situation as Shelby and the teens were.

"Human remains, you say?"

"Yes. There's a shallow grave, and there are bones," Shelby said, her voice quavering.

"Could they be from an animal, perhaps? Someone's pet dog or cat?"

Shelby shook her head violently. "No. I'm quite certain they're human bones. The . . . the skeleton is still intact."

The dispatcher on the other end drew in her breath sharply. "A patrol car is on its way."

"Thank you."

Shelby ended the call and punched in another number.

"Frank McDonald," the husky voice drawled when the call went through.

Frank sounded tired, Shelby thought—as if she had woken him. She felt guilty. The police were on their way—perhaps there was no need to bring Frank out at a time like this.

"Frank." She tried to keep the quaver out of her voice, but she wasn't successful—she was wet, cold, and frightened, and it was obvious.

"Shelby? What's wrong?" Suddenly Frank's voice became brisk and businesslike.

Shelby explained about the teens digging a fire pit and uncovering what looked to her like human remains.

"I'll be right there. You're at Zeke Barnstable's farm, right?"

Relief flooded Shelby. "Yes. Take the gravel drive past his house as far as it goes. We're in that small copse of trees at the end of it."

"Hang on. I'm coming."

"What should we do?" Hannah asked as Shelby stuffed her cell phone back in her pocket.

She'd wrapped her thin arms around herself and was shivering.

"You kids go wait in my car." Shelby pointed toward the road.

"I'll stay here with you," Chip said, raising his chin and squaring his shoulders.

He was a good deal taller than Shelby although as thin as a willow branch, with the faintest suggestion of facial hair on his chin and upper lip.

They waited in silence until, several minutes later, car headlights pierced the darkness created by the canopy of trees. Shortly after that, they heard twigs snapping and leaves rustling. Two uniformed patrolmen burst through the bushes into the small clearing.

Shelby sagged with disappointment. She had hoped that Frank would be the first to arrive.

One of the officers turned on his flashlight and aimed the powerful beam at the shallow hole in the ground.

Shelby turned her head quickly. She'd already seen as much as she wanted to.

Shock set in and Shelby began to shiver. She yearned to go home, crawl under her down comforter, and not come out again until this was all over. She tried not to think of that because it only compounded her misery and unfortunately wasn't an option.

The sound of someone stumbling followed by a muffled oath announced Frank's arrival. He burst through the tangle of bushes, putting up an arm to ward off the

low hanging branches on the saplings nestled between
the larger trees.

"Shelby!"

Shelby moaned and threw herself into Frank's open
arms. He stroked her hair with his hand and tightened his
other arm around her. She stood like that for a few minutes, letting her muscles relax, giving in to the tears that
were hot behind her eyelids. Then she made herself push
away from the warm circle of his arms.

"Frank," one of the officers called. "Come take a look,
would you?"

"Why don't you go wait in the car?" Frank whispered
in Shelby's ear.

She straightened her shoulders. "That's okay. I'm fine.
I'll wait here."

Frank walked toward where the officers were clustered
together without looking back. They talked in low voices,
only an indistinct murmur reaching Shelby.

Frank walked over to Chip, who still stood by the grave,
his posture stoic although Shelby saw the faint tremor in
his limbs. Frank clapped a hand on the boy's shoulder.

"Why don't you go back and wait in your car, son? I'll
be along to talk to you shortly."

Chip didn't need any further encouragement. He gave
a shuddering sigh, turned on his heel, and began thrash-
ing his way back through the bushes toward the road.

Finally, Frank turned to Shelby. "Were you the one
who found . . ." He gestured toward the makeshift fire pit.

"No. Amelia and her friends did."

Frank looked around. "Where are they?"

"I sent them to sit in my car."

"What was Amelia doing out here so late?"

Shelby bristled at the note of censure in his voice.

"She certainly didn't have my permission, if that's what you're thinking."

Frank hung his head. "I'm sorry. I didn't mean to imply . . ."

"That's okay."

"I'm going to need to talk to the kids." He ran a hand along the back of his neck.

The rain had slowed to a mere drizzle, and darkness was descending fast.

Frank went first, holding back branches and making a path for Shelby to follow. Chip was sitting in his own car, his arms folded on the steering wheel with his head resting on them.

Amelia, Brad, Hannah, and Lauren were in Shelby's car, the girls in front—Amelia behind the wheel—and the boys sitting far apart in the back.

"Go sit in my truck," Frank said to Shelby. "You look like you're freezing."

"I'm okay."

Frank shrugged, opened the front door of Shelby's car, and crouched down.

"Are you girls okay? Amelia?"

They nodded their heads, their eyes wide and their lips quivering.

"We only wanted to make a fire pit," Hannah burst out.

"What brought you out here to Zeke Barnstable's farm?"

The girls looked at one another. Finally, Lauren spoke, her voice so tiny, Shelby could barely hear her.

"We didn't have anywhere else to go, and we knew

Zeke wouldn't be coming after us. . . ." Her voice trailed off as if she'd suddenly realized what her words meant.

Frank nodded his head. "How did you choose the spot to dig?"

One of the boys in the back cleared his throat. "We looked for a clearing in the trees and a spot that was pretty flat."

"I take it you have no idea whose remains those are?"

Frank glanced from the occupants of the front seat to the back. They all shook their heads.

Frank's knees gave a loud crack as he stood up. He put a hand on the roof of the car and bent down. "I'm going to send one of the officers over to take down your names. Then you all go on home, okay?"

A look of relief washed over the teens' faces.

"Take Amelia home," Frank said to Shelby. "I'll be by when we're finished here."

||||||||||||||||||||||||||

Shelby was quite certain that never before in her life had she been so grateful to walk through her own back door. She grabbed the old fleece that she kept on a hook in the mudroom and pulled it on, breathing a sigh of relief at the instant warmth that enveloped her.

With a grunt, Bitsy got up from the corner of the kitchen where she was curled up in Jenkins's dog bed, her head hanging off one end and her feet the other. Jenkins ambled in from the living room, yawning widely. They surrounded Shelby, and she bent down to accept their warm, sticky kisses.

Amelia went straight to her room. Shelby decided this was not the time to talk to her; she'd had a bad shock, and she was cold and wet—no good was likely to come of it. She'd save that conversation for the morning.

As soon as she heard Amelia's door close, she tiptoed up the stairs and peeked into Billy's room. He was sprawled on his bed, still in his shorts and T-shirt, a book splayed open on the floor. He hated to disturb him even though his hands and face were grubby and needed washing. She maneuvered the covers out from under him, laid them lightly on top of him, and tiptoed back out of the room.

Back in the kitchen, Shelby filled the kettle with water and plunked it down on the stove. She dug around in the pantry, found a box of chamomile tea, and grabbed a mug from the cupboard.

She jumped when the kettle whistled and quickly pulled it off the stove. It was probably going to be quite a while before Frank was finished at Zeke's farm. She took her tea into the living room and tried to find something to watch on television but nothing held her interest. Too many questions were revolving around and around in her mind: Whose body had the kids found? Was it even human? It had certainly looked like it to Shelby, but she was far from an expert. The medical examiner would be able to tell for sure.

Shelby was dozing when Frank knocked on the front door. For a moment, she couldn't remember why he was there, but then it all came rushing back to her. She hobbled to the door—stiff from being curled up on the sofa—and pulled it open.

Frank looked wet, cold, and tired.

"Can I get you a cup of tea or coffee?" Shelby asked as she held the door wide.

Frank's eyes crinkled as he smiled. "Do you have anything stronger? It's been quite a night."

He followed Shelby out to the kitchen, where she rummaged in the pantry and pulled out a slightly dusty bottle of Knob Creek bourbon. She poured a splash into a tumbler.

"Ice?" She held the glass toward Frank.

He shook his head. "I'll take it neat."

Shelby put the drink down on the table in front of him and took a seat opposite, pulling her legs in to avoid his long ones, which were stretched out under the table.

Dear Reader, Frank looks so comfortable sitting at my kitchen table—as if he belongs there. I'm not sure if that is a good thing or not.

Frank took a big gulp of the bourbon and sighed. "I needed that."

"What did you find out about that grave and the . . . body?"

"The ME confirmed the remains were human. We won't know much more until the autopsy is completed. He promised to get on it right away." He shook his head. "Pathologists get all excited about cases like this. He's going to start on it tonight."

Shelby shivered. "So, you don't have any idea whose body it might be?"

"It doesn't take a genius to come to the conclusion that it's Brenda Barnstable's. She's been missing now for a couple of years and suddenly a body turns up in a shallow grave on Zeke's farm."

"Do you think Zeke killed her?"

"Seems pretty likely, don't you think?"

18

Dear Reader,

The sun is out today. Mist is rising from the puddles
dotting the driveway as they slowly dry up. Yesterday's
rain also brought out the earthworms in the gardens.

Earthworms play an essential role in growing things
by improving the fertility of the soil and helping with
soil drainage by creating channels as they burrow.

I've read that the Maori of New Zealand eat certain
species of earthworms and consider them a delicacy.
I am grateful for the job they do in my garden, but I do
not plan to cook up a batch anytime soon!

Shelby heard a car coming up her drive and peered out
the window to see Bert pulling up outside the mudroom
door. She quickly hid the carrot cake she'd made for

Bert's birthday in the laundry room and then went to open the door.

"Happy birthday," Shelby said as soon as Bert reached the mudroom.

"Why, thanks." Bert grinned broadly. "I'm grateful for every one I have. Although at my age, the sands are about done running through the hourglass, so who knows how many more I have left?"

"You're going to live forever," Shelby said, and she meant it even though she knew it was impossible. She couldn't imagine life without Bert.

The door to the laundry room was open a smidge, and out of the corner of her eye, Shelby noticed Jenkins nudging it open farther. She hurried over, shooed Jenkins away with her foot, and pushed the door closed until she heard the latch click.

Jenkins looked very disappointed and went to join Bitsy in a sunbeam that was throwing light across the kitchen floor.

"You're looking a little peaked," Bert said, examining Shelby's face. "Rough night?"

"You can say that again. Let's have some coffee, and I'll tell you about it."

Bert retrieved mugs from the cupboard while Shelby filled the coffee machine with fresh coffee and water. She pushed the ON button, and the machine gurgled to life. Moments later, she and Bert were seated at the kitchen table, mugs in hand, picking at the remains of a coffee cake Shelby had made two days ago.

Shelby told Bert about Amelia going to Zeke's without telling her, Amelia's arriving home in a panic after finding the body, and Shelby's own trip out to Zeke's farm.

Bert whistled and put her coffee cup down with a clang. "So Zeke did kill his wife after all."

"We don't know that. . . ."

"If it walks like a duck, quacks like a duck . . ." Bert took a sip of her coffee. "Plenty of people thought he did it, but the body was never found. For all anyone knew, Brenda had hightailed it to Alaska, where she was living in an igloo and fishing for her dinner."

"It does seem the most obvious deduction that the body is Brenda's," Shelby conceded.

"Pretty stupid of Zeke to bury the body on his own property. Of course, it doesn't matter now. She was never found while he was alive, and I suppose that means he was successful in covering up her murder." Bert drained the remaining coffee in her mug and put it down with a conclusive bang.

"It does make me wonder about Tonya Perry," Bert continued, picking at the last of the coffee cake crumbs. "She was convinced that Zeke murdered his wife. Maybe she finally decided to make him pay for the crime she assumed he'd committed."

"I think you might be right," Shelby said, thinking of the things she'd heard about Tonya.

But how was she going to prove it?

||||||||||||||||||||||||||

Shelby had decided to let Amelia stay home. The fact that Amelia and her friends had found a body would be all over school, and Shelby wanted to spare her the questions that she'd no doubt have to field. The less said about the incident, the better, and the sooner Amelia could begin to forget about it.

Amelia still hadn't appeared downstairs when Shelby began making some mozzarella cheese. She planned to use it in a white bean, tomato, and mozzarella salad for the church's luncheon for the Women's Auxiliary.

Mozzarella was easy to make—milk, citric acid, and rennet produced a deliciously creamy version of the cheese.

Amelia slunk into the kitchen while Shelby was squeezing the whey from the curds.

"Gross," she said, peering over Shelby's shoulder. "What is that?"

"It's the cheese you love to have on your pizza—mozzarella."

"Oh."

Amelia rummaged in the pantry, pulled out some cereal, and began eating it straight from the box.

Shelby opened her mouth to say something but decided against it. She couldn't decide exactly how to approach Amelia about the previous evening. Of course, the longer she put it off, the harder it would get.

"Do you want to talk about what happened last night?"

Amelia looked at Shelby and tears sprang to her eyes.

"Do I have to? I just want to forget the whole thing. I couldn't sleep. I kept seeing the body. . . ."

Shelby looked at her daughter. There were the telltale bags under her eyes that confirmed her lack of sleep, and her face was white and strained.

Shelby put a hand on Amelia's shoulder, and Amelia briefly put her own hand over her mother's.

"No, you don't. Not right now. I just thought . . ."

Shelby dropped her hand and turned back to the counter. She plopped the ball of mozzarella cheese into a waiting bowl of ice water and poured the whey into a container and put it in the refrigerator—she would use it later to make bread.

When she turned around again, Amelia had disappeared back upstairs, taking the box of cereal with her.

Shelby finished making the mozzarella and put it in the refrigerator to chill. She'd soaked some great northern beans overnight, and they'd been on the stove since she got up to feed the chickens.

All she needed to do was slice some tomatoes, snip some basil from the garden, and assemble the salad.

She looked down at herself. And she'd have to change. She couldn't show up for the lunch in her working-in-the-kitchen-and-garden clothes!

Shelby was about to head upstairs when the front doorbell rang.

Dear Reader, why do people only show up when I'm wearing my grubbiest clothes and I have yet to comb my hair?

"Oh," Shelby said when she saw Frank standing on her doorstep.

"I hope I'm not bothering you."

He had his cap in his hands and was kneading the brim nervously.

"No. Come in." Shelby whirled around. "Would you like something to drink?"

Frank shook his head. "Thanks, but I can't stay. I have some news I thought you'd be interested in."

"Come on. Let's go into the kitchen, and I'll get you a glass of lemonade. I made it this morning."

Frank grinned. "In that case, I won't say no."

Shelby poured glasses of lemonade while Frank sat at the kitchen table and stretched out his legs.

"The pathologist was up half the night examining the remains," Frank said after he'd had a sip of his drink. "He discovered there was an old break in the corpse's femur—the leg bone," he explained.

Shelby nodded. She knew what a femur was.

"He seemed pretty excited about it, and I couldn't see why, but then Doreen—she's the department secretary—pointed out that until Dr. Gregson arrived in town, everyone went to old Doc Parsons."

"I know—we all did."

"Exactly. Seeing as how we already suspected the remains belonged to Brenda Barnstable, Dr. Gregson agreed to check the patient files he'd inherited from Doc Parsons."

Frank leaned his chair back on two legs, and Shelby held her breath.

"Fortunately Doc Parsons kept good records, unlike a lot of medics his age. Dr. Gregson found X-rays in Brenda's file. Upon examination, they showed that Brenda had broken her leg in the exact same spot the corpse's leg was broken."

"Really?"

"Yup. Dr. Gregson had a look and then the pathologist confirmed it. Of course, we'll have to wait on the DNA test results—fortunately Zeke Barnstable had kept Brenda's toothbrush and hairbrush in the bathroom exactly where she'd left them."

"So you don't know for sure?"

"As sure as we need to be at this stage. The DNA

evidence will clinch the deal if and when this ends up in court."

Frank drained his glass. "I won't keep you any longer. I thought you'd want to know."

"Yes, thanks."

Frank walked to the front door and paused with his hand on the doorknob.

"I hope you don't think I'm making up excuses to see you."

Shelby felt her face grow hot. "No, no. Not at all. I appreciate your stopping by to give me this news."

Frank nodded and opened the front door.

"I guess I'll see you," he called over his shoulder as he headed down the walk to his truck.

IIIIIIIIIIIIIIIIIIIIIIIII

Mrs. Willoughby was atwitter when Shelby arrived at the church hall with her salad. Her face was red and shiny with perspiration, and she was panting slightly.

"Move it a bit to the left," she said to a woman who was positioning a vase of wildflowers—they looked as if they'd been plucked from the side of the road—on one of the long tables that had been set up end to end.

The tables were covered in half a dozen mismatched white tablecloths that were on loan from members of the Women's Auxiliary. Places had been set with the church's utilitarian silverware and thick white china.

Mrs. Willoughby pulled a tissue out of her sleeve and sneezed into it.

"Those flowers are wreaking havoc with my hay fever." She tucked the tissue back up her sleeve and pointed to a long table that was apart from the others. "We're setting up the buffet over there. Jenny Hubbard has brought three of her lemon meringue pies." Mrs. Willoughby kneaded her doughy hands. "I do hope no one will put pepper on them this time." She gave a high-pitched giggle.

"I don't think we have to worry about that," Shelby murmured soothingly.

A group of women walked in and stood chatting idly. Mrs. Willoughby bustled over to them and shooed them toward the table.

"It's time to get started," Shelby heard her trill at the group.

Shelby hurried over to place her salad on the buffet table, which boasted an interesting spread of food—meatballs simmering in a slow cooker, a casserole with crushed potato chips on top, a platter of deli meats and cheeses, bread and rolls, and a large pan of lasagna.

Shelby turned back to the dining table, where it looked as if a game of musical chairs was in progress, with much switching of seats and rearranging of chairs. Shelby found herself a seat between Mrs. Willoughby and Coralynne, with Isabel and Jenny Hubbard directly across the table. Isabel's heavy gardenia perfume wafted in Shelby's direction and she felt a slight headache beginning.

Mrs. Willoughby and Coralynne heaped a bit of each of the dishes from the buffet spread onto their plates while Isabel had some of Shelby's white bean, tomato, and mozzarella salad, a plain green salad, and a small square of lasagna. Isabel glanced at the plates of the other two ladies, and Shelby thought she looked aghast.

As soon as everyone had returned to their seats from the buffet line, Mrs. Willoughby banged her spoon against her glass. The chatter dipped to a murmur and finally died out.

"I want to welcome everyone today to our annual luncheon. I want to remind you about the Christmas bazaar. October will be here before we know it. Time is of the essence. We need to have our ducks in a row. If you haven't already signed up to volunteer, please do. We need all hands on deck." She paused. "Now please go ahead and enjoy your lunch."

Dear Reader, Mrs. Willoughby is certainly full of clichés today, isn't she?

Mrs. Willoughby sat down and beamed at Shelby, Coralynne, Jenny, and Isabel. She rubbed her hands together.

"What a delicious-looking meal we have here—don't you think?"

Isabel poked at her salad with her fork. She looked up, her eyes shining. "I heard that Brenda Barnstable's body has been found at long last."

Coralynne paused with her fork halfway to her mouth, a piece of lettuce dangling precariously from the tines. "You don't say!"

Mrs. Willoughby leaned forward, and barely missed planting her considerable bosom in her lasagna.

"Yes. And on Zeke's Barnstable's property," Mrs. Willoughby said, and Shelby envisioned the words printed in bold. "That proves it, don't you agree?"

Coralynne shivered with excitement. "Do you think he felt so guilty that he was forced to take his own life?"

Mrs. Willoughby shot her an impatient look. "By hitting himself over the head with a hammer?"

Shelby stifled a laugh by pretending to be choking on

her food. She cleared her throat loudly and followed it up with a big gulp from her water glass.

Coralynne looked momentarily miffed, but curiosity got the better of her. She turned to Shelby.

"Have you heard anything? After all, your brother-in-law is on the police force."

"No, I'm afraid not."

Both Coralynne and Mrs. Willoughby looked at Shelby as if they didn't believe her.

"I think it's obvious who did it, and it wasn't Brenda's husband," Jenny spoke up abruptly. She leaned closer over the table. "I think it was Tonya Perry."

Mrs. Willoughby sucked in air through her teeth. "I have heard that she threatened Zeke when she found out that Brenda had gone missing. She's a big woman, and although Zeke is a farmer, he's awful skinny and not very tall."

"That type is often surprisingly strong," Coralynne said. "My brother is as thin as a beanpole, but that time I wanted to move my refrigerator, he picked it up as if it was nothing."

"I can't see Tonya getting up the energy to do much of anything," Mrs. Willoughby said. "She's no use as a volunteer. You have to keep after her the whole time, like a sheepdog after an errant member of the flock. I don't know what Daniel sees in her."

Isabel stiffened and her lips thinned into a straight line.

Jenny scowled at Mrs. Willoughby. "Did I ever tell you what Tonya did to my Tracy?"

"Yes," Mrs. Willoughby said decisively.

"Don't you think that proves she's capable of almost anything?" Isabel said.

"But murder," Coralynne protested.

Jenny toyed with her fork, poking at the remains of her lunch and scraping the tines through the last bits of macaroni salad on her plate.

Her face drooped into defeated folds. "I'm afraid that as much as I hate Tonya, she can't have killed Zeke."

"What?" the table gasped.

Jenny nodded. "It's true. My Tracy decided to come to the fair. She said she wanted to see me win." Jenny preened but then her expression grew disappointed. "And I would have if Tonya hadn't doused my pie with pepper."

"Go on," Mrs. Willoughby said rather testily.

Jenny told the story Shelby had already heard—about the suspicion that Tonya had set fire to Tracy's piece in the university art competition.

Shelby noticed Isabel's eyes glittering as Jenny told her story.

Dear Reader, I have the sneaking suspicion that Isabel is going to run straight to Daniel with this story in order to discredit her rival for his affections.

By the time Jenny finished telling her story, her face was red and she was slightly out of breath.

Mrs. Willoughby pursed her lips. "I don't see how that proves that Tonya didn't murder Zeke. If anything, I would say it proves the opposite—that she's obviously capable of it."

Jenny scowled at Mrs. Willoughby. "Well, I'm not finished with the story, am I? I only needed to catch my breath for a minute."

Mrs. Willoughby sat back in her chair, her posture stiff with irritation.

"Like I was telling you"—Jenny shot Mrs. Willoughby

a dirty look—"my Tracy came to the fair for the pie contest. She didn't expect to see Tonya there, and obviously Tonya didn't expect to see her. It was right before Isabel tried that bite of my pie. As soon as Tonya clapped eyes on Tracy, Tonya took off running. If that doesn't say something about her guilt, I don't know what does."

"Did Tracy catch up with Tonya?" Shelby said.

Jenny shook her head. "No, but she followed her all the way to the exit of the fair and even out into the parking lot. Unfortunately Tonya jumped in her car and took off. Tracy said she only wanted to talk to her about the incident. To have what she called *closure*."

Dear Reader, it certainly sounds as if Tonya didn't have time to murder Zeke. She was with me at the pie contest and then in Tracy's sights the rest of the time. Unless the station wagon where Zeke's body had been found was left unattended earlier. I will have to check with Jake.

19

Dear Reader,

I try not to listen to gossip, but sometimes it's the only
way to get information. But as the saying goes, believe
nothing of what you hear and only half of what you see.
I do think Jenny was telling the truth though—she certainly wouldn't go out of her way to give Tonya an alibi.

Shelby stayed behind after the lunch to help clean up. As
she was clearing the dishes away, she noticed a group of
women edging their way toward the door.

Mrs. Willoughby, whose hands were full of dirty
plates, came up to Shelby and poked Shelby with her
elbow. "There they go sneaking out. The same ones every
time. Leaving us to do all the work."

Shelby wasn't surprised. Cleaning up wasn't the most popular volunteer job.

She carried her armload of dishes to the large plastic bus tubs that Coralynne had placed on the now-empty buffet table.

With all the dirty dishes cleared off the tables, Shelby began bundling up the tablecloths.

"Where do you want me to put these?" she asked Mrs. Willoughby.

"If you could take them down to my office, that would be wonderful. The owners can pick them up there." Mrs. Willoughby sighed. "Maybe we can put some of the money from the Christmas bazaar toward buying St. Andrews its own tablecloths."

"Good idea," Shelby said as she headed toward the door.

The old wooden floors in the hallway creaked under Shelby's feet as she walked toward Mrs. Willoughby's office. Shelby found the sound comforting along with the slightly dusty smell wafting from the worn and nearly threadbare Oriental carpet.

The door to Mrs. Willoughby's office was partially closed. Shelby eased it open with her elbow and stepped inside. The light was on in Daniel's office, and the scent of gardenias wafted toward Shelby.

She tiptoed farther into the room and strained to hear the murmured voices coming through the open door. Shelby could tell by the perfume that Isabel was Daniel's companion. And as she listened, she realized her suspicions had been right—Isabel was filling Daniel in on everything Jenny Hubbard had told them about Tonya.

Shelby put the tablecloths down on the chair beside Mrs. Willoughby's desk and tiptoed out of the room again.

When she got back to the hall, the cleanup was done and Mrs. Willoughby was giving the tables a final wipe.

"You go on, dear," she called out to Shelby. "Everything's been taken care of."

Shelby glanced at her watch and then hurried out to her car. She'd invited Bert to come by at three o'clock. She hadn't mentioned the cake, but she was pretty sure Bert would be able to guess what the invitation was all about.

Shelby was pulling into her driveway when she noticed Billy's school bus coming down the road. She walked to the end of the drive and waited for him to get off.

"Hi, Mom," he said before trudging ahead of her toward the house, his backpack slung from one shoulder.

"I'm hungry," he said as soon as they'd walked in the back door.

"Bert's coming over for some birthday cake. Can you wait a few more minutes?"

Billy groaned. "Okay."

Shelby set the cake on the table and added a few candles.

"You'll need more candles than that. Bert is ancient."

Shelby looked up to see Amelia standing in the doorway.

"I wouldn't say *ancient*, and I don't think we want to risk burning down the house."

"I'm here, I'm here," Bert called as she opened the door to the mudroom and wiped her feet on the mat. "What's this all about?" She glanced around and the look of surprise on her face would have done any Oscar-winning actor proud.

When she turned to Shelby, she had tears in her eyes.

"You shouldn't have. And my favorite cake, too."

Shelby smiled to herself. They enacted this little charade every year on Bert's birthday, and neither of them ever grew tired of it.

Dear Reader, I don't think Amelia is amused—I saw her roll her eyes.

"Can we have some cake now?" Billy sat slumped in his chair, his elbows on the table and his chin in his hands.

Bert laughed. "Let me blow out the candles first." She leaned across the table and gave a big huff. "Hand me that knife, would you?"

Bert cut generous slices and pushed the plates toward Billy and Amelia, then handed Shelby one.

Bert turned to Shelby. "So, how was the luncheon? They've been trying to get me to join for years, but the last thing I want to do is hang around with a bunch of church ladies."

Shelby laughed. "They're a good group. Mostly."

Bert grunted.

"Can I go out now?"

Shelby looked over at Billy's plate. It was empty except for a smear of frosting.

"Okay."

Billy shoved his chair back, dropped his plate into the sink, and headed out the door, letting it slam behind him.

"He never stops moving," Shelby said.

"Boys."

"Happy birthday, Bert," Amelia said as she, too, stood up and deposited her plate in the sink.

"Thanks, honey," Bert said as Amelia left the room.

Shelby began to tell Bert about Jenny Hubbard's daughter being able to give Tonya an alibi.

"I guess that rules her out."

"And Isabel made short work of sharing the information about Tonya's past with Daniel. I heard them in his office and she was filling him in on all the gory details."

"You've got to give her credit for determination." Bert cut herself another sliver of cake. "Who's next on our list of suspects?"

Shelby licked the last bit of cream cheese icing off the tines of her fork. "Ryan Archer is still a possibility. He lied about being at the fair and apparently doesn't have an alibi. At least not one he's willing to share."

They sat in silence for a moment, listening to the birds chirping outside.

Suddenly Bert jumped to her feet. "I'll help you with the dishes."

"No, you won't," Shelby said. "It's your birthday. You sit and put your feet up."

"I can tell by the stubborn look on your face that there's no point in arguing with you." Bert sank back onto her chair.

Shelby rinsed the plates and stacked them in the dishwasher.

"Have you done anything about those pots and pans yet?" Bert said.

Shelby felt prickles of guilt. "No. I don't know what to do. I can't possibly endorse a product that's so terrible."

"Send 'em back, then."

"But the money . . ."

"You wouldn't be able to live with yourself if you did anything else."

"Yes," Shelby sighed.

Suddenly there was a rap on the wood of the screen door, and Shelby heard it squeak open.

Jake strode into the kitchen. His expression was stern, and he was grasping Billy by the back of his shirt. Billy refused to meet Shelby's eyes but instead looked down at his feet.

"What happened?"

"I caught this young man egging my henhouse." He gave Billy a slight shake like a terrier might shake a mouse.

Shelby gasped. Billy certainly knew better than that. Eggs were food, and to deface someone else's property . . . What had gotten into him?

"Billy!"

Billy mumbled something that sounded like *I'm sorry, Mom.*

"Why would you do something like that? You know better."

Billy shrugged and continued to stare at his feet.

Shelby looked at Jake. "Billy will clean it all up. Won't you, Billy?"

Jake's lips twitched into a smile. "We've already decided on that, haven't we, Billy?"

Billy grunted.

"I've got a bucket and sponges and some soap." Shelby rushed over to the broom closet.

"Don't bother," Jake said. "I've got all of that myself." He gave Billy's shirt a slight tug. "Come on, buddy, you've got some work to do."

Shelby stood in stunned silence as the door closed behind Jake and her son.

"I don't know what's gotten into him." She turned to Bert. "He's never done anything like that before."

Bert gave her an all-knowing look. "Seems to me he needs a father. Your neighbor"—she jerked a thumb toward the door—"would be the perfect candidate. He's handsome and kind and Billy already likes him."

Dear Reader, I love Bert. I really do, but sometimes I wish she would mind her own business. Especially when she's right. Maybe not about Jake but certainly about Billy needing a father.

|||||||||||||||||||||||||||

Shelby padded out to the garden barefoot. She loved the feel of the earth on her bare feet, warm from the afternoon sun. Her tomatoes were still blooming although they would soon come to an end. She knew from experience that the first frost was just around the corner. One plant was heavy with several large tomatoes. Shelby picked them all and carried them inside.

Tonight was the viewing for Zeke Barnstable. The ME had finally released the body. The closest funeral parlor was in Allenvale, so the body had been sent there originally, but the wake itself was being held in the hall at St. Andrews to make it easier for local people to attend.

Shelby cut the tomatoes in half and squeezed the seeds into the sink. She then grated the flesh and put the resulting pulp into a large saucepan. She added olive oil, salt and pepper, a sprig of basil leaves, and some tomato paste, gave it a good stir, and left it to simmer for fifteen minutes while the water for the pasta boiled.

Billy was watching television in the living room. He was unusually subdued following the incident at Jake's. While Shelby had expressed her disappointment in his behavior, she hadn't said much of anything else. An afternoon in the sun applying elbow grease to Jake's henhouse had taught Billy more of a lesson than anything she could have said or done.

Shelby poured the pasta into the water and lowered the heat. She stuck her head into the living room and called Billy for dinner, then went to the bottom of the stairs and yelled for Amelia.

||||||||||||||||||||||||||

"Why are we eating so early?" Amelia said as she twirled spaghetti around her fork.

"I have to go to church tonight for a viewing."

"What's a viewing?" Billy asked.

She hesitated. How to explain the concept to someone as young as Billy?

"It's when someone dies and everyone goes to check out the body," Amelia said before Shelby could answer.

"Cool," Billy said. "Can I go, Mom?"

"I'm afraid not. You can stay here and finish your homework. Amelia will look after you." Shelby looked across the table at Amelia.

"I don't need looking after. I stayed all by myself the other night, didn't I?"

Shelby raised her eyebrow at him and Billy went back to slurping up his spaghetti.

"Amelia, can you do the dishes? I have to get cleaned up."

"Sure."

⁞⁞⁞⁞⁞⁞⁞⁞⁞⁞⁞⁞⁞⁞⁞⁞⁞⁞⁞⁞⁞⁞⁞

Shelby took a quick shower—her hands smelled like freshly picked tomatoes and who knows what the rest of her smelled like?—and changed into a skirt and blouse she hadn't worn since her brief stint working in Chicago. She was surprised to find that the skirt was loose. She didn't consciously set out to exercise—she didn't have to. Working on a farm was exercise in and of itself.

The viewing was set for seven o'clock and Shelby pulled into the church parking lot at a quarter after the hour. She didn't want to be the first to arrive—that could have been terribly awkward—but she didn't want to be too late, either. She had no idea whether Zeke had any family besides Rebecca, but there was already a respectable number of cars in the parking lot.

Shelby heard voices as soon as she headed down the hallway to the church hall—muted in deference, no doubt, to the solemnity of the occasion.

A shiny wooden casket was displayed at the front of the room with a small spray of flowers in front of it. Shelby stood at the door for a moment and scanned the crowd. She saw Bert talking to Coralynne. Mrs. Willoughby was, as usual, officiously bustling about the room. Jodi Walters was there, too. Her son, Ned, was the one who had broken Amelia's heart. Shelby noticed Rebecca, Zeke's sister, standing with several people clustered around her.

Most of those in attendance were other farmers. While they didn't socialize all that much, they were there for one another and Zeke was one of their own.

Shelby supposed she ought to pay her respects to Rebecca first. By the time Shelby reached her, the small group around Rebecca had broken up and Rebecca was standing alone.

Shelby was surprised to see she had a damp tissue in one hand. The only other time she'd met Rebecca, she had had the impression that Rebecca and Zeke hadn't gotten along. Maybe she had been mistaken.

"I'm sorry for your loss." Shelby uttered the timeworn phrase. "I didn't know Zeke well, but he used to give us corn every summer. We really appreciated it."

Rebecca pressed the sodden tissue to her eyes. "Yes, Zeke was generous to a fault."

Shelby felt like she did when she used to play pin the tail on the donkey as a child and she would be spun around and around until she was dizzy. This new version of Rebecca had her totally confused.

A tall woman, stooped at the shoulders, approached, and Rebecca turned to greet her. Shelby escaped with a barely concealed sigh of relief. She turned around and nearly ran smack into Jodi Walters.

Given the romantic entanglement between Jodi's son and Shelby's daughter, Shelby greeted the woman with a certain coolness that wasn't like her.

Jodi didn't seem to notice. She indicated Rebecca with a nod of her head.

"What's gotten into her? Acting like she gives two hoots about her brother's death when everyone knows she resented him like crazy."

"Why would she resent him?"

"While Rebecca was off gallivanting who knows where, Zeke was taking care of their parents and doing all the work on the farm. Is it any wonder, then, that the farm was left entirely to him?"

Shelby glanced at Rebecca. "Who gets the farm now, with Zeke gone?"

Jodi shrugged. "I would imagine Rebecca does." She jerked her head in Rebecca's direction. "Although I don't know what this big act of hers is all about. It's not like she's fooling anyone. When Rebecca came back from wherever it was she'd been, she and Zeke had a knock-down, drag-out fight over at the Dixie Bar and Grill."

"Were you there?"

"Are you kidding? With three kids at home I don't have time to hang out at the Dixie." She shook her head. "No, someone told me about it. I can't remember who."

A short, dark-haired woman waved to Jodi from across the room and Jodi murmured an apology and moved away. Shelby stood where she was for another moment, thinking. Rebecca had resented her brother getting the farm, but now that he was dead and she was the one to inherit the land, who was to say she hadn't killed him to make that happen?

20

Dear Reader,

As I walked from my car to the church, I noticed the increasing chill in the air even though it's only mid-September. It's already a little cooler than it was last week—which means my onions should be ready for harvesting soon. You will know they're finished growing because the tops dry out and fall over. Left too long, they will spoil in the cooler temperatures.

Once they've been harvested they have to dry for several weeks before going into the cellar for storage. Even though I could never braid Amelia's hair to save my life, I do manage to braid the onion tops, which makes for a nice presentation.

I'm looking forward to baking an onion tart with the first of the crop. It's easy to make and includes bacon.

Anything with bacon is good, right? I will share the
recipe in a future blog post.

Shelby was about to leave the church hall when she remembered that Bert had said her neighbor worked at
the Dixie Bar and Grill. It was probably too much to hope
for that she'd been there the evening Rebecca had had the
fight with Zeke, but it was worth asking.

Bert was standing over by the door, collecting her
purse and sweater from the chair where she'd left them,
when Shelby approached her.

"Zeke got a good turnout," Bert said as she slipped on
her pale blue cardigan and hung her purse from the crook
of her arm. "He would have been pleased, although a
crowd this size would have scared him."

"I was talking to Jodi, and she said that when Zeke's
sister returned after having been off somewhere for years,
she caught up with Zeke out at the Dixie, and they had a
huge fight. Didn't you say your neighbor works there?"

"She does."

"I wonder if she was there when this fight occurred."

"You can ask her.

Shelby glanced at the clock on the wall of the church
hall. "Do you think she'd be home now?"

"Not likely since I saw her leave as I was pulling my
car out of the garage. She was wearing her Dixie Bar and
Grill T-shirt, and as far as I know, she only ever wears
that if she's going to work."

"Maybe I could catch up with her there." Shelby
hesitated.

"Do you want me to pop in and make sure the kids
are okay?"

Dear Reader, sometimes I swear Bert can read my mind.

"I hate to put you out. . . ."

"Don't be silly." Bert smiled. "Is there any of that carrot cake left, by any chance?"

"There is. And put on some coffee if you'd like."

"I don't mind if I do." She shooed Shelby with her hand. "You go on ahead and see what you can find out at the Dixie. I'll stay with the kids."

Shelby started to walk away but then turned around again. "What is your neighbor's name?"

"Doris. Doris Daniels."

With Bert at the farm, Shelby wouldn't have to worry. She didn't like the idea of leaving Billy and Amelia alone at night—especially not after Amelia's escapade the other night.

Shelby had been to the Dixie once or twice with Bill, but neither of them had particularly enjoyed the place. In the summer they preferred sitting in rocking chairs side by side on their front porch, and in the winter, who wanted to go out when you could snuggle together on the couch in front of the fire?

The Dixie was housed in a squat brick building with a neon sign that had several letters that didn't light and a parking lot that desperately needed repaving. Shelby pulled in, jouncing over a giant pothole, and finally eased her car into a space on the end of a row of pickup trucks and cars with more rust on them than paint.

Although the evening was cool, the air conditioner hummed and a pool of condensation dripped onto the walkway to the right of the front door.

The interior was dim, and even though smoking was

no longer allowed, the odor of Marlboros and Kools from earlier, less restrictive times still clung to the walls and the flat carpet that was so worn, it was impossible to tell what the original design had been.

The patrons sitting at the bar were almost exclusively male, but there were a few couples seated at the handful of pockmarked wooden tables in the back. A group of men holding cans of beer clustered around a pool table, shouting encouragement to the players.

A waitress with blond hair and gray roots hurried past, carrying a large tray laden with heavy chipped plates of hamburgers and fries. Shelby didn't see anyone else waiting tables so she assumed this had to be Doris Daniels, Bert's neighbor.

Shelby watched as Doris slid the food in front of customers at two of the tables, then, with her empty tray tucked under her arm, headed back toward the bar and the swinging door to the kitchen.

She must have caught sight of Shelby standing just beyond the entrance, because she changed paths and headed toward her.

"Can I help you?" she asked when she reached Shelby. "As you can see, it's seat yourself." She waved toward the tables, several of which sat empty.

Shelby cleared her throat nervously. "I wanted to talk to you. I'm a friend of Bert's."

Doris looked startled. "A friend of Bert's, huh? Nothing's happened to her, I hope."

"No, nothing like that. I wanted to ask you a few questions."

"Now I'm curious. I've got my break coming up in five

minutes. I usually go outside for a smoke. Meet me out back?"

Shelby nodded, and Doris turned and quickly strode away toward the kitchen.

Five minutes. Shelby couldn't stand the smell and the noise of the Dixie for another minute, let alone five. She would go outside and wait.

Shelby made her way around to the rear of the building. An overflowing dark blue plastic garbage can sat to the right of the door where the overhead light flickered like a strobe.

Barely five minutes had passed before the back door flew open and Doris stepped out, a cigarette at the ready in one hand and a red plastic lighter in the other.

The flash from the lighter was a brief glow against the deepening darkness, illuminating Doris's face and accentuating the lines around her mouth, nose, and eyes.

She exhaled a plume of smoke and smiled at Shelby. "So, what can I do for you?"

Shelby took a deep breath. She should have given some thought as to how she was going to present this to Doris. Maybe plunging in was the best way.

"I understand that Zeke Barnstable used to be a regular here."

"Regular as rain," Doris said, drawing in smoke. "He and that Jim Harris. Every Thursday night for years. But then a funny thing happened—Zeke stopped coming around. Of course, now he's dead."

"That's sort of why I'm here," Shelby said. "I heard that Zeke's sister tracked him down here one night a while back."

"Rebecca?" Doris gave a laugh that ended in a gurgling cough. "Darn right, she did. Disappears for I don't know how long and then the first thing she does after she comes back is pick a fight with her brother."

"Do you know what they argued about?"

Doris attempted another laugh but it was cut short by a cough. "Everyone knew what it was about. She made it plain as day and as loud as could be."

Shelby waited patiently while Doris drew on her cigarette again.

"It was about money. What else? And the fact that their parents had died and had left the farm to Zeke while she was away."

"She blamed Zeke?"

Doris ground her cigarette out under the heel of her sneaker and then kicked it off the walkway onto the grass where Shelby could see a cluster of other extinguished butts.

"She did. She was furious. Talked about getting some lawyer to prove that Zeke had—'unduly influenced' is what I think she said—their parents. Seems to me she'd already talked to a lawyer, or else I don't know where she would have picked up an expression like that."

"Do you think she was really mad? Maybe it was grief at finding her parents had died?"

Doris threw back her head and laughed. "Honey, she threatened to kill him. Sure, I think she meant it."

||||||||||||||||||||||||||

Bert was asleep in front of the television, her knitting abandoned in her lap, when Shelby got home.

Bert woke with a start. "I must have dozed off there."

"Everything go okay?"

"Fine. Billy is in bed. I had to force him to get him into the bath, but he finally had a wash. Amelia went upstairs, but I can't promise she isn't texting her friends on that phone of hers." Bert eased herself out of her chair with a grunt. "There's still some coffee, if you'd like a cup."

"That sounds good."

Bert followed Shelby out to the kitchen and watched while Shelby poured herself a mug of coffee.

"Are the dogs outside?" Shelby said as she blew on her coffee.

"Yes. They were in the mudroom whining, so I let them out."

Shelby went to the back door and whistled. Moments later Bitsy and Jenkins came bounding through the mudroom and into the kitchen, smelling of fresh air, sun, and dirt. They circled around and around Shelby while she scratched their backs and patted their heads.

"So, tell me. What did you find out from Doris?" Bert said when Shelby joined her at the kitchen table.

Shelby cupped her mug of coffee between her hands. The last sliver of carrot cake sat on a platter in the middle of the table.

"According to Doris, Rebecca showed up at the Dixie one night and had it out with Zeke. She claimed he influenced their parents into leaving the entire farm to him."

Bert snorted. "I can't imagine what she'd thought they were going to do, seeing as how no one knew where she was. And she'd never shown a lick of interest in the farm—certainly not when it came to pulling her weight with chores."

"I imagine the property is worth something. Even if you didn't plan to farm it. It's only a matter of time before one of those big, fancy housing developments pops up in Lovett."

Shelby shaved a bit of cake off the remaining piece and popped it into her mouth.

"Land is always worth something. That's why my daddy used to say, don't put your money in the bank—invest it in something you can stand on."

Bert stood up and took her coffee cup to the sink, where she rinsed it out and put it in the dishwasher.

"Do you think I should tell the police about the fight between Rebecca and her brother?"

Bert paused with her hand on the counter. "If by *the police* you mean Frank, I don't see why not. Even they occasionally miss something."

||||||||||||||||||||||||

Shelby sat in the living room, the television muted but flickering in the corner, and stared at the cell phone in her lap. Should she call Frank? She glanced at the clock on the mantle. Maybe it was too late? Maybe she should wait till morning?

But by morning she might have lost her nerve. She gave herself a shake. Frank was her brother-in-law. She'd known him almost as long as she'd known Bill. There was no reason to be nervous about calling him.

Dear Reader, I know perfectly well why I'm nervous— I'm afraid Frank might take the call the wrong way. But I am going to indulge myself a little longer by pretending that I don't realize this.

There was a noise from upstairs and Shelby stopped with her cell phone in her hand. She waited, holding her breath, but all was quiet. It was probably Billy rolling over in his sleep.

Impatience finally got the better of Shelby—impatience with herself—and she dialed Frank's cell phone. He answered on the fourth ring. There was noise in the background—a woman's voice? Shelby forced herself not to examine why that caused her a frisson of distress. It was none of her business who Frank spent his time with. He might have been at the office and it was a colleague. Or perhaps it was Nancy—although their divorce was final they might still have things to discuss.

"'Lo?" Frank's usual laconic greeting sounded dispirited—as if he was tired or discouraged about the case.

"Hello," Shelby said.

"Shelby." The tone of his voice became more cheerful. "What's up? Is everything okay? Billy? Amelia?"

"Everything's fine," Shelby said, then hesitated. "I thought there was something you ought to know. It may have some bearing on Zeke's murder."

"Oh?"

"It's about Zeke and his sister, Rebecca. Did you know that when she arrived back in town, they had a huge fight out at the Dixie?"

"Arrived back in town? Where had she been?"

"No one knows, apparently. She just showed up one day."

"Interesting."

The noise behind Frank had died down. She heard him take a sip of—coffee?

"The waitress out there, Doris Daniels, said Rebecca threatened to kill Zeke."

Frank was silent. She heard the tapping of computer keys.

"Here it is," Frank said. "Looks like Lovett's finest got

involved. Someone filed a police report." He was quiet for a moment. "Seems there was no harm done. Officer Prendergast broke up the fight and that was that."

"Until now."

"What do you mean?"

"Zeke is dead. Isn't it possible that Rebecca made good on her threat to kill him?"

Frank's indrawn breath told Shelby everything she needed to know.

"I think this is worth looking into. I'll get on it first thing in the morning."

"Thanks."

"And, Shelby? Are you sure everything is okay?"

"Yes, Frank, we're fine."

Shelby clicked off the call before she could say anything else.

Because there were a lot of things she wanted to say. She was lonely . . . Sometimes she was scared . . . She wasn't always sure she was doing the right thing.

Instead she went out to the kitchen, made a cup of chamomile tea, carried it up to bed, and slipped beneath the covers.

The windows were open and the curtains billowed into the room on the soft night breeze. Shelby picked her book up off the nightstand and opened it. She paused for a moment, listening to the croak of the frogs outside and the chirp of the cicadas, and then she began to read.

21

Dear Reader,

I'm looking out the kitchen window, watching rivulets of water turn the view as blurry as a Monet painting. The rain began sometime during the night and hasn't let up since. I rather enjoyed its comforting patter on the roof while I was curled up snug in bed.

Most people assume farmers welcome rain, and we do—most of the time. But there is such a thing as too much rain. In a dry spell we can always water, but there's not much we can do if it rains for days on end. Too much rain compacts the soil and causes soil loss. It can cause rot and leech important nutrients from the soil.

And you can't get much work done in a flooded field. So while I don't mind that it's raining today—I only hope it lets up by tomorrow.

Shelby turned away from the kitchen window and came face-to-face with the box of cookware she was supposed to be endorsing on her blog. It would have to go back. She'd thought long and hard about it, but she didn't have it in her to fool her readers into buying an inferior product.

Shelby rummaged in the kitchen junk drawer—didn't every kitchen have one?—for her roll of packing tape. As she was securing the flaps, she heard Billy's feet hit the floor overhead. Good—he was up and getting ready for school. She looked at the clock. She would have to call Amelia if she wasn't up in the next ten minutes.

Shelby finished securing and labeling the box while Billy ate his bowl of cereal. She had to go to the feed store for dog food—she would take the package with her and mail it then.

Amelia came dragging down the stairs at the last possible moment, grabbing a granola bar as she ran out the door to catch the school bus. At least it wasn't a toaster pastry, Shelby consoled herself as she watched her daughter disappear down the drive. She was grateful that Amelia was still riding the bus—in a few years she'd have her driver's license and would no doubt want her own car.

It would come as a great shock to Amelia that if she wanted a car, she was going to have to work for one. There was no way an extra automobile fit into Shelby's meager budget.

Shelby tidied up the kitchen, wiping down the counters, scooping the crumbs from her morning toast off the table, and sponging up the bit of milk Billy had dribbled from his bowl of cereal.

She washed her hands, ran a comb through her hair,

and wrestled the bulky package of pots and pans out to her truck. She would send the company an e-mail alerting them to its imminent arrival and explaining why she couldn't possibly endorse their product on her blog.

The Lovett Feed Store was the first stop on Shelby's list of errands. She turned into the parking lot, found a space, and pulled in the pickup truck. As Shelby was getting out, another pickup truck backed out of a space and shot toward the exit of the parking lot, stopping for barely a second before pulling out into the street. Shelby saw only a flash of red but she knew immediately that it had been Frank.

He must have come to talk to Rebecca Barnstable. Shelby felt a vague prickling of guilt for having mentioned the fight between Rebecca and Zeke. But surely Frank would have found out soon enough on his own?

Shelby was grateful that the rain had slowed to a drizzle and she barely got wet as she dashed toward the open door of the feed store.

Inside, it was dim and smelled of grain. Shelby grabbed a cart and wound between sacks of feed stacked one on top of another. The ancient cart had a stuck wheel so that it pulled hard to the left, and Shelby got a workout trying to keep it on track. She pushed it toward the back of the store, where there was a small selection of pet food.

She found the brand she wanted and loaded the unwieldy bag into her cart. As she approached the checkout counter she was disappointed to see that Rebecca wasn't behind the cash register—it was a middle-aged man with thinning hair who Shelby suspected was one of the Van Enks, who had owned the feed store since it opened in her grandparents' time.

"Is Rebecca here today?" Shelby asked when she approached the counter.

"She's taking a break." The man came out from behind the cash register. "No need to take that out of the cart—it's heavy." He used a portable scanner to read the price on the dog food.

Shelby paid for her purchase and put her wallet back in her purse.

"Take the cart out with you," the man said. "Leave it by the front door and I'll send Dieter out to fetch it."

He wasn't going to get an argument from Shelby—the bag was heavy and she was more than happy to leave it in the cart even if steering the thing felt as challenging as controlling a Formula One race car on the Indianapolis Speedway.

The rain had picked up while Shelby was in the store, and it wasn't long before a huge wet splotch plastered her T-shirt to her back. The rain was cool, and despite temperatures in the mid-seventies, she shivered slightly.

She looked around as she wrestled the bag of dog food into the back of her pickup. The cashier had said Rebecca was having her break. Unless she'd stayed inside, there weren't a lot of places to go to relax for a few minutes—especially not in the rain. The roof on the sides of the feed store had a slight overhang that protected the area underneath—maybe Rebecca was sheltering there?

Shelby caught a whiff of cigarette smoke when she rounded the corner and wasn't surprised to see Rebecca leaning against the side of the weathered building, holding the stump of a butt between her fingers.

Shelby's foot slipped on some loose gravel, sending the stones shooting across the concrete walkway. Rebecca jumped at the sound and looked in Shelby's direction.

Even from a distance, Shelby could tell the woman was in distress—her eyes were red and the hand that held the cigarette to her lips was shaking.

She was hunched over, like a crab about to scuttle away from a predator. Shelby held up a hand to indicate she didn't mean any harm.

"Is everything okay?" Shelby asked, employing the same tone of voice she used to soothe Billy and Amelia when they were upset.

Rebecca threw down the end of her cigarette and ground it into the pavement with what looked to Shelby like unnecessary force. She glanced up at Shelby.

"No, everything's not *okay*. Unless you count being questioned by the police as being *okay*."

"I'm sorry. I didn't mean—"

Rebecca's shoulders drooped. "No, I'm sorry. It's not your fault."

She put a hand over her eyes, and Shelby saw her shoulders begin to shake.

"The police think I had something to do with my brother Zeke's death."

"Why would they think that?" Shelby asked although she was pretty sure she already knew the answer.

Rebecca gave a loud sniff. "Someone told them about that fight Zeke and I had a couple of years ago out at the Dixie." She gave a bitter laugh. "Why would I wait this long to kill him?"

Dear Reader, why, indeed? But the fact remains— without Zeke in the picture, Rebecca inherits some property that could prove to be very valuable in the future.

"But if you have an alibi, all you have to do is tell the police, and they'll realize you didn't do it," Shelby said.

Rebecca played with a piece of lank hair she'd pulled over her shoulder. She mumbled something that Shelby didn't catch.

"I'm sorry—what was that?"

"I do have an alibi," Rebecca said, her expression growing sulky. She sketched a circle on the pavement with the toe of her sneaker.

"All you have to do is tell the police where you were and who you were with and that will be the end of it."

"I can't tell them."

"Why not?" Shelby asked gently.

For a moment the only sound was the splat of water dripping off the edge of the overhang onto the ground.

"Because I promised."

iiiiiiiiiiiiiiiiiiiiiiii

Billy was getting out of school early because of scheduled parent-teacher conferences, so when Jim Harris called to see if Billy would like to earn a little pocket money helping muck out some stalls at the stable, Shelby assured him Billy would be there as soon as he'd had some lunch.

"But, Mom, that sounds icky," Billy protested when Shelby told him about it.

"Mucking out stalls is part of being a responsible horseman. Besides, Mr. Harris is willing to pay. I know you've been saving for a new baseball mitt."

Billy kept his father's old glove in his room. Bill had been a pitcher on the Lovett High School baseball team. His junior year the Bobcats had missed being all-state champs by a hair. Shelby knew that Billy tried on the mitt every couple of months but it would be a long while yet before it fit.

Billy continued to grumble as he ate his peanut butter and jelly sandwich—he was on a kick lately where that was all he wanted for lunch no matter what else Shelby had on hand.

While Billy finished his meal, Shelby took advantage of a break in the rain to snip the tops off her basil plants, which were threatening to flower. She inhaled their delicious scent, knowing that their growing season would soon be coming to an end. She would miss all her fresh herbs when winter came.

Billy was watching television when Shelby carried her bounty back inside.

"Are you ready?"

Billy reluctantly retrieved the remote, his finger pausing over the OFF button.

"Billy!"

"Okay." He switched off the television and followed Shelby out to the car.

It was no longer raining, and the dark storm clouds that had hung over the area all morning were quickly blowing east, leaving behind bright blue skies.

Shelby turned into the Harrises' drive and went past the white farmhouse and around back to the stables.

Jim Harris came out of the stables as Shelby pulled up in front and parked.

"Hey, Billy, how's it going?" He gave Billy a high five.

Billy's face brightened slightly.

"Why don't you go say hello to Blackjack before we get started?"

Blackjack was Billy's favorite horse. Billy's face brightened even more, and before Jim could say another word, he was off at a trot toward the open stable door.

"He's a good kid," Jim said when Billy was out of earshot. "You've done a fine job with him."

"Thanks."

"Not like most kids these days." Jim looked up at the sky. "Sometimes it seems as if the world is spinning out of control. I mean"—he kicked at a piece of gravel with the toe of his boot—"who would suspect we'd have another murder in Lovett? It's not the sort of thing that happens here."

Shelby nodded. "I know what you mean."

"I wonder if the police are any closer to finding out who did it."

Dear Reader, is Jim pumping me for information?

"Poor old Zeke—killed with a hammer. Can you imagine? I can't believe he's gone. I heard it wasn't an ordinary hammer but one of them hammers that farriers use to make horseshoes."

"Really?"

Jim nodded.

Shelby tried to hide her excitement. If that was true, then Ryan Archer was the most likely suspect. He'd obviously lied about not being at the fair. He could have easily stolen the hammer from his father. Hadn't Ryan's father said his hammer was missing the day Shelby and Kelly were at the Harrises' stables? Maybe Ryan was the one who had taken it.

And maybe Ryan was the one who had used it to kill Zeke Barnstable.

22

Dear Reader,

While Billy has been mucking out stalls over at the Harrises' stables, I've been working hard, too. I've been pruning our Brussels sprouts plants—removing any yellow leaves and taking off the lowermost leaves from the sides of the stalks. This helps the sprouts to develop. I've also been topping the plants—cutting off the growing tips—because I've found it helps increase the plants' production.

I've spent some time in the kitchen, too, brewing up tinctures to get us through the winter. Tinctures preserve the chemical properties of herbs for up to several years and are easy to make. I've put peppermint, ginger, and fennel in a glass jar, covered them with boiling

water, then added food-grade alcohol to fill the jar. I'll
keep this mixture in a cool, dark place, shaking daily,
for anywhere from two to six weeks, at which point I
will transfer the mixture to the small glass bottles my
grandmother used to use for hers.

This particular tincture is fabulous for soothing heart-
burn or indigestion or easing nausea. It works wonders
whenever we've overindulged in spicy or fried foods
or if one of us comes down with a stomach virus.

Shelby was tidying up the kitchen when the door to the
mudroom opened and slammed shut. Amelia walked in
and dropped her books on the table with a loud thud.

"How was school?" Shelby asked, turning around with
a sponge in her hand.

She didn't expect much more than a word or two—
Amelia usually answered questions with a *yes*, *no*, or *fine*.

"It was epic," Amelia said, her head half-buried in the
refrigerator.

"Epic? Wow, that sounds great."

Shelby paused. She hoped she was interpreting the
word *epic* correctly.

Amelia turned around with a jar of peanut butter in
her hand. She unscrewed the top and scooped some out
with her finger.

Shelby bit her tongue and didn't say anything. She
didn't want to chance spoiling this rare dialogue they
were having.

"I told Mr. Campbell about Brittany Morse cheating,"
Amelia mumbled, her mouth sticky with peanut butter.
"At first he didn't believe me, but then Connor—he's one

of the coolest boys in school—heard me talking and told Mr. Campbell that Brittany had copied off his paper, too."

"So then Mr. Campbell believed you?"

"Yes." Amelia ran her finger around the nearly empty peanut butter jar. "And get this. Mr. Campbell must have talked to Brittany, because she went around the lunchroom telling everyone I was a liar and a narc and nobody should talk to me."

Shelby held her breath. That was what Amelia had been afraid of.

"Was it awful?"

Amelia shook her head. "No, because apparently everyone told Brittany off. Then they all began coming up to me to tell me they were glad I'd told on Brittany because she'd been cheating off of everybody while acting like she was so smart and perfect."

"I'm glad that worked out," Shelby said calmly, breathing a sigh of relief.

"It was epic," Amelia said again. She looked at Shelby. "You were right. Thanks, Mom."

She clutched the jar of peanut butter and scurried out of the room, leaving Shelby standing openmouthed.

‌‌‌‌‌‌‌‌‌‌‌‌‌‌‌‌‌‌‌‌‌‌‌‌‌‌‌‌

Shelby drove home from the Harrises' stable with all the windows wide open. The smell made no mystery of how and where Billy had spent his afternoon.

"How was it?" Shelby glanced over at the passenger seat.

"It was fun," Billy said. "Afterward, Mr. Harris let me ride Blackjack." Billy stuck his hand in his pocket and pulled out several crumpled bills. "And look, Mr. Harris even paid me. He said I did a good job and next time he needs help, he's going to call me."

"I'm proud of you," Shelby said, reaching out and patting Billy's knee.

She didn't have to look at him to know that he was probably scowling at this seemingly unwarranted display of maternal affection.

Bert was in the kitchen when they arrived home.

"Looks like you've been busy," Bert said, indicating Shelby's glass jar of herbs sitting in a darkened corner on the kitchen counter.

"I got the Brussels sprouts plants pruned and topped, too."

"You're going to have to think about hiring some help come spring," Bert said, cutting up an apple and handing the plate to Billy. "You can't keep doing things by yourself with just the occasional hired hand."

"I know. I hate to do anything that cuts into the farm's profit, slender as it is."

"You would be able to produce more."

"True."

A knock on the door startled them both.

"Maybe it's Jake," Billy said, slipping out of his chair and running to the back door.

"I hope I'm not interrupting anything."

Shelby's heart skipped a beat at the sight of Frank standing in the doorway of her mudroom.

"Not at all. Come on in." Bert picked up the coffee carafe and held it toward Frank. "Coffee? I can put on some fresh."

"No, thanks. I've already had my fifth cup today." He held his hands out in front of him. "I'm getting the jitters from so much caffeine."

"Caffeine is no substitute for sleep," Bert said, grabbing a mug and pouring herself a cup of coffee.

"Tell that to my insomniac brain," Frank said.

"I helped Jim Harris muck out some stalls today," Billy burst out with. "And he paid me, too."

"That reminds me," Shelby said. "Jim told me that the hammer used to kill Zeke was a farrier's hammer."

Frank went very still, his face a blank.

"Really?" he said finally.

"It's not true?" Shelby asked.

"Well, we already knew it wasn't an ordinary hammer."

"Is there anything else new on the case?" Bert said, slipping two teaspoons of sugar into her coffee.

"Nothing to speak of," Frank said.

"So, you didn't want a cup of coffee and there's nothing new on the case . . . Just why are you here, then?" Bert said, but in a teasing voice.

Frank laughed. "I wondered if I could get some herbs from you. Is the basil still growing?"

"Not taking up cooking, are you?" Bert said in disbelief.

"Not exactly. I am trying my hand at some marinara sauce. It ought to be easy enough, right? And to cook the pasta all that's required is to boil water, and even I can do that."

"Tired of microwave cooking?" Shelby said.

A slow flush colored Frank's face. He looked down at the floor. "Actually, I'm having company."

"By the look on your face, I assume that company is female," Bert said, glancing over at Shelby.

"Let me go cut some basil for you," Shelby said, jumping up from her seat.

She grabbed her scissors off the counter and slipped out the back door, letting it slam behind her. She half ran down the walk, then stopped for a moment to catch her breath.

There was no reason why Frank's having a woman over for dinner should have bothered her. No reason at all.

She cut several hefty pieces of basil and forced a smile on her face as she entered the kitchen.

"Here you go," she said, handing the herbs to Frank. "Don't they smell divine?"

"Let's hope I do them justice." Frank smiled. "And now I'd better get to it. Who knows how long this is going to take me?"

Shelby and Bert were silent for several long minutes after Frank's departure. Billy had gone to play outside and they were alone in the kitchen.

"Has that sexy neighbor of yours been by lately?" Bert said.

"Jake? He was here the other day."

Shelby turned her back and began wiping down the already-clean counter. Suddenly she whirled around to face Bert.

"What are you getting at?"

"Nothing." Bert was the picture of innocence. "I don't want to see you hurt, that's all," she added after a minute.

||||||||||||||||||||||||||

After Bert left, Shelby went out to the garden to pick the last tomatoes clinging to the vines. They were bright red and looked ready to burst. She savored the warmth they had soaked up from the sun as she held them in the palm of her hand.

There were too many for her to use, and she wasn't sure they'd last until the next farmers' market. Matt had said he'd be glad to have them.

Shelby carried the basket of tomatoes inside and put them on the counter. She glanced at the clock. She would ask Amelia to stay with Billy while Shelby ran to the general store.

Shelby went to the foot of the stairs and called Amelia. Amelia burst into the kitchen seconds later.

"Is there anything to eat?" Amelia asked with her head in the fridge. "I'm still hungry."

"There's fresh mozzarella, if you want some of that sliced with a tomato." Shelby put her hand on the basket of tomatoes.

Amelia turned around with an appalled look on her face. "I'm starved. There was hardly any peanut butter left in that jar. I need real food. Lunch today was disgusting."

She made what Shelby thought of as her *ewwww* face.

"What was it? Liver and onions?" Shelby said dryly, knowing the school cafeteria did its best to provide food the students would enjoy—such as pizza, hamburgers, and macaroni and cheese.

"Worse. Tuna sandwiches."

While Shelby's children ate things a lot of other children would turn their noses up at, such as Brussels sprouts, kale, and beets, they still had their unique likes and dislikes. Amelia happened to dislike tuna.

"There's some leftover macaroni and cheese. You can heat it up in the microwave."

Amelia had already pulled the container out of the refrigerator and was eating it cold.

"Can I go to the movies with Katelyn on Saturday?" she asked, stuffing another forkful of macaroni into her mouth.

"Katelyn? I thought you two weren't friends anymore. Because of Ned."

Dear Reader, I highly disapprove of girls breaking up their friendship because of a boy. Girls need one another at this age more than they need a boyfriend, don't you think?

Amelia gave an exaggerated sigh. "That was before. She and Ned have broken up."

"Seriously?" Shelby turned around and leaned back with her elbows on the counter.

Amelia slid into a chair at the table and continued wolfing down the macaroni and cheese. "Yeah. It happened right after the fair."

"Why? What happened?"

"I don't know." Amelia picked up a piece of elbow macaroni that had fallen off her fork onto the table and held it down for Jenkins, who was hovering underneath the table, waiting for just such an opportune moment. "She said she'd tell me today."

Amelia's spoon made a scraping sound as she scooped up the last bits of macaroni and cheese in the container. "She even threw away that hideous stuffed animal Ned won for her at the fair."

"What? You mean that stuffed woolly mammoth?"

Amelia looked surprised. "Yeah. They had a fight on the way home from the fair, and Katelyn threw it into some bushes."

|||||||||||||||||||||||||||||

Just because Ryan Archer could conceivably have found that stuffed woolly mammoth that Katelyn had tossed into the bushes didn't mean he hadn't been at the county fair, Shelby rationalized as she carried her basket of tomatoes out to her car.

It wasn't proof he hadn't been there, and it wasn't proof he had. She was back to the beginning.

And she was afraid that Jake was still at the top of Frank's suspect list, but she didn't know what she could do about it.

When Shelby arrived at the Lovett General Store both Matt and Margie Dale were behind the counter. A customer was standing in front of a display of canned soup, and Shelby heard someone else at the back of the store. The general store was never too busy at any given time— except maybe Saturday mornings—but served a steady stream of customers all day long.

"What have you brought me?" Matt said as Shelby approached the counter.

"The last of the tomatoes."

Shelby put the basket down on the counter.

"Those are beauties," Margie said.

"We might get a few more before the first frost, but not many. I'm afraid this is the end of the season."

"It always makes me sad to see summer go," Margie said, straightening a display of herbal cough drops. "But then the leaves start to turn those beautiful reds and yellows, and I forget all about it."

Matt leaned his elbows on the counter. "Has there been any news about the murder?"

"Zeke Barnstable, you mean?" Margie said, her eyes widening.

"I thought I had it figured out, but I was wrong," Shelby said. "Ryan Archer—his father's a farrier—had a beef with Zeke and Zeke was killed with a farrier's hammer. That points a pretty big finger at Ryan."

"But?" Matt said, grinning.

Dear Reader, I don't think he's taking me seriously!

"He claims not to have been at the fair, but I saw he had a stuffed woolly mammoth in his car—"

"A what?" Margie said.

"A woolly mammoth—a long-extinct creature." Shelby picked a tomato out of the basket and began rolling it back and forth between her hands. "Billy tried to win one at the fair. Ryan claims it had been thrown away and he found it, but I think it's more likely that he won it at the county fair."

"Did he win it?" Matt said, frowning.

Shelby shook her head. "No. According to Amelia, her friend tossed it into the bushes after a fight with her boyfriend."

"And Ryan picked it up?" Matt said.

"That's what he said."

"But it's not necessarily true." Matt pulled a basket out from under the counter and began arranging Shelby's tomatoes in it.

Shelby's shoulders sagged. "No. I really thought I'd eliminated him as a suspect."

"I know Ryan Archer," Margie said.

Both Matt and Shelby turned in Margie's direction. Shelby was surprised.

"You know Ryan?"

"Yes. I knew his mother, too, before she passed away. If she had lived that boy would have turned out differently, mark my words."

"Differently?" Shelby said.

"You've heard about what he did at the cemetery—defacing those gravestones. People pay good money for those. Besides, look at what they represent—the memory of their loved ones."

"I understand Zeke was the one who turned him in," Shelby said.

Margie nodded, her mouth set in a grim line. "Zeke's wife's gravestone was damaged, although at the time no one really knew if she was dead or alive." She narrowed her eyes. "I feel bad because I never should have trusted Ryan."

"What do you mean?" Matt sounded alarmed.

"The day of the fair he came in here to buy some beer. I know he's of age but I made him show me his driver's license anyway." Margie looked down and drew circles on the counter with her index finger. "I shouldn't have. He left with two six-packs, and when I looked out the window"—she gestured over her shoulder—"I could see a bunch of kids—they couldn't have been more than fifteen or sixteen years old—waiting outside."

Shelby held her breath although she suspected she already knew what happened.

"Ryan passed the beers all around and then they jumped in his car and took off." Margie looked at Matt. "I'm sorry."

Matt put his hand over hers. "It's not your fault."

Shelby cleared her throat. "What time was this, do you remember?"

Margie shrugged. "About two o'clock?"

Shelby looked at Matt. If Ryan was busy buying some underage kids beer at the Lovett General Store at two o'clock, there was no way he'd had time to get to the county fair, murder Zeke, and stuff his body in that Volvo.

"Poor Ryan," Margie said, her voice breaking. "He was always trying to fit in somewhere. I suppose he thought giving in to those kids would make him a hero in their eyes."

There was a rustling sound and the customer Shelby had heard poking around in the back of the store came around the end of an aisle. She was surprised to see it was Jim Harris. He smiled at Shelby, and put two bottles of weed killer down on the counter.

"Billy was a big help this afternoon," he said to Shelby as he reached into his pocket for his wallet. "He's a good boy."

Shelby felt the glow that a parent does when someone praises their kids.

Margie rang up the sale, and Jim handed her the money.

"Nice to see you," Jim said as he carried his purchase out to his car.

Margie slapped her hands down on the counter and looked at Matt. "Since you're here now, I guess I'll take off."

"Thanks, Margie."

Margie untied her apron, bundled it up, and stuck it under the counter. "Say hello to Bert for me," she said to Shelby as she collected her purse and headed toward the door.

"It sounds as if that effectively removes Ryan as a suspect," Matt said as the door closed behind Margie.

"Yes, and I'm glad. I would hate to think of someone so young doing something so horrible." Shelby glanced at the tomatoes on the counter and they made her think of Frank, his marinara sauce, and his female dinner companion.

Shelby gave Matt a flirtatious smile. "Last time I saw you, you promised me dinner."

A huge grin spread across Matt's face. "I certainly did."

"Are you going to make good on your promise?"

Dear Reader, what on earth has gotten into me?

"You bet."

"Okay," Shelby said with a nervous edge to her voice. "How about tonight?"

"Tonight?" Shelby was horrified by the way her voice squeaked.

"Do you have other plans?"

"I . . . I need to get a sitter."

"I'm sure your friend Bert would be happy to oblige. I'll call and make a reservation at Lucia's for seven o'clock, and I'll pick you up at six thirty."

"Okay."

23

Dear Reader,

Even though the growing season is winding down, there are still lots of things to do on the farm. Soon I will be clearing out some of the beds and planting cover crops. A cover crop protects and enriches the soil. A cover crop also suppresses weeds and helps prevent soil runoff.

I will probably plant oats, which will provide a quick cover but still allow me to plant early in the spring. The plants can become quite tall, and I love watching their golden stalks sway in the wind when everything else is barren or snow covered.

Shelby stumbled out of the store and into the parking lot in a daze. She had just said yes to a date. Her first real, official date since Bill died. Her stomach clenched and she felt nauseated. What had she done?

She headed toward her car, her heart beating hard against her ribs, her breath coming in short gasps as if she had been running.

Someone slammed the door of the car next to hers, and Shelby looked over. Rebecca Barnstable stood next to her dusty and dented Kia. She blew out a stream of smoke, then dropped the butt on the ground and stubbed it out. Her hair was greasy and lank as usual, and she was wearing a tank top and a pair of cutoffs.

She nodded at Shelby as she walked by, heading toward the door to the general store.

On an impulse, Shelby called her name.

Rebecca spun around, a surprised look on her face.

Shelby felt her mouth go dry. What was she going to say? None of it was really any of her business.

"Yes?" Rebecca said, staring at Shelby, her eyes narrowed.

"It's only that I think you should tell the police what your alibi is. They might be wasting precious time when they could be pursuing the real killer."

Rebecca's face crumpled as if she was going to cry.

"I told you I can't."

And she ran toward the door of the general store.

|||||||||||||||||||||||||||

Shelby was relieved when she pulled into the driveway of Love Blossom Farm. She was still in such a daze that she didn't trust her reflexes. She'd driven back to the farm, going five miles per hour under the speed limit and waiting an extra couple of beats at stop signs to be completely sure no one was coming.

Jenkins and Bitsy gave Shelby a warm welcome when she got home—the dogs always acted as if she'd been gone for weeks, not just a couple of hours. Of course they were also anxious for their dinner, so Shelby knew their exuberance wasn't entirely about her return.

She filled the dogs' bowls and then picked up the telephone to call Bert.

Bert's voice was exceptionally gleeful when Shelby asked if she could stay with the kids that evening.

And even though Shelby kept claiming it wasn't a *date*, Bert insisted on calling it one.

Shelby looked at her watch. She'd better hurry if she was going to be ready by six thirty. She was getting out of the shower when Amelia yelled upstairs.

"Bert's here."

"I'll be right down," Shelby yelled back, clutching a towel around her, her hair wrapped turban-style in another towel.

"Take your time," Shelby heard Bert shout from the foyer.

Shelby did take her time—at least more time than usual. Her hair—dark and curly—wasn't easily subdued into the sleek hairstyles that were in vogue, but she did her best. She thought she had at least come close to achieving what fashion magazines had taken to calling *beachy waves*.

Shelby stared into her closet in dismay. Lucia's, despite serving excellent food, wasn't an extremely fancy restaurant, so there was no need to fret about not having designer clothes. But when you had almost no clothes . . .

Shelby bit her lip and pawed through the hangers. She came upon a long, gauzy skirt her mother had sent her, purchased from some hippie commune in California. Shelby had never worn it.

It was a kaleidoscope of colors in a paisley print, so Shelby chose a slim-fitting black T-shirt to top it off.

Bert gave a sharp whistle when Shelby walked into the kitchen.

"You clean up real good," she said as she grated zucchini. She gestured to the pile of zucchini on Shelby's counter. "I thought I'd whip up some muffins for you and the kids." She lowered her voice to a whisper. "I'll sneak some vegetables into them."

"So I look okay?" Shelby said, suddenly feeling insecure.

"You look beautiful."

A car pulled into the driveway and Shelby ran to the window to look out.

"He's here. I'd better get going."

Bert gave her a stern look. "You stay right where you are. He can get out of the car and ring the bell like a gentleman."

Shelby couldn't help but smile.

Moments later the doorbell pealed. Shelby forced herself to wait a couple of beats before opening the door.

The sharp intake of Matt's breath and the way his eyes lit up told Shelby she had, indeed, *cleaned up real good*, to use Bert's words.

⠀⠀⠀⠀⠀⠀⠀⠀|||||||||||||||||||||||

The evening had turned cool and dry, and they made the trip to Allenvale with the windows down, enjoying the lightly scented air that streamed in. Conversation was, as always, easy with Matt, who was interested in a myriad of things and happy to converse about any of them.

"I don't know much about your family," Matt said, quickly glancing at Shelby.

"There's not much to know, really. I don't have any sisters or brothers. My parents were older when I was born. My father had been an electrical engineer and my mother managed an art gallery in Chicago. But then with my grandparents getting older, they decided to come back home to run Love Blossom Farm. By then they'd become very interested in ecology and sustainability even though those ideas were still in their infancy back then."

"Interesting. So they weren't always farmers."

"No, although they did grow up on a farm. But the idea of a simple life, living with nature, appealed to them after the stress and hubbub of high-powered jobs in the city. They leased their pasture to a dairy farmer and concentrated on creating a sort of boutique farm with lots of herbs, exotic lettuces, and enough vegetables to feed their family. And of course they jumped on the organic bandwagon."

Shelby realized she'd been doing all the talking, and turned to Matt. "What about you? Where is your family?"

Matt was quiet for a moment as he negotiated a left turn.

"My father was a lawyer, and my mother took care of the house and their complicated social life. My father passed away from a heart attack—stress induced, most likely—almost fifteen years ago and my mother got remarried, to a writer, a biographer. They live in Westport, Connecticut. I hardly ever see them." He glanced at Shelby and smiled. "Not because I don't want to, but our lives don't intersect much anymore."

"Do you have brothers or sisters?"

"No. You and I have that in common. My parents considered me their *miracle baby*. They were more than happy to stop with one—I'm not sure they even wanted that many children."

Shelby didn't know what to say. She'd been wrapped in a blanket of love from the moment she was born. She couldn't imagine having lived without that.

Matt made a right turn into the parking lot of Lucia's. He pulled the car into a spot, got out, opened Shelby's door, and extended a hand. She grasped it, surprised at how warm it was and how good that felt.

A wave of voices and rattling crockery rushed at them as they opened the door to the restaurant. Lucia's was packed, but the maître d' spotted them immediately and hastened toward them with two oversized menus. He greeted them with a practiced smile and quickly showed them to a table for two in the corner.

"I'm glad I made a reservation," Matt said as he pulled out Shelby's chair.

Shelby looked around. It was hard to believe the restaurant was in an ordinary building in an ordinary strip mall in Michigan—the ambience was so charming, with candles flickering on every table, heavy white linens, dark chairs, and murals on the wall that looked like frescoes from Florence. She felt as if she had entered another world.

Conversation continued to be easy as they waited for their meal—osso buco for Shelby and eggplant parmigiana for Matt.

The food was excellent, and Shelby was contemplating

the dessert menu when she looked up to see two women being led to a nearby table by the maître d'.

"That's Rebecca Barnstable," she said in surprise.

Rebecca had obviously washed and styled her hair, put on makeup, and changed into a pair of plain black pants and a royal blue polyester blouse. A young woman with long dark hair was following her. She was elegantly dressed in a simple black sheath with strappy, high-heeled sandals.

"I wonder who that is with her," Shelby said.

Matt swiveled slightly in his seat. "I've never seen her before, but they look alike. Must be a relative—a cousin or something."

Shelby risked another glance at the women advancing toward them. The younger woman did look a lot like Rebecca—incredibly like her. So much so that Shelby didn't think it was a coincidence.

"I wonder . . . ," Shelby began.

Matt smiled. "You wonder what?"

"You know Rebecca disappeared shortly after high school graduation and no one heard from her again until she returned to Lovett many years later. Her parents were still alive and of course there was her brother, but from what I've heard she didn't contact any of them and none of them knew where she'd gone. They didn't even know if she was still alive or not."

"Do you think there was a quarrel? From what you've told me, this Rebecca is a bit hotheaded." Matt pushed his empty plate away. "I've heard of families having arguments that drove them apart like that."

"That's possible, but I don't think so. There's another reason why a girl might suddenly disappear like that."

Matt cocked his head.

"Because she was pregnant. I think Rebecca had a baby, and that woman is her daughter."

||||||||||||||||||||||||||

As they were finishing their coffee, Shelby noticed the young woman who was with Rebecca headed toward the back of the restaurant.

"Excuse me," she said to Matt. "I'll be right back."

Matt stood as Shelby got up from her chair.

Shelby made her way between the tables toward the restrooms. When she pushed open the swinging door, Rebecca's companion was standing in front of the mirror, touching up her lipstick.

Shelby looked around. The ladies' room was as nicely appointed as the rest of the restaurant, with generously sized mirrors framed in gold, matching gold fixtures, and a plump velvet-covered bench in the corner.

Shelby stood at the sink next to the young woman and turned on the faucet. She washed her hands, and as she was reaching for one of the paper towels stacked next to the sink, she turned to the girl.

Shelby smiled. "You look just like your mother."

The girl's face broke into a grin. "I do?"

"Yes." Shelby pretended to be flustered. "I mean, I assume that's your mother." She gestured toward the dining room. "I'm sorry. I'm being terribly presumptuous."

"Not at all." The girl put her hand on Shelby's arm. "That is my mother. We're only now getting to know each other." She looked down at her feet. "I was adopted shortly after I was born, and my adoptive parents discouraged me from looking for my birth mother. But I'm twenty-two now, and I can do what I want." She raised her chin.

"You must be thrilled to have found her."

The girl's face glowed. "I am. Believe me, I am." She stuck out her hand. "I'm Kate, by the way."

Shelby shook her hand. "Shelby McDonald."

Kate opened her purse and dropped her lipstick inside. "It was nice meeting you."

"You, too."

Shelby stood in the empty restroom for a moment. So she was right—Rebecca had left town because she was pregnant. And had stayed away for a long time—to be near her daughter, perhaps? To catch a glimpse of her now and then?

The thought made Shelby's heart ache. She couldn't imagine having a child and then not being able to be a part of their life. It would have been unbearable.

iiiiiiiiiiiiiiiiiiiiiiii

Shelby wasn't surprised to find Bert asleep in front of the television, her knitting abandoned in her lap once again, when Matt dropped her off after dinner.

As Shelby stepped inside, the dogs raced to the front door, yipping excitedly and wagging their tails furiously. Bert startled awake when she heard the commotion.

"I must have dozed off," she said, rubbing her eyes with the heels of her hands.

"I hope the kids weren't too much of a problem."

"Not at all. They're perfectly good at amusing themselves. Amelia has been upstairs since you left. Billy watched a couple of reruns of *Hawaii Five-O* with me, then went to his room a little while ago. It's been quiet—I suppose he's fallen asleep."

Shelby sank down onto the sofa, where Jenkins and Bitsy immediately joined her.

"So, tell me," Bert said, slapping both palms down on the tops of her knees, "how was your dinner?"

Shelby had known she was going to get the third degree from Bert as soon as she came home. It was the price she had to pay for having Bert as a babysitter.

"Dinner was lovely," Shelby began. "The food was delicious and the restaurant is so charming."

"And your date?"

"Equally charming," Shelby answered evasively.

"Come on," Bert urged. "You can do better than that."

"Matt is very nice—"

"When a woman says a man is nice, that usually means he's as dull as dishwater," Bert said.

Shelby shook her head. "No, no, I mean it in a . . . positive way. He has good manners—he's pleasant and kind to everyone." Shelby thought about how gracious Matt had been with their waiter. "He's interesting."

"Ah, now we're getting somewhere." Bert's eyes gleamed.

"Are you going to see him again?"

"Yes. Behind the counter at the general store."

Bert shook a finger at her. "You know that's not what I mean."

"I don't know. I suppose." Shelby stroked Jenkins's ear. "But I haven't told you the most exciting part."

Bert leaned forward in her chair.

"Rebecca Barnstable was there."

"At the restaurant? Lucia's doesn't seem like the sort of place she would go."

"I know. But she wasn't alone. She was with a young

woman who both Matt and I noticed looked a lot like her. I was able to talk to her when we both went to the restroom." Shelby paused.

"Well, go on," Bert said. "Get to the punch line, for heaven's sake."

Shelby drew out the pause a little longer and then said, "The girl is Rebecca's daughter. Her name is Kate."

"You don't say!" Bert slapped her hand against her leg. "So that's why she disappeared all those years ago. She was pregnant."

"So it would seem."

24

Dear Reader,

I don't know about you, but every time I make a roast,
I seem to end up with a complete mess on the bottom
of the roasting pan that takes a lot of elbow grease to
clean. But fortunately I learned a little trick from my
grandmother.

Sprinkle some baking soda over the bottom of your
pan, add hot water and some white vinegar, and let the
whole mess soak for a while. When you come back, the
burnt bits will lift right off and washing the pan will be
a breeze!

Shelby was tired, but she still found it hard to settle down.
The dogs followed her out to the kitchen, their nails tapping on the wide-planked wooden floor. Shelby filled the

teakettle and put it on to boil. Maybe some chamomile tea would make her sleepy.

Jenkins and Bitsy went to stand by the back door and Jenkins began pawing at it. The paint at Jenkins's level had long since been scraped off, and Shelby didn't see any point in repainting it—Jenkins would only do it again. Shelby opened the door to let them out for their last run of the night.

She took her tea and sat down at the kitchen table. What a stroke of luck it had been to run into Rebecca and her daughter. The evening had provided the answer to one question at least—why Rebecca had disappeared those many years ago.

A thought came to Shelby while she was sipping her tea. Rebecca had done her best to keep her daughter a secret. She was unlikely to run into anyone she knew at Lucia's in Allenvale—unlike at the Lovett Diner, where everyone pretty much knew one another except maybe for the truckers who came through late at night when all the Lovett residents were already tucked up in bed.

Could it be that Rebecca had been with Kate the afternoon of Zeke's murder and that was why she was unwilling to tell the police about it? But surely if she was being suspected of murder . . . Shelby shrugged. People did strange things for strange reasons. Perhaps Rebecca was hoping another detail would emerge to prove her innocent and she wouldn't have to reveal the existence of her daughter.

It was certainly a possibility, Shelby thought as she drank the last of her tea, rinsed out the mug, and put it in the dishwasher.

Shelby opened the back door and called for the dogs. They came running toward the house, Jenkins in the lead and Bitsy lumbering behind. They burst into the kitchen with their tongues hanging. Jenkins had a dried leaf stuck in the fur on his belly, and he rolled around on the floor, trying to dislodge it. Shelby picked it off for him and threw it in the trash.

Bitsy leaned against Shelby's leg, looking to be petted, and Shelby reached over and idly scratched her back. Her hand brushed something unusual and she looked down. A piece of paper was rolled up and tucked under Bitsy's collar.

Shelby stared at it for a moment. Where on earth had that come from? Bitsy couldn't have picked it up herself— someone had to have put it there. Her hands shook as she slid the roll out from under the dog's collar.

She unrolled the paper. There was a message on it written with letters cut from a magazine. Shelby read the note.

MIND YOUR OWN BUSINESS AND STOP NOSING AROUND OR SOMEONE IS GOING TO GET HURT.

All the air rushed out of Shelby's lungs and she felt as if she could no longer breathe. She let go of the piece of paper and it dropped to the floor. Who would have done such a thing?

The murderer, of course. She'd obviously touched a nerve, but whose?

Shelby looked at Bitsy and shivered. The killer had been in her yard—close enough to attach that note to Bitsy's collar. The thought that they might have harmed Jenkins and Bitsy left her weak, and she sank into a kitchen chair.

She had to call Frank. She realized she hadn't thought about him all night. Was he still with his date? Maybe she ought to call the police station instead.

Shelby quickly looked up the number for the Lovett police station. A tired-sounding voice answered on the other end.

Shelby explained the situation and the officer promised to send someone around immediately. As soon as she hung up the phone she checked the locks on the doors and closed and locked the windows on the first floor.

She became limp with relief when she saw the lights of a squad car in the driveway. She looked out the window and watched as two officers got out of the car. Suddenly a pickup truck came roaring down the drive and parked alongside them.

Shelby couldn't see clearly in the dark, but she was pretty sure that was Frank getting out of the truck. He approached the two policemen and they conferred briefly. The policemen then got back in their squad car and headed down the driveway.

Moments later there was a knock on the front door.

Shelby yanked it open. "Frank!"

"I came as soon as I heard. Why didn't you call me?"

"I didn't want to bother you."

Frank fixed Shelby with a stern look. "I've told you before. I promised Bill I would look out for you and the kids. And I meant it."

"Yes," Shelby said in a small voice.

"Where is this note?"

Shelby led Frank out to the kitchen with Jenkins and Bitsy close on his heels. Normally she would have offered him a cup of coffee, but she was so frazzled, she didn't think of it.

Frank took a handkerchief from his pocket and picked the note up off the floor where Shelby had dropped it. He held it gingerly by the corner. His expression darkened as he read it.

"And you have no idea who sent this to you?"

"No. It was attached to Bitsy's collar. I found it when she came in from her last run of the evening"

"And the dogs weren't harmed?"

"No, thank goodness."

Frank's expression darkened further. "They had to have been in your yard—near the house. And you're here all alone. I don't like that."

"Frankly neither do I," Shelby said with a slight return of her usual spirit.

Frank smiled briefly.

"Why would anyone send you a note like this? Why do they think you've been nosing around?"

Dear Reader, this is the part I've been dreading. How do I explain about my snooping?

"You've been asking questions again, haven't you?" Frank said before Shelby could reply. "Don't you see how that can be dangerous? Once someone has committed murder, what's to stop them from doing it again? They have nothing to lose."

Frank's words sent an icy chill down Shelby's spine.

"I haven't really been asking questions," Shelby said. "People talk and I listen."

"Can you think of anything you've heard that might have prompted the killer to send this note?" Frank brandished the piece of paper.

Shelby thought of Rebecca in the restaurant and her daughter, Kate.

She shook her head. "No."

Frank sighed, took a plastic bag from his pocket, and carefully inserted the note.

"We'll see if forensics can lift any prints from this, but the system is so backed up that by the time we get the results, the perp will probably have been tried, sentenced, and locked up in jail."

Frank put a hand on Shelby's shoulder. "I'm going to take a look around outside. Lock the door behind me, and call me if you see or hear anything—and I do mean anything—out of the ordinary, okay?"

"Yes."

"Promise?"

"Promise."

<hr>

"You don't look very perky this morning," Bert said when she showed up at Shelby's back door.

Shelby yawned. "I'm not feeling perky. I didn't sleep well last night."

"Any particular reason?"

Bert took a mug from the cupboard and poured herself a cup of coffee.

Shelby told her about finding the note attached to Bitsy's collar.

Bert gave a loud harrumph. "I don't like the sound of that. I'd feel a whole lot better about you and the kids if you had a man under your roof."

Shelby bristled. "I'm perfectly capable of taking care of myself."

"Of course you are," Bert said soothingly. "But a big,

strong man is a lot more likely to scare someone off than a gal who is only a hair past five feet tall."

"I don't suppose I can argue with that," Shelby said dryly.

"Did you still want to make some watermelon pickles?" Bert said, hooking a foot around one of the kitchen chairs and pulling it closer. She put her feet up. "I could give you a hand."

"Are you sure?" Shelby said. "Are your legs bothering you?"

Bert scowled. "Of course not. I like to put them up occasionally. It helps with the circulation."

Shelby doubted that, but she knew better than to argue with Bert.

"If we start on the pickles today, they should be ready by the next farmers' market. They're always a big seller."

"No time like the present, then." Bert swung her legs down from the chair and got to her feet.

Shelby retrieved the watermelons and put them on the counter. She didn't grow them herself—the Clarks, who had a farm on the other side of Lovett, gave them to Shelby in exchange for some of her root vegetables.

Cutting the rind off the melons was a tedious process, and Shelby was glad of Bert's help. She was saving the pulp to make watermelon granita.

"How are Billy's riding lessons going?" Bert asked. "Is he going to take a blue ribbon in next year's county fair?"

"He certainly hopes so," Shelby said as she peeled the rind off the last piece of watermelon.

"Jim Harris has been teaching for a long time—he's got a string of blue-ribbon winners to his credit. Hopefully Billy will be the next one."

Shelby filled her biggest pot with water and added a generous measure of salt.

"I feel sorry for Jim," Shelby said. "We were there the day of the anniversary of his brother's death. He's still very torn up about it."

"It's always hard when there's no closure," Bert said, cutting the rind Shelby had prepared into one-inch pieces.

"I imagine it's hard not knowing who was responsible."

"I think Jim has always felt a little responsible himself." Bert scooped up the rinds as Shelby cut them and added them to the pot of boiling water.

"Why would Jim feel responsible?"

Shelby set the kitchen timer for five minutes. She would check the rinds then to see if they were tender. Sometimes they needed an extra minute or two.

"Doris—she's my neighbor who you met who works at the Dixie—was waiting tables the night it happened. It seems Jim and Sid were there together enjoying a couple of beers and shots of whiskey when they got into an argument."

"Oh?"

Bert nodded as she scooped a piece of rind from the pot and tested it with the tip of a knife. "She didn't know what it was about, but I guess Sid walked out of the bar in a huff. The two of them had gone to the Dixie together in Jim's truck, so Sid didn't have his car. He began to walk home." Bert dropped the piece of rind back into the pot. "Which is pretty silly, considering it was a good five miles to his farm and he could barely walk a straight line. At least that's what Doris said."

"Why would that make Jim feel responsible? He didn't do anything."

"That's the thing. He didn't do anything—he let Sid walk out and didn't go after him until it was too late."

"Sid was already dead?"

"He hadn't gotten far. He was found barely even a quarter of a mile from the Dixie. Jim always felt that if he'd left the bar sooner and stopped Sid, he would be alive today." Bert measured out sugar, vinegar, allspice, cloves, ginger, and some pickling spices and put them in a saucepan along with two cinnamon sticks. "And who knows? Maybe Sid would be alive if Jim had gone after him. But then you could say he might be alive if they hadn't had the fight or, heck, if they hadn't gone to the Dixie in the first place. You can't go second-guessing things like that."

Bert turned the gas on under the mixture in the saucepan. "Jim also felt that if he'd gotten to his brother sooner he might have at least seen who was driving the car that hit Sid."

<hr>

Shelby stared with satisfaction at the row of glass jars in her refrigerator, filled with green watermelon rind pickles with their slim edges of pink. She'd put Love Blossom Farm labels on them, and they would be ready for the next farmers' market.

Shelby spent the rest of the morning outside cleaning out beds and readying them for their cover crop. It didn't take long before she was hot, tired, thirsty, and very dirty. She'd agreed to meet Kelly for a cup of coffee later in the afternoon—Kelly wanted to discuss the details of her upcoming wedding—and by then Shelby was more than happy to put down her shovel and head inside for a shower.

She was aching and filthy, but fifteen minutes under

the pulsing shower—that was all the hot water her old water heater could crank out at one time—soothed her sore muscles and made her feel like new.

She threw on a clean pair of shorts and a T-shirt and went downstairs. Billy and Amelia's breakfast dishes had been abandoned in the sink. Billy was over at Jake's helping him on the farm—something he would moan and groan about if Shelby had asked him to do it—and Katelyn's mother had picked Amelia up for the day. She was taking the girls to a movie later in the afternoon and for some shopping at a mall forty-five minutes away. Shelby had managed to scrounge up some cash for Amelia's ticket and for her to buy something inexpensive at the mall.

Shelby's cell phone rang as she was pulling into the diner's parking lot. It was Kelly to say she was running a bit late, but she'd be there shortly. A calving both she and the farmer expected to be routine had run into an unexpected complication, but mother and baby were now doing fine and she only needed to clean up a bit before heading to the diner.

Shelby shuddered at the thought of the type of cleaning up Kelly would have to do. Being covered in dirt was a little different from being covered in— Well, it didn't bear thinking about. It was one of the reasons she'd been pleased to lease her pasture to Jake—she didn't mind getting her hands in the earth, but dealing with animals was a whole other ball game.

Shelby left her car unlocked and the windows rolled down—people in Lovett didn't bother much with security. There wasn't much to steal, and if you really needed something the farmers were quick to help you out. There was a deep vein of generosity in the community that Shelby cherished.

The diner wasn't busy—lunch was over and no one was ready for dinner yet. Shelby looked around. She smiled at Jessie Tedford, who was finishing off a piece of the diner's rhubarb pie, and waved to Earl Bylsma, whom she'd known from St. Andrews for ages.

A woman was standing at the take-out counter and Shelby realized it was Rebecca Barnstable. Shelby supposed she was picking up a late lunch to take back to the feed store. She watched as Rebecca paid the clerk and turned to go.

Rebecca passed Shelby's table, and Shelby put out an arm to stop her.

"Hello," Shelby said.

Rebecca looked not unlike a fish caught on a fisherman's hook. Shelby half expected her to begin twisting and turning.

"Hello," Rebecca mumbled, not meeting Shelby's gaze.

"Picking up some lunch?"

"Yes. Treating myself," Rebecca said with an edge of bitterness to her voice.

"The food here is good although it's not fancy. Not like Lucia's."

Rebecca's eyes became wary and she edged away from Shelby's table.

"You were at Lucia's last night. How did you enjoy it?"

For a minute, Shelby thought Rebecca would deny it, but she apparently realized that was futile.

"It was okay."

"Your daughter is lovely," Shelby said.

Rebecca jumped as if she'd touched a live wire.

"How—"

"We ran into each other in the ladies' room. The resemblance is quite striking. She's a beautiful girl."

In spite of herself, Rebecca gave a small smile. "She is, isn't she?"

Shelby nodded. "You must be very proud of her."

Rebecca's smile widened. "She's graduated from college and has a good job."

Shelby thought she could practically see Rebecca's chest swell.

"Why are you keeping her hidden?"

Rebecca looked at Shelby and laughed. "Why do you think? I know people around here talked when I disappeared. I know they put two and two together. Times have changed but not all that much. At least not here. I don't want to put my daughter through that."

"I don't think—"

"Besides, she's not mine anymore. She has another mother, as well as a father—something I wasn't able to give her."

"If she was with you the afternoon your brother, Zeke, was killed, you have to tell the police," Shelby said as gently as possible. "It gives you an alibi."

Rebecca kicked at the table leg. "Why should I tell them when they'll find out who really did it eventually?"

"Because they're wasting time investigating you when they could be looking for the real killer."

Rebecca curled her lip. "Ask me if I care."

Shelby was shaken by Rebecca's attitude. She knew there was no love lost between Rebecca and her brother, but you would have thought she'd have some interest in seeing his killer caught.

Rebecca had an alibi, so she was obviously ruled out as a suspect, and Shelby was left with no further ideas.

〰〰〰〰〰〰〰〰〰〰〰

Shelby was still a little rattled when Kelly arrived, all smiles, smelling of hay, fresh air, and farm animals.

"I have some great news." Kelly slipped into the booth opposite Shelby.

Shelby eyed the waitress who was fast approaching with her pad at the ready.

"What can I get you to drink?" the waitress said, slapping some menus down on the table.

"Just an iced tea for me," Kelly said, handing back the menu.

"Same for me."

Kelly was practically bouncing in her seat as the waitress walked away.

"You're about to burst," Shelby said. "What is your news?"

"Seth has agreed to have our wedding at Love Blossom Farm," Kelly squealed.

"That's wonderful. I'm so glad. It's going to be so much fun." Shelby frowned. "So, does that mean that Seth finally talked to his mother?"

Kelly ran a hand through her tangled red curls, dislodging a piece of hay that fluttered to the floor of the diner.

"Seth said it's our decision, not his mother's."

"Good for him." Shelby leaned back as the waitress slid a frosted glass of iced tea in front of her. "I wonder what Mrs. Gregson will say, though."

Kelly fiddled with the wrapper from her straw, pleating

it between her fingers. "I'm a little scared—scared that she'll talk Seth out of it."

"Seth seems like a man who knows his own mind."

"He does, but that woman is like a bulldozer."

Shelby giggled.

"What's so funny?"

"I have this vision of Mrs. Gregson wearing a cocktail dress, a long strand of pearls, and gloves, and sitting atop a giant bulldozer, chewing up the land around the barn at Love Blossom Farm."

Kelly erupted in laughter. "You always know how to make me feel better."

"Have you decided on a month yet?"

Kelly wrinkled her nose. "I still have to talk to Seth, but I was thinking May—before it gets too hot."

"And after the snow melts . . . hopefully," Shelby said, remembering one of the terrible winters they'd had when the mounds of snow piled more than a story high in parking lots hadn't completely melted until nearly the beginning of May.

"I'd like to make flower chains for my bridesmaids to wear in their hair," Kelly said, her eyes turning dreamy. "And carry a bouquet of wildflowers." She scowled. "Mrs. Gregson will probably complain that they exacerbate her hay fever."

Kelly grabbed Shelby's hand. "And you'll be my matron of honor, of course. And Lancelot can be the ring bearer. If we can get him to behave."

Lancelot was Kelly's golden retriever. He was a high-spirited dog, and Shelby couldn't quite picture him walking demurely down the aisle.

"And Amelia as a bridesmaid if she's willing, and Billy

a junior groomsman." Kelly paused to take a sip of her iced tea. "We don't want to have a huge wedding party. Seth's brother will be his best man."

"I think both Amelia and Billy would be thrilled to be included."

Dear Reader, I think I am almost as excited about this wedding as Kelly is.

"Enough about me," Kelly said. "Do the police still think that dreamy neighbor of yours killed Zeke?"

"I don't know. I haven't heard anything new." Shelby shivered. "Did I tell you about the note?"

Kelly leaned forward, her eyes wide. She took her straw out of her iced tea and sucked the liquid out from the bottom. "No. What note?"

Shelby explained about the paper warning her to keep her nose out of things that had been attached to Bitsy's collar.

Kelly drew her breath in sharply. "That's terrible. Who would do such a thing?"

"The killer, I suppose."

Kelly put a hand on Shelby's arm. "You have to stay out of things. You could get hurt."

"I've shown it to the police, and believe me, I have no intention of getting involved any further."

25

Dear Reader,

I love weddings, don't you? I like simple ones, fancy ones, small ones, big ones. I've heard some people go in for those destination weddings, and I think that's wonderful if that's what you want, but to me the most important thing is to be surrounded by family and friends. And how many of your family or friends can afford to fly to one of those exotic Caribbean islands or Hawaii or even Florida?

I love the idea of a big tent in someone's backyard or a reception in the church hall where you've celebrated so many things—baptisms, communions, confirmations, even funerals.

Or even standing up in front of the justice of the peace and a meal at the Lovett Diner afterward—there's nothing wrong with that, either.

I'm so excited for Kelly's wedding. I'm going to do everything I can to make it just the way she wants it.

When Shelby got home, she changed back into her old clothes and headed out to the garden. She ought to have been able to finish the bed she was clearing out before it was time to make dinner.

Bitsy and Jenkins trotted over to see what she was doing but obviously found it boring, because they soon ran off to chase a rabbit that had dared to cross their field of vision.

Shelby worked to pull out a particularly tenacious plant, grunting and groaning and sweating profusely. She worked her hand weeder around the roots again and then grasped the plant with both hands. Finally the roots gave way and she went tumbling backward, landing on her rear. At first she was stunned, but then when she realized how silly she must have looked she began to laugh.

"What's so funny?" a male voice drawled.

Shelby looked up to see Jake smiling down at her. He held out a hand. She grasped it and let him pull her to her feet. She brushed off the seat of her shorts with an embarrassed grin.

Shelby heard a noise behind her and Billy ran past, yelling "Hi, Mom" as he went by. He was no doubt headed for the old apple tree he loved to climb.

"I hope Billy was more of a help than a hindrance today," Shelby said.

Jake grinned. "He was great. He's a hard worker when he puts his mind to it. I hope it's okay—I gave him a couple of bucks."

"That's very generous of you, considering what he did to your henhouse and the waste of those eggs."

Jake shrugged, and stuck his hands in his pockets. "He cleaned it all up, so as far as I'm concerned it's forgotten."

"Have the police been around again?" Shelby asked. The sun was catching her in the eyes and she squinted up at Jake.

He held up his hands and wiggled his fingers. "I had my fingerprints taken. An interesting operation, or at least it would have been if I wasn't scared out of my wits for being suspected of murder."

"Why take your fingerprints?"

"Now that they've found the murder weapon they've been able to dust it for prints." He kicked at a loose stone. "Although any criminal worth their salt knows enough to wear a pair of gloves before handling anything that could incriminate them." Jake gave a short bark of laughter. "Like the murder weapon."

"I heard it was a farrier's hammer," Shelby said.

"Really? You mean, the kind they use to make horseshoes?"

"Yes."

"I wonder where the killer came by one of those."

"I thought Ryan Archer might have been the killer, but it turns out he has an alibi. He was at the general store buying beer for a bunch of underage boys."

Jake shook his head. "Some people never learn. Ryan's on probation—he needs to keep his nose clean, and it doesn't sound like that's what he's doing."

"I suppose it was a stupid thing to do, but at least he gave himself an alibi."

"True. Breaking your probation is a lot less serious than being suspected of killing someone." Jake scratched his head. "What about that father of his? He would have access to a farrier's hammer. He probably has a whole bunch of them."

Shelby thought back to that afternoon at Jim Harris's stable when Ryan Archer had had to bring his father a hammer because the one in his truck was missing.

"Do you know anything about Dick Archer?" Shelby asked.

"Sorry. Not really. I know people think he's a bit odd. But I don't really know him."

"I wonder who does."

"Your friend Bert seems to know every single person in Lovett." Jake laughed.

"Bert did mention Dick Archer. She said the same thing—that he's considered a bit of an odd duck." Shelby thought for a moment. "But maybe I should talk to her again. She might know more—maybe something she doesn't realize could be important."

||||||||||||||||||||||||||

Shelby thought about what Jake had said as she scrubbed the dirt out from under her fingernails while standing at the kitchen sink. She'd suspected that Zeke's murder had been committed by Ryan Archer. But was it possible Ryan's father had taken Ryan's side and blamed Zeke for his son being sent to jail?

Shelby dried her hands, grabbed the phone, and quickly dialed Bert's number. The phone rang more than half a dozen times, and Shelby was about to end the call when Bert finally picked up.

There were voices in the background—female. It sounded as if Bert was having a party.

"I'm sorry," Shelby said. "It sounds like I'm interrupting something."

"Just an impromptu card game with some friends."

"I can call back."

"Nah, that's fine. I had a losing hand anyway. What can I do for you?"

"You said you knew Dick Archer."

Shelby grabbed the damp sponge sitting by the sink and scrubbed at a spot on the kitchen table that looked like dried sauce from macaroni and cheese.

"Yes," Bert said, drawing out the word, her tone wary.

"Did he blame Zeke for Ryan having to go to prison? I mean, if Zeke hadn't turned Ryan in, the police might never have found out that he was the one defacing the gravestones."

Shelby put the sponge down and scraped at the spot with her fingernail.

"Jeez, I don't know. I suppose it's possible. Although Dick Archer never struck me as the type to do something like that." Bert paused. "I think he would be more likely to march his son down to the police station himself."

"Can you think of any other reason why Dick Archer might have had a grudge against Zeke?"

"Nothing comes to mind. Of course, I don't know everything that goes on."

Dear Reader, don't believe Bert. Very little happens in Lovett that she doesn't eventually hear about.

"I wish you wouldn't play detective," Bert said. "You could get hurt. Can't you leave it to Frank?"

"I will. Don't worry," Shelby said, her fingers crossed behind her back. "Listen, I've got to go. I'll talk to you later."

Shelby hung up the phone. A drop of sweat was making its way down her back. She didn't like lying to Bert, although she was pretty sure that Bert hadn't believed her anyway.

Dear Reader, does it count as a lie if the other person knows you're not telling the truth?

iiiiiiiiiiiiiiiiiiiiiii

Shelby realized she hadn't eaten. Her stomach was growling loud enough for her to hear, and she was getting a headache. She opened the refrigerator and peered inside. The contents were pathetic. Here she was, a blogger offering enticing recipes, and she had hardly any food in the house. The saying about the shoemaker's children came to mind as she prowled around in the produce drawer.

She found a head of tender butter lettuce she'd picked earlier in the week, the remains of a tomato so ripe it was almost purple, and half a cucumber. She had some fresh mozzarella left from the batch she'd made, along with some homemade croutons—so easy to make and a wonderful use of stale leftover bread.

She threw together a salad, whipped up some vinaigrette, and took her plate to the small table where her computer was set up. She had to write to the cookware company and let them know she'd sent back their pots and pans and that she wouldn't be able to endorse their product.

She scanned her e-mails—there were several from fans of her blog who wrote regularly. She breathed a sigh of relief—no complaints this time.

She began writing her e-mail and had gotten as far as the first sentence when her phone rang.

Shelby stretched out an arm, reaching for the receiver that sat on the kitchen table. She clipped a glass full of water, and it overturned, sending a cascade of liquid onto the floor. Shelby stared at it in dismay as she pressed the button to answer the call.

"Hello?"

Kelly's muffled voice came across the line. "I'm so upset." And she burst into tears.

"What's wrong?"

Shelby reached in the other direction, grabbed a towel hanging from the oven handle, and dropped it on top of the puddle on the floor. She used her foot to swish the towel around and absorb the spilled water.

Kelly gave a loud sniff. Shelby could hear her blowing her nose.

"Seth told his mother about our wedding plans, and she's all upset. She's insisting on having the wedding at their country club up north. And when Seth told her that was out of the question, she said we could go ahead and have the wedding without her."

Shelby frowned. "What did Seth say?"

"He told her that that was her choice."

Shelby pumped a fist in the air. *Go, Seth!*

"But now he's feeling terribly guilty. His mother said his father isn't well. He has some sort of heart problem. It's not serious . . . yet. But it could be."

Shelby exhaled sharply. "It sounds like his mother is using that to try to persuade you. Has Seth talked to his father himself?"

"No."

"Maybe it's not as bad as she's making it sound."

Kelly gave another loud sniff, and Shelby waited while she blew her nose.

"You're probably right. I'm getting all upset for nothing."

"At least Seth is sticking to his guns."

Shelby jiggled her mouse just in time to prevent her computer from going into sleep mode.

"That's true," Kelly said, ending her sentence with a hiccough.

"Changing subjects a bit," Shelby said, "do you know anything about Dick Archer?"

"The farrier?"

"Yes."

"Not much. People seem pleased with his work."

"Do you think he might have had a grudge against Zeke? After all, Zeke turned Archer's son in to the police."

"Ohhhhh," Kelly said. "You're thinking that maybe Dick Archer is the murderer?"

"He doesn't seem like the type, but Zeke was killed with a farrier's hammer."

"That was on Sunday, right? At the fair?"

"Yes—middle of the afternoon."

"Let me think." Kelly was silent for a moment. "No, I don't think so."

"Don't think so what?"

"That Dick Archer could be the killer. The day of the fair I was called over to Randy Meyerling's farm to check on one of his cows that he thought might be pregnant—like I had to do for the Mingledorfs that time. Sometimes it's hard to tell."

Dear Reader, what a shame the cow can't just pee on a stick and be done with it.

"Anyway, Dick Archer was there banging out some new shoes for Randy's old mare. That was midafternoon. And he was still there when I left. And it wasn't long after that I heard about Zeke's murder."

"You're sure he wouldn't have had time to—"

"No way."

Shelby groaned. "That rules him out, I guess. I'm back to square one."

Shelby stared at the screen saver that had popped up on her computer—a picture of Amelia and Billy when they were younger, curled up on Bill's lap. A wave of grief washed over her and she turned away quickly. Maybe it was time to replace the photograph with something that didn't bring back painful memories.

"Are you still there?" Kelly asked with laughter in her voice.

"Yes. Sorry. I was . . . daydreaming."

"Oh."

"Don't you think it odd that both Brenda and Zeke Barnstable were murdered?"

"I find it odd that anyone in our little town has been murdered. Farmers are quiet people—I certainly don't think of them as homicidal maniacs."

"What I'm wondering is—is there a connection of some sort between the two murders? They were husband and wife. . . ."

"It's possible."

"The problem is, I can't imagine what the connection could be."

26

Dear Reader,

I had an exciting e-mail this morning. Another company is asking me to promote their cookware. They sell cast-iron pots and pans for very reasonable prices.

Cast iron offers durability (I have my grandmother's Wagner Ware set and still use it!) and excellent heat retention, making it the perfect choice for searing or frying.

And it goes from stove top to the oven with no trouble.

Some pans come preseasoned and others will need a bit of oil rubbed into them. Be sure to clean them with mild soap so as not to remove the seasoning—a popular method of cleaning is to use coarse salt and a paper towel to rub out the pan.

Shelby sat for a moment after hanging up with Kelly. Was there a connection between Brenda's and Zeke's murders? An idea—little more than a wisp—floated just out of reach. She sighed. Perhaps if she turned her mind to something else, she would be able to grasp the idea—whatever it was.

She jiggled her computer mouse, and her computer sprang to life again. She devoted time every Saturday afternoon to writing at least two or three blog posts in case the week became too busy and time got away from her.

She was a creature of habit, she supposed—like the other people in Lovett Bert had mentioned: Jim and Zeke at the Dixie on Thursdays, then Jim with his brother, Sid, there on Friday nights—the same night Brenda and her friends headed to the Dixie for their weekly girls' night out.

Shelby paused with her fingers hovering over her computer keys. Something had suddenly struck a chord. What was it? The thought came to her so swiftly, she almost jumped—Jim, Sid, and Brenda all at the Dixie on the same night of the week. Was there any significance in that?

She picked up a pencil and began tapping it against the desk. Bitsy and Jenkins obviously took that as some sort of signal, because they both showed up at her side, panting heavily against her bare legs.

"Sorry, guys. False alarm. It's not time for dinner yet."

Jenkins tilted his head this way and that as if he was really listening. Bitsy made her way through the tangle of chair legs and plopped down under the table with a deep sigh that Shelby imagined signaled her disappointment.

For a moment Shelby lost her train of thought and nearly groaned in frustration. She'd been thinking about Brenda, Jim, and Sid at the Dixie . . . That was it. She snapped her fingers, but this time the dogs merely lifted their heads and stared at her quizzically.

What if . . . Shelby got so excited, she jumped up from her chair and began to pace up and down the kitchen. What if Brenda saw who hit Sid the night he was killed? And what if that person knew she'd witnessed the hit-and-run? Had they tracked her down and killed her to keep her from going to the police?

Of course it was possible that Brenda hadn't even been at the Dixie that night. She might have stayed home, laid up with a headache, the flu, or a stomach upset. Shelby picked up her pencil and began drumming it again. Who would know? She dropped the pencil suddenly, and it rolled off the table and onto the floor. Bitsy and Jenkins both watched it with curiosity but without stirring from their comfortable spots under the table.

Tonya Perry would know. She and Brenda had been best friends—surely Tonya was part of the group that went to the Dixie every Friday night.

Shelby almost reached for the phone but then thought better of it. It would be awkward enough approaching Tonya with these questions—it might be better to do it in person.

Shelby had learned from her mother and grandmother never to go somewhere empty-handed. She would need an excuse to call on Tonya. She'd pick some Macs from the tree out back. Tonya was a whiz at baking—surely she would appreciate having the fruit for a pie.

Shelby sighed as she looked at the blank screen on her computer. She'd not gotten very far with her blog. She'd have to forgo some reading tonight in order to make up for it. She turned off her computer, grabbed a wicker basket from the kitchen counter, and went out the back door with Bitsy and Jenkins happily trotting at her heels.

Shelby took a deep breath and inhaled the scent of apples that drifted toward her on the breeze long before she even reached the small group of fruit trees.

It didn't take her long to fill her basket with ruby red Macs—enough for at least two apple pies. She hoped Tonya would be pleased.

Shelby washed her hands, transferred the apples to a brown paper bag, refilled the dogs' water dishes, and headed out the door.

|||||||||||||||||||||||||||

Tonya's house wasn't far from what passed for downtown Lovett. Kelly had said that Tonya had inherited it from her grandmother. The house was fairly close to the street, with weathered white paint and scrubby grass in the front yard. Shelby headed up the cracked concrete walk and rang the bell.

The door creaked as Tonya opened it. If she was surprised to see Shelby standing on her doorstep, she didn't show it. She put up a hand to fluff her blunt-cut bangs as she pulled the door wider and gestured for Shelby to go in.

"I've brought you some apples." Shelby held out the paper bag. "I thought you might like them for some pies."

Tonya took the bag and held it to her chest as if she

feared Shelby would snatch it back again. They went into an old-fashioned parlor at the front of the house. It looked as if Tonya had inherited her grandmother's furniture along with the house. The sofa was stiff and the fabric scratched the backs of Shelby's thighs.

"Would you like some lemonade?"

"Yes, thank you, but please don't go to any trouble."

Tonya smiled. "It's no trouble."

Shelby heard Tonya opening and closing the refrigerator door and rummaging in the kitchen cupboards. Moments later Tonya reappeared with two sweating glasses of lemonade. She handed one of them to Shelby.

Shelby hadn't worked out how to broach the reason for her visit. She stalled, taking several sips of her drink.

Tonya's smile was beginning to wear thin when Shelby finally brought up the subject of Brenda's death.

Tonya lifted the hem of her shirt and dabbed at her eyes.

"I still can't believe she's gone."

"Do you still go to the Dixie on Friday nights?"

Tonya shook her head. "It's not the same without Brenda. I haven't been there since the night she died."

Shelby looked around for a place to put her empty glass, but there weren't any coasters so she continued to hold it.

"Were Sid and Jim there that night, too? Do you remember?"

Tonya was already nodding her head. "Yes. They were always there on Friday nights. One of Brenda's friends—I didn't know her real well—used to talk to Sid. I think she was hoping he would ask her out, but he never did."

"Had Sid had a lot to drink that night? I understand he and Jim had a fight."

"That's what he and Jim fought about. Sid was ordering another beer with a whiskey chaser—his usual—when Jim tried to tell him he'd had enough. They began quarreling and got quite loud. I remember the bartender shot Sid a look, and that's when he got up and stormed out. He bumped into this couple's table on his way to the door, and knocked over the woman's beer. It spilled all over her lap, and she was furious. But Sid didn't even stop to say he was sorry or anything."

"Brenda was still there when that happened?"

"Yes, but she said she had to go. Zeke would be waiting for her."

"She drove herself to the bar?"

Tonya squirmed in her seat, obviously uncomfortable. "We didn't want her to leave. She'd had a couple of beers over her usual limit. Our friend Kathy said she'd take her home, but Brenda insisted she was fine and would drive herself."

Shelby was silent while Tonya chewed her bottom lip.

"Brenda was all worked up about Zeke—I think that's why she drank more than her usual. She was complaining about how he didn't pay any attention to her and didn't appreciate her and how all she did was work all the time. I think she was unhappy at that Laundromat, where she had a part-time job, and wanted to quit, but Zeke wouldn't hear of it."

Tonya paused to take a breath.

"Afterward we were . . . we were worried that Brenda might have . . . We were afraid that Brenda might have done it. That she might have been the one who hit Sid."

Tonya pulled at her bottom lip with her fingers. "Next thing we hear that Brenda's disappeared."

"Was that right after—"

"No. It was a couple of days later. On the Wednesday after Sid's funeral."

"She didn't tell anyone where she was going?"

"Not that I know of. She didn't tell me—I know that. Not Kathy, either, or any of her other friends, or they would have said."

Tonya put her empty glass down on the carved wooden coffee table, and Shelby winced. She was afraid it was going to leave a ring.

"It sounds terrible, but we figured she might have run away because—you know—she was the one who'd killed Sid."

Tonya tugged at the hem of her shirt. "And here she's been dead all along." She wiped her sleeve across her eyes. "I always said that Zeke must have done it. Brenda made it sound like the two of them weren't getting along. Maybe Zeke decided to do something about it." Tonya sniffed. "With all that property Zeke had, he probably figured they'd never find the body."

IIIIIIIIIIIIIIIIIIIIIIIIII

Shelby was so preoccupied while making dinner that she nearly set fire to the bacon fat she was heating for the creamed corn. Amelia rescued the pan just in time and gave her mother an appraising look before going back upstairs to her room.

Shelby couldn't stop thinking about what Tonya had told her. Had Zeke killed Brenda and then buried her body, telling everyone that she had run off somewhere?

Or had Brenda witnessed the hit-and-run accident that killed Sid and the driver had come after her, killing her and then burying her on her own property? If her body was found, Zeke would have been the first and most logical suspect.

But then who had killed Zeke and why? Maybe the two murders weren't connected after all, and she was wasting her time.

Shelby stood over the stove, stirring the corn mixture. She looked at the situation from every angle she could think of. She was ready to give up when a thought came to her. It was so startling, she accidentally hit the side of her arm against the frying pan.

She quickly shoved her arm under cold running water, watching as a thin red line formed on her forearm. She grabbed a paper towel, blotted off the water, and picked up the phone. She waited breathlessly for Kelly to pick up.

"Kelly," Shelby said when her friend finally answered. "Are you up for an adventure?"

"Is it dangerous?"

"Mmmm, not really," Shelby said as she stirred the creamed corn in the skillet.

"So, what is it?"

"I'd rather tell you in person."

"This is beginning to sound very mysterious. Count me in."

"Can you come by after dinner? Around seven thirty? I want to make sure Billy has a bath tonight."

"Sure. As long as none of the animals in my care inconveniently decide to give birth tonight and need my assistance."

Shelby laughed. "Okay, I'll see you then."

"Can you give me a tiny hint, at least? My curiosity is killing me."

"I'll tell you everything when you get here."

Shelby heard Kelly groan and then the click as she ended the call.

⚞⚟⚞⚟⚞⚟⚞⚟⚞⚟⚞⚟

Shelby began to doubt the advisability of her plan as she sat at the kitchen table, staring at the clock, waiting for Kelly to arrive.

On the one hand, they would probably be perfectly safe—Zeke was dead, after all. On the other hand, it would be hideously embarrassing if they were caught, and she had no idea how she would explain what she and Kelly were up to.

Dear Reader, that should be what I was up to. Poor Kelly is merely along for the ride. If things go south, it will be all my fault.

Shelby had pleaded, argued, and bargained with Billy until she finally got him in the tub and made him promise to actually use soap while he was in there. She sniffed him as he ran past her, wrapped in a towel, his hair wet and dripping down his back, and she thought she caught a whiff of Ivory Soap. She breathed a sigh of relief. Billy's idea of bathing was to spend half an hour playing with his toy boats and then getting out of the tub nearly as dirty as when he got in.

Amelia had promised to watch Billy while Shelby was out of the house. Shelby was a little nervous about leaving Amelia in charge at night, but she didn't anticipate things taking longer than an hour. Amelia had promised to leave her bedroom door open so she would hear her little brother if he needed anything.

Shelby jumped when she heard Kelly's car come down the driveway and pull up outside the mudroom door.

"Where are we going?" Kelly asked as she burst through the door.

Her red hair was haphazardly pinned into a knot on top of her head, and her cutoffs were fraying badly on the bottom. Shelby regarded her friend with affection—even with no makeup and her hair in a jumble, she was a beautiful woman. A light that spoke of kindness and empathy shone from her eyes.

Shelby heard a noise in the hall and put her finger to her lips.

"I'll tell you when we're under way," she said as Amelia walked into the kitchen.

Amelia nodded at Kelly and wrinkled her nose at the smell that seemed to follow Kelly around no matter what she did.

"We're heading out," Shelby said, her purse slung over her shoulder and her car keys in hand.

"Where are you going?" Amelia asked, her head in the open door of the refrigerator.

"Out," Shelby said.

She heard her daughter sigh and sensed Amelia's frustration as she let the mudroom door close behind her and Kelly.

Touché, she thought with a certain amount of glee.

"Now will you tell me where we're going?" Kelly asked as she buckled her seat belt.

"We're going to Zeke Barnstable's farm."

"Why?" Kelly said, swiveling around to face Shelby.

"I have a hunch." Shelby put on her blinker and turned right.

The road was deserted, although they soon met up with a farmer driving an ancient tractor at a speed that even a snail could have outpaced. Shelby put on her brakes and slowed her car to under twenty miles an hour, trying not to fume with impatience. There was a double yellow line, so she couldn't even pass.

She breathed a sigh of relief when the farmer finally turned onto a dirt road and she was able to step on the gas again.

"You're being quite maddening, you know," Kelly said.

Shelby laughed. "I'm sorry. It's just that I'm going to feel really stupid if I'm wrong. And I want to put that off as long as possible."

"Hmmph," Kelly said, settling into her seat.

Shelby flipped down her visor—the sun had dropped lower in the sky and was shining directly through the car window. It was still light out, but shadows were deepening as dusk fast approached.

Shelby's heartbeat sped up as she turned down the rutted lane that led to Zeke's farm. There was no reason to expect anyone to be on the property, but what if Rebecca had decided to move in now that the house was hers?

There were no signs of life in Zeke's old farmhouse. No lights glowing from the windows, no voices or sounds of music. Shelby jounced down the rutted drive, past the house, toward the garage in the back.

The garage looked as if it had originally been a storage

shed. There were two bays, each with double doors that opened outward and were crisscrossed with wood like an old stable door. Shelby was relieved to see that neither door was padlocked.

"Now will you tell me what we're looking for?" Kelly stood next to Shelby's car with her hands on her hips.

"We're looking for a car," Shelby said as she approached the garage.

"I guess we're looking in the right place, then, this being a garage." Kelly pointed at the weathered and worn structure.

Shelby put her hand on the door handle, closed her eyes, and said a short prayer. She pulled and the door opened. She exhaled in a rush as dust motes wafted on the stale air that billowed out.

The bay on the right of the garage was empty except for some old and rusted rakes and hoes propped against the wall. A car was in the left bay—an older model Chevrolet TrailBlazer.

"Is this what you were hoping to find?" Kelly whispered. She looked over her shoulder. "I don't know why I'm whispering. No one is about."

Shelby made her way around to the front of the SUV. Its bumper was nearly touching the back wall of the garage and she had to squeeze into the small space inch by inch. She pulled a flashlight from her shoulder bag and shone it at the front of the car.

She couldn't restrain a shout of triumph as she examined the TrailBlazer.

"Look." She motioned for Kelly to join her.

Shelby pointed at the front bumper of the car.

"The headlight is smashed." She ran her hand along the dent in the fender. "This car has been in an accident."

"So have a lot of other cars," Kelly said, examining the damage. "What does that have to do—"

"I think Zeke's wife, Brenda, is the person who hit Jim Harris's brother, Sid, while she was on her way home from the Dixie Bar and Grill. Sid had had a fight with his brother and, in a fit of anger, stomped out of the restaurant. Brenda's friends said she'd been drinking more than usual. They were concerned about her driving. And with good reason, it seems." She traced the dent with her finger.

Shelby heard the sharp intake of Kelly's breath.

"So Brenda is the one who ran Sid down."

"And didn't even stop." Shelby turned to her friend. "I thought maybe Brenda had seen the accident and the driver had come after her and killed her. But that obviously wasn't the case. Brenda had been the driver herself."

"Do you think Zeke helped her hide the car?"

"He must have. I don't see how she could have kept it from him. I imagine he didn't want her to go to jail—she cooked his meals, cleaned the house, helped out on the farm, and worked part-time to bring in some extra money."

"So . . ." Kelly held her hands out in front of her and spread her fingers wide. "What does this have to do with Zeke's murder?"

"I don't know." Shelby's shoulders slumped. "I got so caught up in finding out if my theory was right."

"It's one mystery solved, at least. Are you going to let Frank know?"

Shelby shuddered. "I have to. Although I know I'm

going to get a lecture about snooping around—something I promised I wouldn't do."

"Frank is right. It could be dangerous."

"Don't worry. I'll be careful. Nothing is going to happen."

27

Dear Reader,

I love garlic. Don't you? I grow it in my garden, so I always have plenty on hand. If you're buying garlic in the store, look for bulbs with firm tissuelike skin. The garlic shouldn't be shriveled or dried out.

If your garlic has sprouted—meaning you find slender green shoots inside when you cut it—remove the shoots. They add bitterness to a dish when cooked.

While I love garlic, I don't love smelling it on my hands after I've been cutting or slicing it. Here's a neat trick to get rid of the odor: Wet your hands with cold water (not hot), pour a generous amount of salt into your palm—kosher salt is best, if you have it—then rub your hands together as if you were washing them. Finally, rinse with cold water.

Voilà! The only garlic smell will be the delicious scent coming from your cooked dish.

Shelby looked in the mirror. There were dark circles under her eyes. She'd spent too much time last night tossing and turning, trying to make sense of Brenda and Zeke Barnstable's deaths.

She took a quick shower—their ancient water heater didn't allow for long, luxurious ones—then briefly switched the water to cold. She gasped. The bracing spray shocked her awake more efficiently than several cups of coffee would.

Shelby rummaged in her closet for what she thought of as her church outfit. It was one of four—two for the summer and two for the winter. This time she chose her coral-colored A-line skirt and a cream blouse in a fabric that could almost pass for silk. The weather was turning cooler in the mornings, so she added a cardigan sweater and opted for pumps instead of sandals.

Billy was ensconced in front of the television, watching Sunday morning cartoons when Shelby got downstairs. He was still in his pajamas, and his persistent cowlick was more obvious than usual.

"Billy, go get dressed. I've put your clothes out on the bed for you."

Billy dragged his feet—which Shelby noticed were getting bigger and were quite dirty on the bottom—but finally she got him upstairs to change. She could hear Amelia moving around above and hoped that meant that she, too, was preparing for church.

Shelby was sweating by the time she hustled everyone into the car. Amelia sat in the front seat, her fingers flying over her cell phone while Billy bounced around in the back as far as the limits of his seat belt would allow.

Shelby breathed a sigh of relief when they pulled into the church parking lot. They were early enough to get a decent space since Amelia had to get to church ahead of the service in order to change into her choir robe and warm up with the choir.

Billy shot out of the car almost before Shelby had it in PARK, throwing a "See ya, Mom" over his shoulder as he headed toward his Sunday school classroom.

Shelby took a deep breath and made her way down the path and into church in a leisurely fashion. She always enjoyed the Sunday service—the familiar hymns, the beautiful voices of the choir, the soothing repetition of words she knew by heart. Reverend Mather's sermons were always surprisingly both thoughtful and thought-provoking, leaving Shelby feeling uplifted for days.

Shelby was surprised to see Earl Bylsma standing in the back of the church, a clutch of programs in his hand. She smiled as she approached him. "I thought you had stopped ushering," she said, holding her hand out for a program.

Earl smiled. "I had, but I decided to take it up again. I love greeting everyone on Sunday mornings. I missed it."

Shelby squeezed his arm and followed him down the aisle to her customary pew. It was funny how people tended to gravitate to the same seat every Sunday—almost as if the church had assigned them their own spot. Shelby knew the family in front of her—the Pecks, whose daughter was in Amelia's class and whose son had a speech impediment that he was getting therapy for. And behind her sat the Van Duzers, an elderly couple whose

children had decided to pursue careers in Chicago. They'd
had to sell their farm, since it was impossible for the two
of them to manage it alone. They'd moved into a local
retirement community and, much to their surprise, were
enjoying it thoroughly.

The organist struck a chord, the doors swished open,
and the choir marched in. Shelby always felt a thrill when
she saw Amelia in the procession, her curly blond hair
giving her the look of an angel.

Shelby opened her hymnal and joined the choir in
song. Before she knew it, the service was over, the pews
rattling as the congregation stood up to leave. Shelby
followed on everyone's heels as they filed out of the
church and crossed the courtyard to the church hall for
coffee and cookies.

The soft murmur of adult voices, punctuated occasionally by a child's shout, drifted toward Shelby as she
neared the hall. Knots of people were clustered around
the large coffee urn and platter of cookies that sat out on
a cloth-covered table at one end of the room. Shelby made
her way toward it.

The coffee smelled heavenly, and she could do with a
second cup. This morning she'd only had time to heat up
what was left over in the carafe from yesterday, so the
idea of a freshly brewed pot was doubly enticing.

Delicate oval-shaped cat's tongue cookies—golden
brown around the edges and pale in the center—were
arrayed on a doily-covered platter.

Mrs. Willoughby sidled up to Shelby as Shelby's hand
hovered over the plate.

"Lovely, aren't they?" she said as she palmed two for
herself. "Isabel made them."

"Isabel?" Shelby raised her eyebrows.

Mrs. Willoughby let out a gusty sigh. "Yes. She's taken over as the provisional rector's wife." She nibbled the end of one of the cookies. "Poor Daniel. He didn't stand a chance."

Shelby glanced toward the door, where Daniel was greeting parishioners. Isabel was standing close by his side, her expensive silk dress and high-heeled sandals out of step with the garb of the rest of St. Andrews' congregation.

Her arm was linked possessively through Daniel's, and her beatifically smiling face was turned toward his.

Mrs. Willoughby nodded her head in their direction. "See what I mean? She won't let anyone come near him."

"He doesn't look unhappy," Shelby mumbled with her mouth full of cookie.

"He's intoxicated."

"Must be her perfume," Shelby said, referring to the heavy gardenia scent Isabel was known to drench herself in.

Mrs. Willoughby gave a shriek of laughter and then quickly covered her mouth with her hand.

"We'll see if it lasts," Mrs. Willoughby said, adjusting her belt around her broad waist. She reached out a hand toward the cookie tray. "I really shouldn't, but I can't resist. These are delicious." She gave a girlish giggle.

Someone bumped into Shelby from behind and she whirled around to see Billy fly past with another boy in hot pursuit. Both of their shirts were coming untucked and Billy had red punch down the front of his. They weaved in and out through the assembled crowd, bumping more than a few people on their way.

"Excuse me," Shelby said to Mrs. Willoughby. "I think it's time to leave now."

Shelby took off after Billy and his friend as they continued to run in a circle around the room. Finally Shelby got close enough to grab Billy's shirttail. He came up short, squirming and panting.

"That's enough," Shelby said. "It's time to go home."

The other boy, whose cheeks were bright red, quickly took off.

"It would be a shame to waste all that energy."

Shelby looked up to see Jim Harris standing in front of them. Mrs. Harris was deep in conversation with Cora-lynne.

"How about you come over to the stables after you've had your lunch and lend me a hand?" Jim said.

"Can I ride Blackjack after?" Billy said, his face lighting up.

"Sure thing. As soon as we finish with the stalls." Jim smiled at Shelby. "I'm sorry. I should have asked you first. Is it okay with you?"

"Sure. Billy loves being around the horses."

"I'll see you after lunch then, buddy." Jim lightly punched Billy on the arm.

Billy's grin broadened until his whole face lit up.

Shelby watched as Jim turned, went up to his wife, and slipped an arm through hers. She turned to Billy.

"Have you seen your sister?"

"She was over there." Billy pointed across the room. "She's talking to some boy," he said in tones of great disdain.

The crowd shifted, and Shelby caught a brief glance of curly blond hair.

"Can we go now, Mom? Mr. Harris is going to be waiting for me." Billy tugged on Shelby's arm.

Shelby ruffled his hair and Billy quickly ducked away from her hand.

"Sure, let's round up your sister and then we'll be off."

||||||||||||||||||||||||||

Billy could barely sit still long enough to eat the sandwich Shelby made him. Shelby had gotten him to change out of his church clothes first—she wanted to treat his fruit punch–stained shirt as soon as possible, before the stain set.

Dear Reader, why do they make punch in such bright fluorescent colors? Don't the manufacturers know how hard it is to get those stains out?

Billy finished his lunch in record time and was already in the car when Shelby walked through the door to the mudroom, her keys in hand. She slid behind the wheel, started the engine, and headed down the drive.

Billy was quiet on the drive out to the Harrises' stables. He spent the ride leaning forward against his seat belt, as if that would get him to the stables faster.

Shelby glanced at him out of the corner of her eye and smiled.

"You really like working for Mr. Harris, don't you?"

"He's nice," Billy said, swinging his legs back and forth. "He's teaching me lots of stuff."

"Like what?"

"I don't know. Just stuff."

"Sure," Shelby said. "Stuff."

Billy already had his hand on his seat belt clasp as Shelby pulled into the Harrises' drive.

"Mr. Harris said to go around back to the stables."

Shelby drove past the farmhouse where the American flag hung listlessly from its pole—the air was still and calm with no noticeable breeze.

Shelby continued down the drive and pulled up to the stables. Billy bolted from the car as soon as Shelby came to a stop.

Jim came out of the stable and walked toward Shelby's car. He'd changed out of the suit he'd worn to church and into jeans and a T-shirt. He leaned an arm on the roof of Shelby's car and bent down to speak to her.

"It's wonderful having such an enthusiastic helper." He turned toward the stable door, where Billy was waiting eagerly. "He's a good boy."

"I know." Shelby smiled, thinking of all the times Billy drove her crazy. "What time shall I pick him up?"

"Is three o'clock okay? That will give him some time to ride."

<hr>

Bert's car was in the driveway when Shelby got home. Shelby found her in the mudroom, obviously looking for something.

"You're back," Bert said. "I was looking for some gardening gloves. That herb patch isn't going to weed itself, you know."

"Gloves? I'm sure I have a pair around here somewhere." Shelby moved some terra-cotta flowerpots around. "What's with the gloves, though?" She turned to Bert. "I've never known you to bother with them before."

Bert held up both hands, which were brown from the

sun, covered in age spots, and rough from years of hard work. She wiggled her fingers.

"I've got my manicure to think about." She let out a wheezy laugh.

"What manicure?" Shelby laughed with her.

"I've got a bit of eczema on my fingers, and I thought maybe wearing gloves while I garden might help."

"Let me see what I can find."

Shelby glanced surreptitiously at her own hands. She could have done with a manicure herself, and a liberal application of hand cream.

Shelby moved some more pots out of the way and seized a pair of flower-printed gloves. "Here you go." She held them out to Bert.

"What about you?" Bert asked as she slipped them on.

"I'll be fine—don't worry."

They carried their tools out to the bed where Shelby grew parsley, thyme, sage, rosemary, and other herbs.

The sun was warm on Shelby's back as she knelt on the rich earth and began pulling weeds. She looked up at Bert.

"I didn't see you in church today."

"I went to the early service," Bert said, shaking the dirt off a clump of weeds.

"It looks as if Isabel has finally managed to snare our poor, hapless rector. She was glued to his side during the coffee hour."

"That poor man has gone from being henpecked by Prudence to being henpecked by Isabel."

"Oh?" Shelby raised an eyebrow.

Bert snorted. "Isabel may be all flirty and feminine around men, but I was on the Christmas bazaar committee with her last year, and that oh-so-delicate, well-manicured hand is really an iron fist."

"Poor Daniel."

"I don't think he would know what to do if he didn't have someone to lay it out for him."

Shelby yanked out a weed, only to discover she'd pulled up a section of thyme. She realized she was preoccupied— wondering whether she should tell Bert about finding Brenda's car in Zeke's garage.

"Got something on your mind?" Bert asked, pointing at the clutch of herbs in Shelby's hand.

Shelby sighed. She couldn't hide anything from Bert— that was obvious.

"I made an interesting discovery last night."

Bert paused with a trowel in her hand. "Uh-oh. Something about Amelia?"

"No, nothing like that."

Thank goodness, Shelby murmured to herself.

"I started thinking about Zeke's murder."

Bert shot her a stern look.

"Thinking about it doesn't count," Shelby said, lifting her chin. "It struck me as odd that both Zeke and his wife were murdered. Was there a connection?"

Shelby sat back on her heels and wiped an arm across her brow, which by now was beaded with perspiration.

"I got to thinking about Sid Harris being killed in that hit-and-run accident. I know you said Jim and Sid went to the Dixie every Friday night for a couple of games of pool. It stands to reason, then, that the hit-and-run must have taken place on a Friday night—unless Jim and Sid broke their routine, and that seems unlikely. I also knew that Brenda and her girlfriends had their night out on Fridays at the Dixie."

By now Bert had stopped working entirely, all her concentration focused on Shelby.

"I wondered if there wasn't some connection between the two. And then it came to me—what if Brenda had seen the person who hit Sid and they had killed her to keep her quiet?"

Bert pointed a finger at Shelby. "I don't think that ever occurred to anyone—not even the police."

"But I was wrong."

Bert looked like a child who'd had a piece of candy yanked from their grasp.

"Wrong?"

Shelby nodded. She took a deep breath—this was the part Bert wasn't going to like.

"I had a hunch."

Bert made a low grumbling noise in her throat.

Shelby thought about retreating, but it was too late now.

"Yesterday, Kelly and I went over to Zeke's farm and looked in his garage."

"And?"

"And we found a car."

"Imagine that."

Shelby shot Bert a look.

"It was Brenda's car—covered in dust and cobwebs. It obviously hadn't been out of the garage since she died."

"I wonder that Zeke didn't sell it. I'm sure the money would have come in handy."

"There's a good reason why he didn't. There was heavy damage to the right front fender. And the headlight was smashed."

Shelby heard Bert's indrawn breath.

"So it was Brenda who hit Sid that night."

"Don't you think that makes sense? Why else would Zeke hide the car?"

"It still doesn't explain Brenda's disappearance and murder. Or Zeke's murder, for that matter."

"I know. But at least it's one mystery solved."

"I assume you've told Frank about this," Bert said in a slightly sarcastic tone.

Shelby tilted her chin up. "I called him and left a message, but he hasn't called me back yet."

Bert looked up sharply. "Maybe he's busy with whoever that was he was cooking dinner for on Friday night."

28

||||||||||||||||||||||||||||||

Dear Reader,

"Waste not, want not" is pretty much the motto of every farmer I know. You may not even realize you're being wasteful—for instance, do you throw out the leaves on your celery, the ends of the carrots, and your vegetable scraps? Don't—save them instead! Keep them in a sealed plastic bag in your freezer, and when the bag is full, make vegetable broth. It won't cost you a penny, and the broth will be so much better than the canned stuff you buy in the store.

With Bert's help, Shelby was able to finish weeding the herb garden before she had to leave to pick up Billy. She even had time to wash her hands and face and run a comb through her unruly curls.

A storm was slowly moving in as Shelby headed toward the Harrises' stable. The skies overhead were thick with gray clouds that appeared almost black when she looked toward the horizon.

Shelby's conversation with Bert was still on her mind. She'd been positive that Zeke's death was somehow linked to Brenda's disappearance and ultimate death. But where was the connection between the two?

Brenda had to have been the one who hit Sid that night as Sid walked home from the Dixie. Poor Jim Harris had spent all these years wondering who had killed his brother, when the answer was hidden in Zeke Barnstable's garage.

Shelby thought about the day she'd come to the stables on the anniversary of Sid's death. Poor Jim had been so worked up about it—still in pain and mourning his brother. The phrase Jim had used—*"an eye for an eye and a tooth for a tooth"*—went through her mind. Now Jim would never see justice done.

The thought came to Shelby so quickly that she almost slammed on her brakes.

What if justice *had* been done?

Jim had left the Dixie to go after Sid that night they'd had the argument. What if Jim had nearly caught up with Sid and had been close enough to see the car that ran his brother down? Certainly he would have recognized it as Brenda's.

Had he killed Brenda and then buried her body on Zeke's property in order to incriminate Zeke? Anyone who watched television knew that the spouse was always the first to be suspected in a case of murder.

Shelby's stomach began to tighten. Billy was with Jim right now. Was he in any danger? Shelby reflexively increased the pressure of her foot on the gas pedal and the car lurched forward.

As soon as she had Billy in the car, she would call Frank again, she decided. She would tell him about finding Brenda's car and about her own suspicions as to what had happened. But not until she and Billy were well away from the Harrises' stables.

Shelby was pulling into the Harrises' drive when a bolt of lightning zigzagged across the sky and the first plump rain drops landed on her windshield. She turned on her wipers and continued toward the farmhouse. A car passed her on the way down the drive. Dawn Harris waved from the window and Shelby waved back. She felt a frisson of fear—she and Billy would now be alone with Jim.

But maybe she was being ridiculous—jumping to conclusions that had no basis in fact?

As soon as Shelby pulled up outside the stable, her cell phone began to ring. She prayed it was Frank.

"Shelby? This is Frank."

"Frank." His name came out sounding like a cry of relief.

"Are you okay?"

"Yes. Fine."

"Do you remember telling me that Jim Harris told you that the weapon used to kill Zeke Barnstable was a farrier's hammer?"

"Yes. Yes, I do."

"There's no way Harris could have known that. I've checked all around the office and everyone swears that they kept that information confidential, as we'd requested. The only way Harris could have known that is if—"

"He was the killer," Shelby finished for him, her voice breaking into a sob on the last words.

She heard Frank's sharply indrawn breath.

Shelby thought she heard the crunch of gravel behind her, and she whirled around, but no one was there. It must have been nerves.

"Where are you?" Frank said.

"I'm at the Harrises' stable and—"

"What are you doing there?" Frank's voice was sharp.

"Billy's here. I came to pick him up."

"Is he in the car with you?"

"No." This time Shelby sobbed in earnest.

"Get Billy in the car. Don't do or say anything to Harris. I'll be there as fast as I can."

Shelby heard the click as Frank ended the call. She put her cell phone on the passenger seat next to her, where it would be easier to reach. Her hands were shaking, and she gripped the steering wheel momentarily to try to stop their trembling. She had to look normal—as if nothing was wrong—or Jim might begin to suspect something.

Shelby strained her ears for the sound of police sirens, but all she could hear was the drone of a tractor in a distant field and the buzzing of bees bunched around a cluster of clover at the edge of the gravel drive.

Shelby got out of the car and shut the door as quietly as possible. There was no reason to be afraid, she chided herself. Jim couldn't possibly have been aware of her suspicions. All she had to do was act naturally.

She shoved her hands in the pockets of her shorts and tried to slow her ragged breathing. She felt the perspiration under her arms and on the back of her neck even though the day was mild and the misty rain falling had a chill to it.

The stable door creaked open slowly, and Shelby was about to call for Billy when Jim walked out.

"I'm here to pick up Billy." Shelby tried to make her voice sound as normal as possible, although she suspected she hadn't succeeded particularly well.

Jim smiled—a smile that wasn't the least bit welcoming.

"Billy is . . . Well, you could say Billy is tied up at the moment."

"We need to leave now." Shelby feigned looking at her watch. "We have to be somewhere."

"That's a shame," Jim drawled. "Because you aren't going anywhere at all."

Shelby felt her stomach drop to her feet.

"What do you mean?"

Jim hooked his thumbs through the belt loops of his worn jeans. "Just what I said. You're not going anywhere."

Shelby tried to summon some righteous indignation but was defeated by the trembling in her arms and legs. "You can't keep me here."

Jim sighed and tilted his hat back. "I can't let you go now that you know the truth."

"What truth?"

"Don't play dumb with me," Jim snapped. "I heard you on the phone with that detective."

"So it's true. You did kill Zeke," Shelby said.

She hoped that if she kept Jim talking—if she stalled long enough—the police would arrive. Once again she strained her ears for any hint of police sirens, but there was nothing.

"Zeke was bleeding me dry. He decided to clear that back acreage on his property. He'd barely begun to dig when he found Brenda's body." Jim scowled. "That land had lain uncultivated for years—there was no reason to suspect the bastard would suddenly decide to make use of it."

Jim turned his head and spat. "Zeke put two and two together—Brenda's damaged car, my brother's death—and he realized I was the one who killed Brenda."

"Couldn't you have gone to the police—"

"And what would they have done? I remembered that time Doug Hickory ran down that fellow on his bicycle. And what did he get? A slap on the wrist, that's all. Six months in jail and two years' probation. Where's the justice in that?" Jim shook his head. "I wanted justice done and the only way to do that was to do it myself."

"Zeke was blackmailing you?"

"Yes. Trust Zeke to find a way to take advantage of the situation."

"So you killed him."

Jim grinned in earnest this time. "He never saw it coming. Just like Sid never saw Brenda's car coming. One time Dick Archer was here shoeing Dancer—my Appaloosa mare. It was easy enough to lift one of his hammers."

"So, you planned to kill Zeke at the county fair?"

"It wasn't planned out—not like with charts and timetables and such. I waited for the right moment, and then I struck."

"Why put him in that Volvo station wagon the firemen were using?"

"I thought it would be amusing. Not to mention fitting. Zeke helped Brenda hide her car instead of doing the right thing. At the time I didn't realize that leaving Zeke's body in that old wreck would point a finger at that neighbor of yours. That was pure luck."

"Did you mean to implicate Dick Archer in the crime? The murder weapon belonged to him."

Jim shrugged. "I didn't plan on it, but it was convenient it worked out that way. I knew that son of his had had a run-in with Zeke."

Shelby knew she couldn't stall much longer. Where was Frank? And where were the police?

"Where's Billy?" Shelby demanded, horrified to hear her voice shake.

"Like I said, he's tied up at the moment."

Jim opened the stable door and motioned for Shelby to go ahead of him.

Most of the horses had been turned out, but Shelby could hear one stamping its hooves and snorting in the far stall. Jim led her over to it.

Blackjack was in the stall, tethered with cross ties attached to the wall. His nostrils flared and his dark eyes were rolling in the sockets, as if he was spooked.

And Billy was seated atop the majestic stallion. His eyes were wild and there were tears pooling at the corners. His hands were tied to the saddle pommel with twine, and a gag—a navy blue bandanna—was tied loosely across his mouth.

29

Dear Reader,

I still can't believe what happened. I'm in shock. I will
tell you all about it later.

Shelby had to restrain herself from dropping to her knees
when she saw Billy. She rushed toward the stall.

"Billy! Are you all right?"

Billy could only mumble with the kerchief tied around
his mouth, but he managed to nod. Shelby knew he was
trying to be brave, and that nearly broke her heart.

Shelby whirled around. "How could you do this?" She
pointed at Billy and then held out her hands toward Jim.
"Take me instead. Let him go, and take me."

Surely her chest would explode, Shelby thought as
blood pounded in her ears so loudly, she could barely hear.

"You'll get your turn. Don't worry," Jim said, moving toward the stall.

"What are you doing?"

"I'm going to turn Blackjack out. Let's see how long Billy can stay seated. He's a good rider. I give him a minute or two."

Jim opened a trunk that sat outside Blackjack's stall. When he turned around he had a gun in his hand.

"At least until the gun goes off, I should imagine. Then Blackjack will spook and . . ."

He waved the gun toward Shelby and she winced.

Shelby glanced around wildly. She had to do something, but what? Blackjack continued to stomp his hooves, clearly getting more and more impatient. Would he burst out of the stall the moment the door was opened? Would Billy be able to stay on his back?

Shelby looked at her hands. She had nothing to use as a weapon. Certainly nothing that would stop someone with a gun.

Jim reached for the latch on the stall. So much blood flooded Shelby's head, she felt faint and her vision grew hazy.

A flash of red in her peripheral vision caught her eye. A fire extinguisher. It was leaning against the wall between the stalls. Jim's back was turned as he fiddled with the latch on the stall. Could she possibly . . . ?

Shelby tried to tame the trembling in her hands and legs long enough to reach for the fire extinguisher. She stepped backward as quietly as possible and held her breath as she bent down.

The canister was heavy and cool in her hands. Fortunately she knew how to use it. She kept a fire extinguisher in her kitchen and had once had to grab it when one of her pot holders caught fire.

The latch on Blackjack's stall must have been stuck, because Shelby heard Jim swear as he fiddled with it. Shelby was able to pull the pin on the canister and aim the nozzle.

"Jim?"

Jim turned around. Shelby took aim and squeezed the lever on the fire extinguisher, releasing a cloud that obscured Jim in a swirl of powder. He immediately began to cough. Shelby continued to spray until the canister was empty.

Jim bent over with his hands on his knees, his body racked with hard, incapacitating coughs.

Shelby wasted no time. She undid the latch and yanked open the stall door. Blackjack was wild-eyed, stamping his hooves and shaking his head. Shelby struggled to untie the twine that bound Billy to the saddle. Her fingers felt fat and clumsy trying to tease out the tight knot.

Shelby heard Jim coughing. She didn't dare waste time checking to see if he was still leaning against the wall, bent over, the way he had been. She had to focus on getting Billy out of there.

Finally the knot in the twine gave way, and Shelby pulled it loose. She helped Billy down off the stallion and untied the bandanna that was over his mouth.

"Mom," he wailed, reaching out for Shelby.

Shelby wanted to hold him forever—to never let him go. But he needed to get out of there to safety. She cradled his head for a moment and bent to kiss it. Finally she shoved him toward the door. "Run!"

Shelby was about to do the same when Jim grabbed her arm in a grip that made her wince.

"Not so fast. I'll catch up with that boy of yours, but first I'm going to take care of you."

Shelby tried to pull her arm free, but Jim held on tight. She could see her skin turning white around the indentations made by his fingers. She struggled briefly but soon realized it was futile when he waved the gun in front of her face.

As long as he had the gun, she would have to do what he said. She just prayed that Billy had had the sense to run down the drive and out to the main road, where the police would surely see him when they got there.

What was taking them so long? Shelby wondered. They ought to have arrived by now. Once again she listened for sirens, but all she could hear was her own ragged breath. Jim was still wheezing, but the vicious coughing had stopped.

The police might get there too late for her, but at least she'd been able to rescue Billy. She knew Frank would take care of the kids if something happened to her.

And it looked like something was going to happen to her. Shelby stifled a sob at the thought, and then squared her shoulders. She wasn't going down without a fight.

But how could she defend herself against a man with a gun? Shelby thought in despair. This wasn't a fair fight, like two kids taking each other on in the playground using only their fists as weapons. Jim was armed, and she wasn't. The deck was clearly stacked in his favor.

Loud noises were coming from Blackjack's stall, and Shelby saw him straining against the cross ties. The stall door was open, but she was too far away to reach it, and if she moved she didn't know what Jim would do. His teeth were clenched, and a muscle twitched along his jawline.

He forced Shelby out of the stable. She'd forgotten it was raining and was surprised to feel the drops on her head and face and running down her back. She looked around quickly, but didn't see Billy. He was a smart boy and she knew he could take care of himself.

"Come on, move."

Jim had the gun at Shelby's back now and was forcing her farther and farther away from the stable, into the pasture, where uninterested horses continued their grazing, barely glancing up at Shelby and Jim's passage.

"You know," Jim said conversationally, as if they were standing across from each other at a cocktail party, "when I found this sinkhole on my property I was really angry. It won't be easy—or cheap—to fill it in. It sure wasn't something I'd been planning on. Money got pretty tight, what with Zeke demanding his blood money every month. But now that hole is going to come in very handy."

"Sinkhole?" Shelby said. She stumbled, trying to slow their progress across the field. "What's a sinkhole?"

"When the property was cleared"—Jim waved a hand toward the horizon—"trees were cut down and some of them were buried in the ground. It was probably easier than hauling them away. Only, trees rot over time and slowly decompose."

A pebble had worked its way into Shelby's shoe. She stopped to shake it out, but Jim grabbed her arm again and yanked her along. The rain was coming down in earnest now, making the hard-packed dirt surprisingly slippery. Shelby stumbled and twisted her ankle and had to bite her lip at the sharp pain that shot through her leg.

"See, as the trees began to decompose, the ground on

top of them began to sink. Pretty soon the whole mess caved in, and bingo, you've got yourself a giant sinkhole."

Shelby looked back over her shoulder. The stable had retreated into the distance, and even the handful of grazing horses in the pasture looked like miniatures. When the police did arrive, would they even know where to look for her? Shelby wondered.

The ground underneath their feet was stubbly with weeds and the sharp prongs of tree seedlings. Blood slowly trickled into Shelby's shoe from a cut on her ankle, and there was a nasty scratch cutting a swath across her left calf.

Her light T-shirt was soaked and clung to her back where her wet hair hung in dripping strands. Shelby shivered both from the chill and from fear.

She stared into the distance but couldn't see the sinkhole Jim was talking about and was surprised to suddenly find herself on the edge of it. It was deep, with sides made muddy from the rain. Bits of branches poked up from the bottom and were interspersed with beds of decaying leaves.

Shelby backed away from the edge, and Jim let out a maniacal laugh that chilled Shelby even further.

"Don't think you're going to get away." Jim waved the gun at Shelby.

Shelby put up her hands. She had no choice but to placate Jim while he had the gun.

"Come on. You're going to go into the hole. And you might as well get nice and cozy, because you're not coming out."

Jim began to push Shelby toward the edge of the sinkhole. The ground was slick now from the rain, and her feet kept slipping. She didn't see how she could keep herself from going over.

Shelby's resolve strengthened—she wasn't letting Jim get the better of her. She managed to hook a leg around Jim's ankle and with a mighty tug was able to send him crashing to the ground.

She was poised to run, but before she could move Jim grabbed her ankle and she went down with a thud that knocked all of the air out of her.

By now Jim was on his feet. He began pushing Shelby toward the sinkhole with his foot. She grabbed at a clump of weeds and held on, but eventually their roots gave way. Shelby tried to grab for Jim's foot, but he danced out of her reach just in time.

By now she was tired—exhausted—from the struggle. Surely even if Jim got her in the hole, the police would arrive before he had time to bury her? Shelby listened hard again, but there were no sirens in the distance. Maybe the police were planning a silent attack? That thought gave her hope and she renewed her efforts, snatching at Jim's pant leg.

Suddenly the ground beneath them began to thunder and quake. The sound stopped Jim in his tracks, and for a moment he became still, listening.

"What the . . . ?"

She only had seconds, but Shelby was able to scramble to her feet.

The thundering was becoming louder. Jim still stared toward the stables, and Shelby turned to look in that direction.

Blackjack pounded across the area where the other horses had been turned out. He easily leapt the fence between the pasture and the uncultivated ground where Jim had led Shelby.

"The cross ties must have broken away," Jim mumbled as he watched the horse approach, steam coming from its nostrils and its flying hooves a mere blur.

It was now or never, Shelby thought. She had to strike while Jim was occupied watching his horse.

Jim had the gun held loosely at his side. He was standing at the edge of the sinkhole, half turned away from Shelby. He appeared not to notice that she'd managed to stumble to her feet.

Shelby stretched her arms out, striking Jim in the back and giving him an almighty push. He flailed his arms as his feet slipped out from under him, and he tumbled head over heels into the sinkhole. The gun went flying and landed in some tall grass a couple of yards away.

For a moment, it was quiet. Shelby was breathing hard from the effort, and Jim lay stunned at the bottom of the sinkhole. Then Jim began to swear. He scrabbled to his feet, shaking his fist at Shelby.

"You're not getting away with this."

He began trying to climb the rain-slicked muddy walls of the hole, but his hands and feet kept slipping out from under him. His face turned red with frustration.

Shelby was poised to run when she heard someone call her name. A man was racing toward her in the distance, his loping stride as familiar as her own face. It was Frank.

Shelby ran toward him.

30

Dear Reader,

There is some good news amidst all this drama and tragedy. Seth talked to his mother and she agreed—albeit reluctantly—to have his and Kelly's wedding at the farm! I can't wait to sit down with Kelly and begin planning. I want it to be perfect, but most of all I want it to be fun!

Shelby stifled a sob as she fell into Frank's arms. Several uniformed men ran past them, shouting, toward the hole, where Jim was still imprisoned.

"Billy?" Shelby cried, clutching at Frank's arms.

"He's fine," Frank said soothingly. "He's in the squad car with Officer McDermott. Last I heard, he was asking McDermott if he could turn on the siren."

Shelby smiled. That certainly sounded like her Billy.

He'd been through a horrible experience, but he was young and would hopefully soon put it behind him.

By now the rain had stopped and a shaft of weak sunlight was shining through a gap in the clouds. One of the officers had managed to corral Blackjack and was leading him back toward the stable. Several of the other officers had managed to pull Jim from the sinkhole, and Jim's hands were now handcuffed behind his back. They were marching him across the rutted pasture toward the squad cars waiting in the driveway.

Frank put an arm around Shelby, and they began walking in the same direction.

Three squad cars were parked in the driveway. Shelby held back and watched until she saw Jim safely ensconced in the backseat of one of the cars.

The passenger-side door of another car flew open and Billy tumbled out. He ran toward Shelby and wrapped his arms around his mother's waist.

Shelby held him tight. Billy was momentarily transformed into the little boy that Shelby swore was growing so fast, he was disappearing before her very eyes.

Frank smiled and ruffled Billy's hair.

"You okay, champ?"

Billy lifted his head briefly and nodded before burying his face in Shelby's T-shirt again.

"How about we get you two home?"

The three of them began walking toward Frank's pickup truck.

〰〰〰〰〰〰〰〰〰〰

Bert was waiting for them in the kitchen when they got back to Love Blossom Farm.

"Amelia was worried when you didn't come back from picking up Billy, so she called me," Bert said as she measured coffee into the coffeemaker.

Shelby glanced at her daughter in surprise. Amelia's head was bent over her phone and Shelby couldn't see her expression.

Shelby collapsed into a kitchen chair and Bitsy and Jenkins immediately strolled over to get their heads scratched. Shelby reached down a hand and stroked their soft fur.

"I imagine you all could do with a warm drink after being soaked to the skin like you are."

Bert bustled around producing mugs, spoons, and sugar and cream. When the last drop of coffee had gurgled into the carafe, she filled the mugs and pushed them toward Frank and Shelby.

"Would you like me to make you some hot chocolate?" Bert asked Billy, who was sitting at the kitchen table fiddling with some LEGOs.

He shook his head. "No, thanks."

"I made some zucchini muffins to kill the time while we waited for you. I couldn't stand to just sit here and worry. Besides, the vines are still producing, so I figured we ought to take advantage of it. You can freeze the extras."

Bert put a platter of golden brown muffins on the table, along with a crock of sweet butter. She poured herself a cup of coffee and sat down opposite Shelby and Frank.

Billy reached for a muffin, and Shelby noticed his hands were filthy but decided not to say anything. On one wrist there was a raw mark that must have been made by the twine that Jim had used to tie Billy's hands to the saddle pommel. The sight of it made a white-hot blast of fury surge through Shelby.

"So. Are you going to tell me what happened?" Bert said slightly petulantly, her patience obviously having worn thin.

Shelby explained about Jim Harris and how she'd been right that he'd killed Brenda to exact what he viewed as justice. And then, when Zeke began blackmailing him, he had to kill him as well.

When Shelby got to the part about Billy being tied to the horse, her voice broke, and she had to stop for a minute. She noticed Bert reach out an arm and put it around Billy's shoulders. For once, Billy didn't try to squirm away.

Amelia looked horrified. She stared at Shelby with her large blue eyes and then turned to look at Billy.

Shelby finished her story and then sat quietly for a moment, sipping her coffee and relishing the peace of her own kitchen with the lowering sun shining through the window and glancing off the pots on her pot rack. When she thought about how close she'd been to never coming home again . . . it didn't bear thinking about.

"I just remembered something," Shelby said, putting her coffee cup down. "Did anyone ever find out who put the pepper in Jenny Hubbard's pie at the Lovett County Fair? We all thought it might have been a diversion to cover up Zeke's murder, but it seems as if that wasn't the case."

Bert laughed. "I can't see Jim Harris carrying a tin of red pepper around in his pocket, waiting for the perfect opportunity."

Frank held his hands up. "Don't look at me. That's a domestic matter, not a police matter."

Bert fixed him with a glare. "Someone could have been hurt."

"And fortunately no one was." Frank smiled back at Bert.

"Someone has to have done it." Shelby broke off a piece off her zucchini muffin and slathered it with butter.

"This is what I heard," Bert said, leaning across the table. She shot a glance at Amelia, who shot one right back.

Shelby hid a smile. For once Amelia wasn't bolting to the sanctuary of her room, bored to tears by the grown-ups' conversation.

"Don't keep us in suspense," Frank said, then drained the remainder of his coffee.

"Rumor has it that Isabel herself put the pepper in Jenny's lemon meringue pie. And that she'd misjudged what the effects would be . . . badly. She thought her reaction would be milder—"

"And less unattractive," Shelby added.

"And that Daniel would sweep her into his arms, terrified that he was going to lose her."

Shelby burst out laughing. "That certainly didn't work out as planned."

"She did get carried off by some hunky firemen, though, from what I've heard," Bert said.

Frank pushed his chair back with an apologetic smile. "I'd better be going. They'll be waiting for me down at the station."

"I'll walk you out." Shelby put her dirty mug in the

kitchen sink and followed Frank through the living room and out the door to the front porch.

The air had turned even cooler while they were inside and Shelby felt goose bumps prickle up and down her arms. The heavy, dark clouds that had sat low in the sky all day were gone—blown away by the wind and replaced with clear blue skies.

The wind was blowing from the direction of Jake's dairy farm and was tinged with the scent of manure. Shelby relished the smell—to her it signified home and Love Blossom Farm. She would never take them for granted again.

Frank hesitated on the front porch. "I was so scared today. I really thought I was going to lose you."

Shelby didn't know what to say.

Frank smiled, and the dimple to the right of his mouth deepened. "I should have known you could take care of yourself."

Shelby thought back to the frantic and heart-stopping moments when she thought Jim was going to succeed in shoving her into the sinkhole, and shivered.

"I'm glad you came" was all she said.

Frank hesitated and then took a step forward. He put his hands on Shelby's shoulders and looked into her eyes, then tilted her chin up with one hand.

Shelby was barely aware of the fact that his head was lowering toward hers and that she was stretching up to meet his until their lips met.

Shelby closed her eyes and allowed herself to be swept away for the moment. Kissing Frank felt so right—and so wrong at the same time.

She felt adrift when he finally let her go. The breeze on her bare arms was frigid, and she began to shiver.

"You'd better get inside. Shock is probably setting in," Frank said as he turned toward the steps.

"If there's anything you need . . ." he added, turning back briefly.

"I'll call you," Shelby said with a smile.

RECICES

APPLE CRISP

INGREDIENTS

6 to 8 apples, peeled and quartered
½ cup white sugar
½ cup brown sugar
¾ cup flour
1 teaspoon cinnamon
½ cup unsalted butter

Arrange apples in a greased casserole dish or 10-inch pie plate. Mix sugars, flour, and cinnamon and cut in butter. Pack over apples. Bake at 350 degree for 45 minutes or until golden on top.

LOVE BLOSSOM FARM
PEACH KUCHEN

INGREDIENTS

2 cups flour
¼ teaspoon baking powder
½ teaspoon salt
½ cup white sugar and ½ cup brown sugar, mixed
½ cup unsalted butter
12 fresh peach halves pitted, peeled, and cut in half
　　or canned
1 teaspoon cinnamon
2 egg yolks, beaten
½ cup cream
½ cup sour cream

Preheat oven to 400 degrees. Grease an 8 x 8–inch baking dish or 10-inch pie plate.

Sift together flour, baking powder, salt, and 2 tablespoons of the sugar. Cut in butter until mixture resembles cornmeal. Pat evenly over bottom and halfway up sides of baking dish. Arrange peach halves over pastry. Sprinkle cinnamon and remaining sugar over peaches. Bake 15 minutes.

Meanwhile, mix egg yolks, cream, and sour cream. Remove baking dish from oven and pour egg-cream mixture over peaches. Return dish to oven and bake 30 minutes more.

TURKEY TETRAZZINI

INGREDIENTS

4 tablespoons butter, plus more for topping
  if desired
1 small onion, chopped
½ lb. mushrooms, sliced
1 tablespoon sherry
4 tablespoons flour
1½ cups chicken broth
½ cup cream, half-and-half, or milk
salt and pepper, to taste
½ pound linguine or spaghetti, cooked al dente
3 cups cooked turkey, cut into small cubes
½ cup Parmesan cheese

Preheat oven to 350 degrees. Heat 2 tablespoons butter
in a sauté pan. Add onion and sauté until softened. Add
mushrooms and sauté for 2 to 3 minutes until tender.
Deglaze pan over high heat with sherry.

In a saucepan, heat 2 tablespoons of butter. Stir in flour
and cook, stirring, for a minute. Whisk in chicken broth
and bring to a boil. Cook over low heat until mixture is
thickened. Remove from heat, add cream, half-and-half,
or milk, and season to taste with salt and pepper.

Cook linguine or spaghetti until al dente and drain.
Add sauce to turkey and mushrooms and mix well. Butter
a casserole dish and put half the linguine in the bottom
of the dish. Add a layer of the turkey-mushroom mixture,

another layer of linguine, and the final layer of turkey-mushroom mixture. Scatter Parmesan over the top and dot with more butter if desired. Bake 45 minutes or until hot and bubbling.